Clever
Little
Thing

Clever
Little
Thing

Helena Echlin

Pamela Dorman Books / Viking

VIKING
An imprint of Penguin Random House LLC
penguinrandomhouse.com

A Pamela Dorman Book/Viking

LIBRARY OF CONGRESS CATALOGING-IN-PUBLICATION DATA

Names: Echlin, Helena, author.
Title: Clever little thing / Helena Echlin.
Description: [New York] : Pamela Dorman Books/Viking, 2025.
Identifiers: LCCN 2024018874 (print) | LCCN 2024018875 (ebook) |
ISBN 9780593656075 (hardcover) | ISBN 9780593656082 (ebook)
Subjects: LCGFT: Thrillers (Fiction) | Paranormal fiction. | Novels.
Classification: LCC PS3605.C45 C54 2025 (print) |
LCC PS3605.C45 (ebook) | DDC 813/.6—dc23/eng/20240515
LC record available at https://lccn.loc.gov/2024018874
LC ebook record available at https://lccn.loc.gov/2024018875

Printed in the United States of America
1st Printing

Designed by Cassandra Garruzzo Mueller

For Jordan

I imagine the corruption of myself running through her tracts, into her veins and recesses. I long to withdraw my sting from her innocent body.

RACHEL CUSK,
A LIFE'S WORK: ON BECOMING A MOTHER

Clever

Little

Thing

1.

On a table by the window is a bowl of fruit that confusingly also contains ceramic fruit. Shiny porcelain Bartlett pears are jumbled with dull green ones notched with brown, too imperfect not to be real. I feel a strong urge to sort the fruit, just to take control of *something*. I'm about to move them when the door springs open. A cheery young woman introduces herself as Kelly, and says, "Just to let you know, we have to take your shoelaces, my love. It's regulation."

"Fine." I take off my shoes and hand her the laces. Lose the battle, win the war. I am going to get out of here.

"We already got your sharps," she tells me.

"Sharps?"

"Anything sharp, love. Razors, nail files. In your case, it wasn't much. Just a pencil."

"I don't have anything to write with?" Not that I have anything to write, and my right hand is still bandaged, my cuts throbbing. I could barely scrawl the word *help*.

In any case, I agreed to stay here for two nights. Not that I had much choice.

"You can write in the lounge. It's lovely and cozy in there, they've got the fire on. Peaceful too: they put the moms who came with their babies in the other wing, so you won't be disturbed." She gives me a pointed look, as if I've forgotten that Luna, three days old and born just before Christmas at thirty weeks, is in the NICU in London. But she's getting the best possible medical care. Stella is the one who's in danger.

Kelly surveys the room. Is she checking to see if I've examined the fruit? Maybe the fruit bowl is a test: If I don't sort it, she'll say I can't tell what's real and what's not. But if I do sort it, she might say I've got an obsessive need to control my surroundings.

Pete says anxiety is my natural mode, and I look for things to worry about. Maybe I do worry too much about what other people think. I force myself to take a deep breath, blow out slowly. I turn away from the fruit, paint on a bright smile for Kelly. "Now what?"

"Pop on your comfy clothes," she says. "I'll wait outside." She closes the door and leaves me. Laid out on the bed is a long-sleeved white cotton T-shirt and white fleece-lined tracksuit bottoms. They have a uniform here.

This could be an upmarket B & B, with its oak beams, comfortable armchair, and big bed with crisp cotton sheets and decorative mound of pillows. On the wall opposite the window hangs a still life: bleached shapes of bottles and jars on a darker background. Empty vessels. Perhaps this is what we mothers should aspire to be.

Someone has unpacked the bag Pete brought. My toothbrush and contact lens solution are in the bathroom. The breast pump is on the table by the window, plugged in and ready to go. The dresser drawers contain my underwear but no sign of other clothes. Did Pete forget them?

Win the war, I remind myself. And my phone's still in my pocket, so I'm not helpless. I change into the clothes Kelly laid out. I go into the bathroom, where there's a basket of soaps individually wrapped in pretty paper, and change my pad too, afraid of bleeding through the pale tracksuit bottoms.

When Kelly returns, she gathers up the clothes I removed. She tells me someone will bring my lunch shortly and to have a nice sit-down while I wait. When she's gone, I stand by the window, staring at the peaceful view of bare winter trees and hills dotted with sheep. Pete didn't stint on this place, I'll give him that. I promised I would relax, but I can't. I can't choose an organic lavender-and-geranium soap and run a soothing bath. I wrap my arms around myself and rock back and forth.

Kelly knocks and enters without waiting for me to invite her in. "Almost forgot." She holds out her hand. I stare at her, wondering if she expects a tip. "Your phone," she says. "We find it helps guests with their rest and relaxation if they don't have their phones to worry about."

"I need my phone."

"You can still use it whenever you want," Kelly says, but I shake my head and grip my phone with both hands. She mutters something about having to run this by management, but doesn't fight me.

When she's gone, I go back to staring out the window. I'm terrified that Pete doesn't understand the danger that Stella is in. I promised to stay, but I could break my promise. I'm no more than a couple of hours from London, although I have no coat and no shoe-laces. I do have my phone, so I can call a taxi. But they might not let it through the gates. In any case, I'm afraid that if they know I'm leaving, they'll do something to stop me. But I have to get back to Stella.

After her birth, eight years ago, I was exhausted, but I lay awake in wonder at the glorious smell that emanated from her, like vanilla pudding, like caramelizing sugar, like honeysuckle. This is the smell of something greater than human, I thought, the secret sweetness at the heart of it all.

Stella no longer smells sweet. When I look back on it, I see that by the time I found out what happened to Blanka, Stella had already begun to change.

THEN

2.

When Stella and I spotted my friend Emmy, her daughter Lulu was already racing towards the sea. But Stella clapped her hands over her ears. "Too loud," she moaned.

"What is, sweetie?" I asked as Emmy unfolded a blanket, laying her baby, Madeleine, on top. When she sat down, she took care to spread the skirt of her white Breton striped dress so it wouldn't get creased. It was a perfect August day, the sky a rare, deep blue. I wanted the girls to run around together. But Stella clutched her head and grimaced as if a military jet screamed overhead, even though the only sound was the surf and the cry of gulls.

Emmy pushed up her oversized sunglasses and studied Stella with concern. "Does she have a headache?"

I shook my head. "I think she doesn't like the sound of the waves. She's got very acute hearing." She also didn't like the sound when I ran her a bath.

Stella sat down and drew her knees up. The broad brim of her sun hat cast her face into shadow. She seemed subdued. Maybe she was more upset about Blanka leaving than I'd realized. She had resigned abruptly a week ago. After four years of working for us, she'd sent a brief text: I cannot come anymore. When I tried to get a reason out of her, she ghosted me. After all that time she'd spent with Stella, playing with her, bathing her, feeding her, apparently my daughter was still just a job to her, one she cast aside like a used tissue.

"Maybe Stella needs a snack," Emmy suggested. "How about a piece of your mom's homemade banana bread, sweetheart? Or I've got some carrots somewhere."

With her hands still glued to her ears, Stella shook her head. "No, thank you."

"She might be getting a bit hot in that sunsuit," Emmy said to me.

"With our Irish coloring, you can't be too careful," I said. Stella had inherited my pale complexion, along with my hair, the dark red of saffron threads.

Emmy's daughter Lulu attempted a cartwheel at the edge of the sea, her flaxen hair twisted into a pretty crown braid. Emmy herself had a fashionably messy side plait. I'd looked at videos on how to do both, but Stella hated me touching her hair. I wished that Stella would go and play too. Year four started in a few days, and Stella still struggled to fit in. I organized this end-of-summer trip to a beach in Kent so Stella could spend time with another kid in her class. Instead, Stella sat in her self-imposed bubble of silence.

Lulu finally turned a perfect cartwheel and then did one after another. My chest felt tight. Lulu looked so joyful and free. Stella had never done a cartwheel in her life. But I reminded myself that other mothers had trouble getting their kids to read, whereas Stella read happily for hours. I tapped her shoulder and made sure she could see my lips. "I love you," I said. Her gaze met mine, but I couldn't tell what she was thinking.

Emmy attached her baby to her breast, though thanks to a clever opening in her dress, you couldn't see a thing. She managed to look chic even when breastfeeding. She caught me looking at her, and I turned away and folded my arms over my own chest, clad in a nondescript white T-shirt. My breasts were swollen, and Emmy didn't know I was pregnant. I was hopeful this time, but I'd lost pregnancies before, and I didn't want to jinx this one by making it public. Not yet. Luckily, I was barely showing.

Emmy placed a hand on my arm and murmured, "I'm so sorry about Blanka. I only found out this morning, or I would have messaged you."

I murmured back, "It's fine. Stella liked her, but she actually wasn't very good at babysitting."

Emmy looked reproachful. "Well, she's gone now."

"She moved?" I laid a palm over the back of my neck. I'd recently had my hair cut short, a practical bob, and it felt like the sun was burning the newly exposed skin.

Now Emmy was staring at me too. "Oh my god, you haven't heard?" She looked at Stella, who still had her hands clapped over her ears, then leaned closer to me and whispered, "Are you sure Stella can't hear?"

I wasn't. Then I had an idea. I took a tissue from my tote, tore it down the middle, and folded each half until I had two tiny wads. I wet the wads and squeezed them out. I pulled Stella's hands away from her ears. "Ta-da! Earplugs." Once I got them in, her whole body relaxed. "Now you can go and have fun," I said. Stella clambered to her feet and ran to join Lulu.

"Genius," said Emmy. I smiled. It seemed like we were going to have an actual, real conversation, instead of just administering sunscreen and snacks. Best of all, Stella was at last playing happily with Lulu.

"Blanka's dead," Emmy said.

I shook my head. The surf rushed into my ears, smashing, pummeling, grinding. Stella was right: the noise *was* unbearable. Emmy's mouth kept moving. When the noise finally retreated, I thought I had the gist: an accident of some kind. Emmy didn't know the details.

"But I just saw her," I said absurdly, as if the fact that she'd just been alive could disprove her death. "When did this happen?"

"On Thursday. Just before the weekend. Look, I'm so sorry you're finding it out from me. I can't believe you didn't know."

"How do *you* know?"

"I ran into my friend who lives on the same street," Emmy said. "She saw them taking her away."

Blanka had died just before the weekend, a few days after she quit. If she hadn't stopped babysitting for us, would she still be alive?

I closed my eyes and saw Blanka shuffling along the pavement in her long black skirt and grey hoodie, shoulders drooping as if she carried all her worldly belongings on her back. She'd only been in her thirties, and had a round, girlish face, but she had moved like an old woman.

"Was it a car accident?" I asked, feeling sick.

Emmy shook her head. "My friend didn't know."

"Her poor mother," I said. I had never met her mother— Blanka was a very private person—but I knew they lived together. I wondered if the accident had happened at home.

"Blanka was with you for a long time, wasn't she? I'm so sorry, Charlotte. This must be awful for you."

I nodded, although in fact Blanka was never one of those babysitters where people say, "She's part of the family." Stella liked her, but Pete and I never quite understood why. We used to joke that she was the nondairy creamer of babysitters: the only good thing you could say about her was that she was better than nothing.

Now I felt terrible for every bad thought I'd ever had about her.

A shriek tore the air. Lulu charged towards us, face crumpled. She threw herself on the blanket, wailing, and Emmy set her baby down and squeezed Lulu tight. Stella stood at a safe distance, clutching something behind her back. My heart sank.

"Stella, what is that?" I called. She shook her head and pointed to her earplugs.

"We went to the rocks," Lulu choked out. "Stella said she had something to show me, and it was a—dead—" She resumed her wailing.

"Oh my god," said Emmy as Stella finally presented what she held: a mass of bones and quills, some kind of seabird. A piece of it fell to the sand. "Oh my god." She snatched up her baby and, clutching Lulu's hand, retreated several yards.

"Get it away!" Lulu whined.

"Don't worry, Lulu," Stella called. "It can't hurt you. It doesn't even have a head."

Lulu buried her face in Emmy's waist. "I don't want that thing near the baby," Emmy called, clutching her infant to her chest. "It could have a disease."

"OK, OK." I walked over to Stella, leaving Emmy consoling Lulu. I pulled out her earplugs, but she didn't complain about the noise of the surf anymore. She was too excited. "Why do you have that seagull, sweetie?" I asked.

"It's not a seagull, it's a gannet. I want to look at it. Please, Mommy?"

I softened. Stella loved investigating. It never even occurred to her that Lulu might not share her scientific interest.

"You can study it at home," I said. "But it's going in the boot. And you're apologizing to Lulu." Luckily, I had a spare plastic bag in my tote. I helped Stella stuff the thing in, and marched her back to the blanket, where Emmy was placating Lulu with banana bread. "I'm sorry you felt scared, Lulu," Stella said, hanging her head. Lulu sniffled and kept on eating. Nobody offered any banana bread to Stella, even though I was the one who made it. I used almond flour because Emmy claimed Lulu was allergic to gluten.

Emmy looked at Stella, her face wary. With a shock, I realized that she was thinking about what Stella had done at her eighth birthday party. My face grew hot.

This skin Stella and I had: you really couldn't be out in the sun for a minute.

Stella insisted on having the bag on her lap on the way home, and I didn't have the energy to argue with her. As I started the drive back to London, my heart ached. She was so different from her peers. She read at an adult level: her bedtime reading was *Birdflight as the Basis of Aviation* by Otto Lilienthal. No wonder it was difficult for her to socialize. And the hard part was, she didn't yet understand the gulf between her and other kids.

Stella was murmuring something under her breath, but the noise of the motorway made it impossible to catch her words. I glanced over my shoulder. Her window was wide open, so wind filled the car, making her hair float as if it were underwater. Whatever she was saying, it was the same phrase, over and over.

Someone swerved into my lane right in front of me, and I hit the brakes. Shaken, I pulled the car onto the hard shoulder, just as my brain made sense of her words: "*Poor* Blanka. *Poor* Blanka. *Poor* Blanka."

"Why are you saying that, darling?" She'd been well out of earshot when Emmy had told me, so there was no way she knew Blanka was dead. But why was she bringing up Blanka now? She'd gone into freak-out mode when I told her Blanka wasn't coming back, but then abruptly stopped mentioning her.

Stella gave me a patient look. "I was saying, 'Poor Mommy,' because it seemed like you didn't have a nice time at the beach."

I'd misheard her, that was all. Of course, she didn't know that Blanka was dead. And she was so sensitive, there was no way I could let her find out.

Pete worked late at his company, Mycoship, which made packing foam out of mycelium, the root system of mushrooms. He wasn't home until ten, long after Stella was in bed. I was reading in the bedroom, and I heard him putting his bike in the bike shed and then opening the front door. He would likely go to the freezer to get something to eat. He wasn't a fan of takeaway, because of the single-use plastic.

I decided I'd let him eat before telling him about Blanka. Suddenly I remembered about the gannet. I leaped out of bed and sprinted to the kitchen, but I was too late.

"Jesus, what is that?"

I explained.

"So you stuck the thing in our freezer—with our food?" was all he managed to say. When I met Pete in California ten years ago, he was thirty-eight, but had looked much younger, with his blue eyes, his swimmer's shoulders, his head of tight blond curls. Now the overhead light showed up the bags under his eyes. I wished he didn't have to work so hard.

"I triple bagged it," I said. "You can still eat your veggie lasagna." Because my morning sickness made cooking difficult, Pete had stocked up on readymade food from the gourmet place we liked. He stuck the lasagna in the microwave and pulled me into his arms. "How are you feeling, my love?" he asked. I was the one who had pushed for a second baby so Stella could have a brother or sister, but now Pete was as eager as I was. He checked the Pregnant Dad app every day.

"I still feel sick." I'd tried everything: motion sickness wristbands, B6, promethazine, you name it.

Pete nodded. "But the other times, when we lost the pregnancy, you felt great. So maybe this is a good sign."

I followed him to the dining table, and we sat down at one end. When we bought this big Edwardian in coveted Muswell Hill—one of the five best places to live in London, according to *The Sunday Times*, we'd ripped out most of the walls downstairs so it was one huge, open space. We kept the period detail—the mantelpieces and wall moldings—but we had sleek, modern furniture and huge black-and-white photos of surf pounding the beaches of Northern California, where Pete grew up. The table was reclaimed oak from an old barn, big enough to seat twelve when you pulled out the hidden leaves. We both loved entertaining. A few days after we met, we threw a Dungeness crab party for twelve. We pushed together borrowed tables and covered them with butcher paper. I served Negronis while Pete wrestled the crabs into the pot. Guests cracked claws and dipped the flesh into my champagne-shallot butter. Then we rolled back the rug and danced until dawn.

After Stella was born, we still entertained, but less and less. We stopped eating crab when the crab population declined due to ocean acidification. And now, after her birthday party, it was hard to imagine any guests ever coming over again.

I'd felt awkward about inviting Blanka to that party. I was worried it might feel too much like working without pay, and that Blanka would feel shy about socializing with our friends. So I didn't ask her. But if I had, would the party have turned out differently? Would Blanka still be alive?

I couldn't shake the feeling that I had failed her.

"What's the matter?" said Pete, seeing my face, and I knew I couldn't put off telling him any longer.

"Blanka's dead."

Pete blanched. He pushed his lasagna away. "That's terrible. She was just here—what, last week? Jesus Christ."

"Emmy said it was an accident, but she didn't have the details."

"What a tragedy. I can't believe it. God—how does Emmy know?" He asked a few more questions, and I told him the little I knew. We were both silent. Then Pete said, "Are you OK, baby? It's terrible news, but it's not a good time for you to get stressed. Here, give me your feet." He pulled them into his lap and began to massage them.

"What kind of accident could it have been?" I said. "Do you think she got run over?" She did cross the road very slowly, apparently never having developed city smarts, even though she'd moved to London with her mother when she was a teenager. Before that, they'd lived in Armenia, and before that, they fled from some country I no longer recalled, some place with a spiky name like Kyrgyzstan or Uzbekistan. But I forgot where, and as time passed, it became more and more embarrassing to ask her again. Besides, questions seemed to make Blanka uncomfortable.

"Or perhaps it was a freak accident of some kind," I continued. "Though it's not like Blanka went skydiving. I used to ask her every Monday what she'd done on the weekend, and she always said, 'Not much.'"

Pete bent the toes of my right foot gently back and forth. "We'll send flowers to her mother. I'll do it, since you're sick."

"She must feel awful," I said. "Do you think it's strange she didn't call me to tell me?"

Pete was frowning at me. "You look very pale. Have you eaten today?"

14

"Rice cakes."

"You have to eat." He served me some lasagna, and I smiled, swallowing down nausea.

"Listen, this bird obsession of Stella's worries me." Pete cut his portion into neat squares. "Year four starts the day after tomorrow. I'm concerned she's not going to fit in."

I frowned. "Marie Curie probably didn't fit in either. If Stella was a boy, Emmy wouldn't have made such a big fuss about her picking up the dead gannet. The problem is that Stella's a girl and so her interest in the thing comes across as macabre."

Pete looked skeptical. "How was everything before that?"

I had to admit that Lulu had mostly played alone while Stella sat with her hands over her ears. "But it's not her fault. She's got very acute hearing."

"She has to learn how to be with other kids," Pete said. "We need to be proactive, especially since—you know."

We both shuddered, thinking of the birthday party, and I tried not to look at that one spot on the kitchen floor, which Pete had scrubbed so aggressively that it was paler than the surrounding wood.

"It's not just other kids," Pete continued. "She hates baths. She hates noises. She hates food, unless each item is separate. And what about freak-out mode?"

I said nothing. Freak-out mode *was* frightening. Late at night, I'd watched videos other parents had posted of their kids' meltdowns, hoping to feel solidarity. Instead, I thought, If you can take a step back and film it, it's not that bad.

Pete squeezed my hand. "I just want to help her. I love her too."

Having finished eating, he pulled out his iPad. "Look, I've been collecting recommendations. I made a spreadsheet of different doctors and therapists."

"But she had her checkup recently," I said. Here in the UK, parents only took kids to the doctor if they were actually ill, but Pete, being American, believed in kids having annual checkups, so I took Stella for the sake of marital harmony. "She's healthy as a horse."

"Physically," Pete said.

"It's not that hard to accommodate her needs," I said. "I would rather do that than take her to a doctor who is only going to slap some label on her that might not fit. And how's she going to feel about seeing a doctor? We don't want her to think there's something wrong with her." Pete looked at his spreadsheet, marshalling another argument, and I offered, "Look, I only stopped working last week. More time with me is going to help her relax. I really think I can help her much better than any doctor. If she gets worse"—which she wouldn't—"then, I promise, we'll get her evaluated."

Pete fiddled with his glasses while I searched desperately for a change of topic. Usually, just the word *Brexit* was enough to get him going, and by the way, why didn't Boris Johnson ever brush his hair? But I didn't think that would work today. "I can't believe Blanka is dead," I said, hating myself for using her death as a segue.

At that, Pete's face filled with compassion. "It must be really hard getting this news so soon after losing your mom."

"I'm upset about Blanka," I said. "This is not about my mother."

My mother, Edith, had died six months earlier: of a stroke, in the night, at home at her terraced Victorian house in Oxford. She slipped away without saying goodbye, exactly as she would have wanted. She and I were very different people. Still, I expected a wave of grief to hit me, but it never did, not like the way Pete got sideswiped when his dad died. Sometimes I'd give a little start, like when you realize, I've forgotten to do something: the kettle is screaming, the smoke alarm needs a new battery. Then I'd think, No, I didn't leave the kettle on, but my mother is dead.

At two in the morning, I was wide-awake, feeling as if the sea still pummeled my eardrums. We met Blanka when Stella was four. I'd been looking for a babysitter to pick her up after school. I was going back full-time to my job at *Design Your Life*, a lifestyle portal, where I churned out content about entertaining and gave etiquette advice in my column, "Charlotte Says." I'd worked there since my late twenties, when an editor at *Design Your Life* had spotted my blog about stress-free dinner parties, *The Reluctant Hostess*, and offered me a job in San Francisco. Luckily, they let me work remotely when we moved to London. "Everybody already knows all this," my mother said, nonplussed, when Pete persuaded her to read my column.

"Americans don't feel they know everything about etiquette," I said. *Design Your Life* had a primarily US audience.

"Well, they wouldn't." Edith was the mistress of the poison dart. A professor of nineteenth-century literature, she spent her last afternoon on earth alone, editing her book on illness and femininity in the mid-Victorian novel. Although Edith thought my job was silly, I loved it. The way I saw it, etiquette wasn't about what fork to use. It was about making other people feel good—with a handwritten thank-you note, a wonderful dessert, or maybe a white lie. This seemed simple on the face of it, but judging by the number of letters I received, common social situations tripped a lot of people up, and made them anxious. As an etiquette expert I gave them a road map: a way to navigate any interaction.

Unfortunately, finding a babysitter good enough for Stella was brutal. One applicant wanted to be picked up *and* dropped off. A second needed to schedule the babysitting "gig" around her shamanic therapy classes. A third said any house she worked in had to be completely free of artificial scent. When I met Blanka at the door, her hair was in two clumsy black plaits secured with elastics decorated with pink plastic bobbles, and her olive-skinned face was childishly round. She was fairly overweight, noticeable in Muswell Hill, with its yummy mummies in Pilates gear, and had heavy eyebrows that needed attention. She slowly lowered herself onto our slender-legged midcentury modern sofa.

I asked, "What do you like about working with kids?"

"I like taking care of kids," said Blanka.

"What do you like *about* that?" She smiled, and I wasn't sure if she'd understood the question. I decided to move on. "You have to keep everything separate when you serve her meals." I showed her Stella's compartmentalized melamine plates.

"Oh yes." She sounded matter-of-fact, not skeptical like the other babysitters.

Encouraged, I continued. "Also, you have to slice her fruit nicely, or she won't eat it. Apples, especially."

"Oh yes." Blanka nodded vigorously, like nobody in their right mind would expect a four-year-old to tackle an unsliced apple. I went through Stella's whole routine, and Blanka agreed with everything I said. Maybe it was because her English wasn't very good, but it was relaxing. I went up to Stella's room and coaxed her out to meet Blanka. As with all the interviewees, Stella marched straight over to Blanka and studied her. The other women had chirped out their names or inquired as to Stella's favorite color. Blanka just held Stella's gaze. Several seconds passed. Then, to my astonishment, Stella climbed onto the sofa and nestled up to Blanka's pillowy body. Our savior.

Now I gave up on sleep and crept into the kitchen. I stuffed a handful of pretzels into my mouth. I'd forgotten about that first meeting with Blanka, when she'd seemed so perfect for the job. Yet somehow things had changed so much that she had left without saying goodbye. That was one mystery I would never solve now. But maybe I could solve the mystery of how she died.

I grabbed my laptop and sat on the sofa. Perhaps she had a Facebook page, which might have more information about her death. But when I typed in "Blanka Hakobyan," there was no Facebook page. No Blanka Hakobyan on Twitter or Instagram. When I googled her name, I got no results. There was a faint twang in my abdomen, and I felt afraid. In years of trying to get pregnant, I'd miscarried three times. But I kept going, because if Stella had a sibling, it wouldn't matter so much that she didn't really have friends and, worse, didn't seem to care. A sibling, I hoped, would teach her how to get along with others.

I walked to the window, hoping a change of position would help. The whole back wall of the house was glass, showcasing our view over London, a sea of lights with the Shard on the horizon, the dull glow of the light-polluted sky. At night, things looked different than they did in the day, but I always felt like I was seeing things as they really were: the night truth. I was going to lose this baby, and Stella would always be alone.

I went into Stella's room and listened to the ebb and flow of her breath. Maybe it was my fault she didn't turn cartwheels on the beach, and I didn't deserve to have another child.

"Oh yes," Stella said, quite clearly, and I gave a start. But her breath was deep and regular: she was talking in her sleep. Blanka used to say, "Oh yes," in response to everything I asked her, always in exactly the same way, like a two-note birdcall. I shivered. It was an innocuous phrase, but still, it was uncanny how perfectly Stella captured Blanka's singsong tone.

3.

I compose my face, trying to appear calm, but not too calm. I must appear exactly as calm as a sane person would in this situation. I am sane, I remind myself. Still, it's hard to look sane when I'm forced to wear what amounts to pajamas. I sit up straight on the edge of the sofa, feet planted on the floor. Dr. Beaufort, my new therapist, has a round, earnest face, greying brown hair cut sensibly short, and a navy poncho that looks like it has dog hair on it. "Sorry about this old thing," she says. "I feel the cold. Do you? Snuggle up in the blanket, why don't you."

"I'm fine." A blanket isn't going to help me right now. On the wall is a painting of a woman standing in a river, facing away from the viewer. She looks like she's trying to hold her ground, but any minute a mighty current will sweep her away.

"Do you need the tissues?" Dr. Beaufort asks. "I moved them onto that side table there. I used to have them on the coffee table, but then a patient said they made her feel like I wanted her to cry. I don't want you to cry. That is, not unless you want to."

"OK?" I say. She's babbling. Maybe she's new to this job. Perhaps she got her qualification after her kids started school. To the right of her is a bookcase, which has heavy psychiatric diagnostic manuals, but also *Mind Over Mother* and *Good Moms Have Scary Thoughts*. Is she a mother who has had scary thoughts? On a side table at her elbow sits a misshapen vase of dried spear thistles. There are no family photos, but that ugly vase definitely looks like it was made by a child.

"Charlotte?" Dr. Beaufort has asked a question.

"Sorry?"

"Can you tell me why you're here?"

I stroke my throat. When I was seven, my mother took me to see a doctor about a persistent cough. Three doctors later, we learned it was thyroid cancer, and I endured surgery and radioactive iodine treatment that left my throat sore, my mouth tasting of dirty coins. Even though they'd cured me, I'd disliked doctors ever since.

"Why are you here?" Dr. Beaufort repeats gently. I stare at the bowl of marble eggs on her coffee table.

"My husband thinks I need a rest."

Dr. Beaufort nods. "What mother doesn't, right?"

I chuckle obligingly.

She studies me with her serious gaze. "The intake form says you're concerned about your daughter Stella."

A headache blooms on the right side of my forehead. Pete has filled her in already. She will likely report on our sessions to him. I probably gave permission on the form I signed when I was so distraught. I have to convince him of my sanity so he will take me seriously and help me save Stella. But if Dr. Beaufort is reporting to him, I need to get her on my side too.

I pick up a marble egg and weigh its coolness in my good hand. I want to roll it over my brow, to soothe its ache. But I must remain calm, polite, composed—while also making her believe me. I need to choose my words carefully, share the monstrous truth a little at a time. "Yes, I am worried about Stella," I say.

Dr. Beaufort nods. "It can be very hard when a new baby comes."

"Stella's not herself," I say. Literally, I think.

"And what about you?" she asks. "You just gave birth, and ten weeks early at that. Hormones can have a powerful effect on the brain, especially when coupled with stress. Have you noticed any change in yourself?" She looks at me, kindly, gently, seeming to take in every detail. I haven't eaten properly for months. Blood oozes from between my legs, and my stitches throb. Dr. Beaufort looks at me, as if she knows that becoming a mother sends your pain tolerance sky-high, and that isn't always a good thing.

She wears no makeup, and her complexion is reddened. She looks like she washes her face with soap and water and rushes out of the house, too busy for a glance in the mirror. On her finger is a Peppa Pig plaster. She is a mother. Maybe she will help me.

"You're right," I tell her. "I have been stressed, and the pregnancy and birth were difficult." Horrendous, in fact. "But I'm still the same person. Stella isn't." The cancer that killed Pete's dad began small, with an ache in his lower back. My childhood cancer started small, with a cough that wouldn't go away. Stella's transformation also began quietly. The first signs were subtle, so subtle, but something was taking up residence inside her, biding its time.

"I'm listening," says Dr. Beaufort, and I begin to talk.

THEN

4.

The day after the trip to the beach, I woke up feeling terrible. "I brought you some peppermint tea," Pete said, setting the cup by my bedside before he left for the office. "I'm sorry I have to leave you on your own with Stella."

I was nearly a week into my second trimester, but the morning sickness seemed to be getting worse. After Pete left, I stumbled to the bathroom and dry-heaved in the sink: nothing. I risked a glance in the mirror. I looked ghastly. I am the kind of redhead who appears washed-out unless I wear makeup, my eyebrows barely there, my lashes pale as a pig's. But because my face is such an indistinct canvas, I can draw on smoky eyes and mulberry lips and look va-va-voom. I didn't have the energy for that today, but I did my best to make myself look respectable.

Stella was sitting at the dining table, drawing a mighty fortress with swallowtail battlements. "Good morning, Mommy," she said. I longed to squeeze her tight and bury my face in her hair, but she'd always had an aversion to snuggling. I gazed at her instead. We'd agreed that if we gazed at each other for three seconds that would be our version of a hug. Stella gazed back at me. One Mississippi. Two Mississippi. On three, she looked away. "Is Blanka coming back?"

I stared at her. "Why are you asking, honey pie?"

"She promised she'd come back and see me," Stella said.

I frowned. When would Blanka have had the chance to make this promise? As far as I knew, she never even said goodbye to Stella.

I dolloped porridge into a bowl, careful to let it cool before I gave it to Stella. She was focused on her picture, her little face intent. Unlike mine, her features were distinct, with a straight nose, rosebud mouth, and big green eyes. I always thought her face like one you'd find in a seventeenth-century portrait, the face of a child reared to think that children should be like little adults. I could see her in a velvet dress with a lace collar, holding a spaniel on her lap. Not that she would ever permit such an outfit.

Could she have checked last night's search history on my laptop? She did know my password, and even though she was only eight, she knew her way around my computer better than I did.

"So *is* Blanka coming?" Stella asked.

"Blanka moved back home," I said.

"But England is her home. She's lived here since she was a teenager."

I decided to brazen it out. "She wanted a change."

After that, Stella barely touched her breakfast. Maybe she was hurt to learn that Blanka had moved abroad. I felt a pang for her, but I didn't regret my lie. Stella wasn't squeamish about death itself, as evidenced by the rotting gannet. But she could not handle dying: the tiniest loss was tragic. When slugs attacked his kale, Pete drowned them in beer traps, and Stella always wept when she found one. There was no way she could deal with Blanka dying, which was hard enough for adults to wrap their heads around.

After breakfast, as I was clearing away the dishes, I noticed a mark on the kitchen wall: a penciled cross, at about the height of my chest. It looked like someone had been planning to bang in a nail there—maybe to hang something from.

"Stella, did you do this?" I asked, pointing to the mark on the creamy paint.

She looked solemn. "The only thing you draw on is paper."

I wet a sponge and carefully removed the cross. I would ask Pete about it later. It felt like a reminder of an incomplete task, which was not his style. If something needed doing, Pete took care of it at the earliest opportunity. He'd already texted to say that, as promised the previous evening, he'd sent lilies and a note to Blanka's mother.

I stepped back to make sure I'd removed every trace of the mark: the wall was pristine. But instead of feeling satisfied, I had a nagging feeling of incompleteness, like I was the one who had abandoned a task halfway through.

Around five, Pete texted to say he'd be home for dinner for once. I wasn't in the mood to think about food, and he said he'd pick up a takeout pizza. I used to love cooking, layering flavor and texture. But when I prepared Stella's food, cooking felt like it stopped one stage short of what it should be, ingredients rather than an actual meal. Maybe that was why Blanka never accepted my invitation to partake. She brought her own food in old yogurt pots from home and left the microwave smelling of meat stew. Though for some reason, she never took a bite in front of me.

"Remember the wacky pizza night we used to host in San Francisco?" Pete said as he brought the pizza box to the table. "We were so determined to make a unique pie every time."

"We did that save-the-ocean pizza with squid ink and anchovies," I said.

"And what was that dessert one? Birthday-cake pizza: Cool Whip, sprinkles—"

I laughed. "Please stop talking before I throw up."

"Those pizzas do not sound delicious," Stella said. I'd made her preferred meal: pasta and sauce, served in separate bowls.

Pete squeezed my hand. "But they were delicious. Always." He traced a finger along our beautiful oak table. "We all had to squash round that tiny IKEA table in those days. Do you remember—"

"Stella, take a few more bites," I said. She wasn't eating.

"Sweetie," Pete said to me, and I knew what he was saying. We'd agreed we'd never pressure her to eat. Better for her to listen to her body's natural cues. But what if something was wrong? Juvenile thyroid cancer wasn't necessarily hereditary, but her face did look a little puffy. I leaned across the table to feel her neck.

"You're tickling me." She pulled away. "Daddy, can I be done?"

"You don't have to eat any more if you've had enough," Pete told her. "Go and read if you like."

"She's barely eaten today," I said. "Do you think she could be coming down with something?"

"She'll eat when she's hungry. And she looks fine to me."

Once she'd gone upstairs, I asked Pete if he had drawn the cross on the wall.

"Definitely not."

"That's weird," I said. "Stella says it wasn't her. Who was it then?"

"Could've been that guy who fixed the fridge," Pete said.

"Why would he draw a cross on the wall opposite?"

"Then I guess it *was* Stella."

"But Stella never lies to me," I said, although she also hadn't denied it.

After dinner, Pete volunteered to do her bath and bedtime. I wasn't sure. In recent months, he'd still been working when she went to bed. If he was home, he always went in to say good night, but he didn't know the details of her current routine. It was easier for me to do it. But maybe I needed to let him take care of her more. Time with Stella would remind Pete that her strangeness was part of what made her wonderful and that our job was to love her as she was. "Remember to run the water with the door closed," I told him. "She doesn't like the sound of the taps running."

While Pete ran the bath, I decided to call Blanka's mother, Irina. She answered the phone on the first ring.

"I wanted to let you know how sorry I am," I said. "We were very fond of Blanka." There was a long silence. "Hello?"

"This happens last week," Irina said. "Thursday."

"I'm so sorry," I said, stricken. "I only just found out. I'm so sorry."

"Nobody tells you."

I wasn't sure what point she was making. Was she saying it was OK I hadn't called earlier? Or maybe suggesting that nobody had

told me so I should stay out of it? Charlotte Says: In a conversa-
tional impasse, when you have no idea what to say next, simply repeat what the other person has said. At least they know you're
listening.

"Nobody told me," I said.

"I have met your daughter," Irina said, changing tack abruptly.
"Blanka brings her to visit sometimes."

"Oh?" That was odd. Why had Stella never told me about these
visits?

"You have beautiful daughter," Irina said.

I nervously began to say thank you, but Irina interrupted.

"She drown," she hissed.

The room turned murky. I couldn't see for a moment. "Stella?"
I whispered, but Irina had hung up. Then I heard Stella crying.

"Daddy! No! No! Please, Daddy, no!"

I rushed upstairs to Stella's bathroom. Pete was holding her,
naked, over the bath, her feet pedaling over the water. "Mommy!
Help!"

"What are you doing to her?" I burst out.

Pete had his arms locked around Stella. She had a look of panic,
like a horse in a burning barn. "What am I *doing* to her?" Pete
placed Stella back on the floor. "Seriously?"

"She doesn't like it when you hold her like that," I said, heart
banging in my chest. Pete had never actually experienced freak-out
mode. So far, it had only happened when I was alone with her,
which was most of the time because I did the bulk of the childcare.
He thought freak-out mode was essentially a tantrum. But it was so
much more than that. She was deathly pale: a warning sign.

"Stella, you can skip the bath," I said.

Pete rolled his eyes. "She needs discipline. We can't just give her whatever she wants. We need to stand firm—"

"Here, baby." I wrapped Stella in a towel.

"You interrupted me," Pete said.

"Because you weren't listening to me," I murmured, keeping my tone gentle in Stella's presence. "She doesn't want a bath."

I knew it was irrational, but Irina's words were still ringing in my ears. Pete sighed and left us to it. I heard the thud of the front door. He was heading out for a bike ride, which he sometimes did at night to unwind. Stella agreed to stand on the bathmat and submit to a soapy washcloth. I dimmed the bathroom light, and that seemed to help. I touched her as gently as I could. Her skin was as delicate as the membrane inside an eggshell, as if she lacked an essential protective layer.

"Are you angry with me?" she said.

"Never," I said. "Never, my darling."

I was proud of the fact that I'd never once lost my temper with Stella, even during freak-out mode. I never wanted Stella to feel afraid of me, as I'd been afraid of my mother, whose rages came out of nowhere. When I was seven, I complained about dinner—fish fingers with margarine—and Edith threw a bag of flour at my head. The bag burst, and my eyes were irritated for days. When I was nine and said I was too tired to wipe the counters, Edith pushed me outside and locked the door. I stood in the snow for twenty minutes without shoes.

Childcare and housework seemed to be what made Edith angry. My existence, basically. My father, who had been her Victorian literature professor, pushed for a child, then died of a heart attack before Edith even gave birth. All she had wanted was to finish her PhD thesis and get on the professor track, but now she had to deal with a newborn alone.

Sometimes after she lost her temper, she went to an academic conference or to teach a course for a couple of weeks, and Maureen, our weekly cleaner, watched *Neighbours* with me after school and slept over. She was a doughy woman with dyed blond hair. She lived in a run-down neighborhood and had brought up her three kids alone. But she seemed to pity me, mixing my Ribena extra sweet and calling me "duck." When I thanked Maureen for making my supper or ironing my school uniform, she said, "You're welcome, duck." Edith didn't believe in saying, "You're welcome," in response to being thanked. She said it was unnecessary. Edith also never apologized: I assumed she believed that was unnecessary too.

From the minute Stella was born, I knew that I would be nothing like Edith as a mother. When I brought her home from the hospital, I lay in bed with her and inhaled her glorious smell. I tallied the sacrifices I'd make: a limb, my eyes, my whole body. I imagined how, to save her life, I'd gladly fling myself in front of a train. I made a promise to myself that night: I would sacrifice anything for her.

Now I wrapped Stella in a thick, warm towel and then got her into her soft flannel pajamas. I tucked her into bed with a book about the history of fortification. When it was time to turn out the light, we did our special stare. This time, she didn't look away too soon. Other parents kissed their children good night or even cuddled them until they fell asleep. I told myself this solemn gaze was more intimate.

I took my laptop, intending to do something useful, but I was so tired I slumped on the sofa. "She drown." Irina's warning filled me with dread. Stella had a swimming lesson in a few days—I'd had to fork out for private classes because the noise of the group class had been too much—should I cancel it? No, that was absurd. Irina didn't have the power to hurt Stella.

But why hadn't Stella told me that she'd visited Blanka's house? Did she know why Irina seemed to have such animosity for me? Surely, she was simply deranged by grief, and who wouldn't be? The problem with that theory was that Irina didn't seem deranged. She seemed calm and matter-of-fact. Maybe she was simply in shock— or maybe she had a good reason for hating me after all. Blanka could have said I didn't pay her enough. I'd paid her the going rate for babysitters in North London. It was true that I didn't pay her what the professional babysitters charged, the ones advertising on childcare apps. But they wouldn't have put Stella to bed in her day clothes with chocolate from my secret stash smeared all over her face. And I didn't fire Blanka even for that. She was the one who left.

"I cannot come anymore."

I texted her and called her a few times after that, but because she didn't reply, it was obvious she had made up her mind. I decided I would give up my job instead. We didn't need the money, and part of me thought that if I'd lost three pregnancies while working, maybe not working would do the trick. Edith had mocked Victorian medical thinking that if women exerted themselves intellectually, it diverted the blood supply from their reproductive organs to the brain. It amused me to think that in giving up work to focus on my pregnancy, I was subscribing to the doctrine she had criticized.

The previous week had been busy, as I tied up loose ends at work and dashed off a farewell "Charlotte Says." Still, I should have gone round to see Blanka. I shouldn't have let her end our relationship with her cryptic text. I should have pushed until she revealed the reason she quit so abruptly.

Now I wondered if she had wanted to discuss it with me at our final parting. As always, she refused my offer of a snack or drink, but took her time putting on her large grey hoodie and locating her bag. I didn't bother making chitchat, because I'd tried in the past, and she barely replied.

I walked her to the door and told her to have a good weekend. Then she just stood there. This wasn't the first time I'd endured this awkward pause. It was almost like she expected something from me, but I had no idea what.

Then she trudged down our front steps, turning to wave at the gate. She had her own special way of doing it, always the same for hello and goodbye, her palm rotating in a circle, as if there were an invisible pane between us and she was wiping it clean.

5.

The day after my conversation with Irina, I went to the fanciest boutique in Muswell Hill and sifted through gift options while Stella read in the corner of the shop. I settled on an expensive blanket of soft grey recycled wool. On second thoughts, I put it back and bought the larger size.

I dropped Stella off with my friend Cherie, another mom from Stella's primary school. Her nine-year-old, Zach, was in the year above Stella, though he often refused to go to school. He was an expert on the chemistry of slime but needed a thirteen-point checklist to brush his teeth. When Cherie and I hung out, we didn't expect the kids to do normal kid things. Stella usually read some hefty tome while Zach stirred non-Newtonian fluids in various mixing bowls.

Then I walked to Blanka and Irina's place. There was an ache in my low belly that I tried to ignore. It was hunger, I told myself. Or nerves.

They occupied the bottom half of a terraced house. The North

Circular roared two streets over. A half-dead purple-leaf plum tree strewed dark leaves outside their front window.

I gave a start. A woman sat inside, so colorless and still that I hadn't immediately spotted her. She wore a grey cardigan, and her greying hair was pulled back in a bun. She sat in a big armchair, staring at nothing.

I raised a hand, but she didn't react. Still, I was almost certain she'd seen me, and I had no choice but to walk up the front path. I ventured a tentative wave. She rose and stared at me through the glass.

Then she tottered off, and I waited. Nothing. I was just deciding that she couldn't face visitors when the door opened. She had Blanka's olive skin and round cheeks. Her face was weathered, her gaze startling in its frank misery. I wanted to turn and run away. But I couldn't stand the thought that I'd done something wrong without even realizing it. If an apology was needed, I was determined to deliver one.

"I'm Charlotte, Stella's mother? I came to say how sorry I am and . . ."

Irina stared at me, and I thought she was going to berate me for daring to show my face. She'd ended our phone conversation on such a hostile note.

But she just opened the front door wide, and waited.

My insides clenched tight. If I was going to lose this pregnancy too, I didn't want to do it in a stranger's house. But I could see that the pale garment I'd taken for a skirt was actually a nightgown, and the cardigan over it was wrongly buttoned up. She was a wreck: I couldn't refuse her.

Inside, the squat, dark furniture was too big for the tiny front room. Every surface was covered with an embroidered cloth or crocheted doily, and every shelf was laden with painted figurines, dolls and carved animals. I proffered the blanket, tied with a grey silk ribbon. Its luxe minimalism was out of place here, and instead it looked drab and utilitarian. Irina nodded but didn't take it.

A black-and-white photo of Blanka in a silver frame stood atop a bureau. She looked about eighteen. She was smiling weakly. The photo made me feel sad. Someone should have told her the thing to do in photos is flash your teeth, *Strictly Come Dancing*–style. That way you look happy and no one can tell the difference.

Irina cleared a mess of wool and needles off the sofa. "I make tea." She trudged off. I looked around for somewhere to put the blanket. An icon hung on the wall above the sofa: a saint with a disappointed face. My body upgraded the bad feeling in my abdomen from an ache into pain, and I sank onto the sofa, still clutching the blanket. I examined the pain's nature and location, trying to discern if it was the same as the pain that heralded my three previous miscarriages. My most recent had been at fifteen weeks. Today, I was fourteen weeks and five days pregnant.

"You like jam?" Irina called from the kitchen.

"Um, whatever you're having," I called back. I'd assumed that she'd tell me what I'd done and I'd apologize profusely, and then I'd leave, my duty fulfilled. Her hospitality unsettled me. Perhaps that was her intention. She'd keep me here until I lost this pregnancy all over her velour sofa. Sweat broke out on my chest.

Or perhaps she expected me to share fond recollections of Blanka. I searched my memory desperately.

Irina returned with a clinking tray: gold-rimmed teacups, a

floral teapot, a dish of jam. She sat down very close to me, and I realized I had the blanket pressed to my midsection. She held out a plate of small, flaky pastries. "Blanka's favorite."

I let her take the blanket and put a pastry on my plate. "Yum," I said, though I couldn't eat a bite right now. I crossed my legs and squeezed my thighs together, hoping nothing was going to gush out. The house smelled thickly of frying oil and some kind of spice like cinnamon. Irina studied me. I realized I had one hand on my belly, the back of the other hand under my nose.

"Sick?" she said gently. I nodded, and she said, "With Blanka, I have sickness all day too."

I was nonplussed. I wasn't showing. Irina saw the surprise on my face. "Here, I am nurse at hospice. But in my own country, I am midwife. I know pregnant woman smells everything." She wrinkled her nose. "Like dog." Then she touched my knee. "But bad smells are good. This means baby is healthy." She compressed her lips in a way that was almost a smile.

The pain in my belly eased: She didn't hate me. I hadn't done anything awful to Blanka. And she was right: smell sensitivity was a pregnancy symptom. I felt a surge of hope, and my eyes filled.

"I'm sorry," I said. "I'm really very sorry." My voice broke.

My tears seemed to satisfy Irina, and she nodded. "You do not have to be sorry. I am sorry for not telling you the day Blanka dies. But for three days, I cannot speak to one single person."

Of course. *Grief* was what had made her so bitter when we'd spoken on the phone. She had lost her only child: the worst had happened. What a narcissist I'd been to think her misery had anything to do with me.

But if she hadn't cursed Stella, what had she meant? "She drown." Meaning dawned on me. "Blanka drown—I mean, drowned?" I said, as gently as I could.

Irina inclined her head in the smallest of nods. "We run from our home to Armenia. There, we are refugees. Many times, we have only bucket for washing. So after we come here, Blanka loves hot bath."

"It happened in a bath?" I'd never even seen Blanka allow herself a glass of water. It was a surprise to learn that same woman loved to indulge in long soaks. And I'd never heard of anyone drowning in the bath.

Irina stood up. "I show you."

Show me what? Though my stomach had mostly stopped hurting, I still felt nauseated. But she took my arm, and her grip was surprisingly strong. I realized she was much younger than I'd thought, perhaps not even sixty. She drew me through the kitchen and into a meagre back garden—mostly concrete, a plastic table. She gestured me towards a narrow gate in the fence between their garden and that of the neighbors. I hesitated.

"Neighbors do not mind. They are gone," said Irina briskly. The neighbors had a tasteful, low-maintenance garden with perky succulents in beds of bark chips. Irina gestured towards a plastic hot tub with the cover off.

I gasped. "In there?"

Irina stood by the tub. "Last week, Blanka is guarding their house when neighbors go on holiday. Blanka decide to go in water. But she stays too long, and I do not know this but she has sickness.

38

Here." She placed her hand over her heart. She paused. "She pass out and goes under."

An undiagnosed heart condition. Poor Blanka. That would explain her lethargy. Sometimes she huffed when she climbed stairs; I'd thought it was her weight that made her breathless. I felt awful. To think I'd felt impatient with all her huffing, had even wondered why she didn't exercise.

Irina climbed the two steps that led up to the hot tub and gestured for me to join her. I was uneasy. Why did she want me to look inside? Surely you would want to avoid the place where your child died. But I had no experience of such grief. Maybe this felt like a way to honor her daughter. My legs felt shaky as I climbed the steps and looked over the edge. The neighbors had not refilled the tub, and there was nothing to see but its bland white plastic interior, smelling faintly of chlorine.

A life had been cut short here, and there was nothing to show for it. There should be some kind of marker of what had happened. Blanka had sat on the ledge that ran around the inside, and all she'd wanted was the small pleasure of a hot soak. Then: a freak accident, a random tragedy. You couldn't make sense of it. It hadn't happened for a reason.

We went back into Irina's house, and she showed me a grape-leaf tin on the mantelpiece. "This is Blanka," she said.

It took me a second to realize what she meant. "Her ashes?" I couldn't think of anything to say in response. "Lovely" wasn't going to cut it. It felt impossible that a living, feeling person—her only daughter—could be reduced to fit inside a grape-leaf tin. There was nothing I could say that would make the situation any better, but I was clearly expected to say something. Then I remembered my mirroring technique. "This is Blanka," I repeated solemnly.

My phone pinged: Everything OK? I'd told Cherie I'd only be gone an hour. I explained that I had to leave, and Irina insisted on putting the remaining pastries into a cookie tin decorated with troika-pulling horses. She handed it to me. "Thank you for coming. These are Blanka's favorite. For your little one."

"Thank you," I said, moved. I had my daughter and another child inside me. I had riches beyond compare. But still she wanted to give me a gift.

Now she was studying me. "Blanka takes good care of your daughter."

I stared at her. Had grief unbalanced her, so she'd temporarily forgotten Blanka was dead? Then I realized that of course, she meant Blanka *took* good care. Irina was more comfortable using the present tense, as if everything that had happened was still happening and would continue to happen.

"Yes, she took good care," I said, even though it wasn't true. Blanka became sloppy in the last few weeks: dirty dishes on the table, uncapped markers on the floor. But there was no need for Irina to know this. Let her think Blanka had been a veritable Mary Poppins.

On impulse, I said, "May I ask why she stopped babysitting Stella? She didn't give me a reason."

Irina shrugged. "She love Stella."

"Yes, Stella loves—loved her," I agreed. "So why did she leave?"

Irina threw her hands up as if to say, "Who knows?" There was something ancient and resigned about it, as if she included all of human suffering in the gesture.

But there must have been some impetus for Blanka to give up her job. "Do you think she wanted more?" I asked. "More of a career?" This was hard to imagine, but it was the best explanation for her departure.

"A career?" Irina looked doubtful.

"Maybe not. Anyway, I'm so sorry." It was time to leave. I gave Irina a suitably sad smile. I *did* feel sad, of course I did, but I could let go of my guilt. I'd never know her reason, but Blanka didn't leave because of anything I did.

But Irina wasn't finished. "My husband wanted to call her Roza or Anna, but she is such a beautiful baby, she deserves special name. Such a good girl when child," she said. "I used to punish her only with cross. I tell her, 'Hold your nose to cross until I say.' Blanka is such a good girl. Always she stay there until I say."

"A cross?" I was startled. That cross on the wall at home was about the height of Stella's nose. Obviously, Stella knew about this childhood punishment of Blanka's, and that was why she'd put it there. But why wouldn't she admit it? She'd happily confessed after drawing on the wall in the past. And if the cross was a punishment, who was it for?

6.

When I got to Cherie's, Zach was playing with a lump of putty-colored gunk in a large metal bowl. I didn't bother greeting him, because he never responded. Stella sat at the other end of the dining table, glued to *Birdflight as the Basis of Aviation*.

Cherie made coffee for herself and tea for me and carried the mugs into her breakfast nook, where the kids couldn't hear us talk if we spoke in low voices. We both agreed that we were dreading tomorrow, the first day of school. I told Cherie about yesterday's dead-bird incident, and she laughed and then said, "Neurotypicals can't understand kids like ours."

I burned my tongue on the tea. "Kids like ours?" Stella had her obsessions, but unlike Zach, she paid attention to the people around her. Zach never met anyone's gaze, but Stella looked you straight in the eye.

Cherie placed a hand on mine. "Listen, I've been mulling over this a lot, and I think you should get Stella tested. I dreaded it too, but when I confirmed that Zach's autistic, it was actually a huge relief because then I had a way forward. And you're lucky—you've got the money to go private. You don't have to worry about NHS waiting lists."

"Stella *is* different," I agreed. "But that's not a reason to take her to a doctor."

Cherie leaned closer. She was skinny and energetic, always dressed in exercise gear, as if parenting were one long triathlon. Usually she was like a coach, always there to say, "Great job!" and "Keep it up!" whatever I did. But not today. "Charlotte, this is coming from a place of love, but Stella has so many of the signs. The sensory processing issues. The difficulty socializing. The hyperlexia."

"Hyper what?"

"The way she won't stop reading. And she started talking late, didn't she?" Cherie said, sitting back as if to rest her case.

Cherie was right that Stella had been a late talker, her first words at seventeen months. She hated the stringy bits on bananas, and her first words were "I don't want yucky stuff on my banana."

I felt a pressure building inside my chest. I hated it when other people thought they knew Stella better than I did. "I know that speech delay is a sign of autism. I've researched this. Stella does have some of the signs—who doesn't? But she doesn't have—"

"But girls are so good at masking," Cherie said. Her breath hit me: coffee and watermelon gum. I pressed my hand under my nose. She saw, and her face darkened.

"I'm sorry, Cherie, I've got a very sensitive sense of smell right now," I said. It wouldn't help to explain that everyone smelled awful to me right now except Stella and Pete.

Cherie opened her mouth, but Stella rushed into the breakfast nook. "Mommy, get it off. Get it off now! It's disgusting!" She held up a hank of hair, matted with gunk. She was trembling, her face blanched. My muscles turned rigid.

"Where are the scissors, please?" I asked Cherie, but she just stepped in front of Zach, like he was the one who'd been slimed.

"I think you should do nothing and let her have her meltdown."

"No way." I couldn't handle freak-out mode right now.

"Are you OK, honey?" Cherie asked Zach, but he was focused on drawing out his slime into long, stretchy strands. Nobody seemed to think he had anything to apologize for. I remembered that Cherie kept her scissors in her junk drawer. I told her we had to go, then grabbed them and rushed out of the house with a trembling Stella in tow. But Cherie rushed after us and seized my arm as I was halfway down the front path.

"Charlotte," she panted. "Those scissors are part of our Calming Clipper kit. We need them. Come back inside and let her scream. That's how kids like ours release tension."

"I just told you: Stella isn't like Zach!" I snapped. "She's absolutely nothing like Zach."

At that, Cherie's eyes bulged and she got right in my face, so close I could see the bleached down on her upper lip. I put out my hand to make her back off. Then she was sitting on her front path with a gasp that was more surprise than pain. We stared at each other: What just happened?

But the countdown to freak-out mode hadn't stopped. I rushed

Stella to the car. I was so upset that it was hard to keep my hands steady when I snipped off the offending clump of hair. I'd have to drop off the scissors later. At least Stella didn't fuss. She was now completely calm. "Why did you push Zach's mommy?"

"I didn't push her. I put out my hand to stop her from intruding in my personal space," I said. My chest felt tight. I'd only wanted to make Cherie move away, but *had* I pushed her?

At home, Stella went up to her room, and I gnawed on a rice cake over the sink. I couldn't lose Cherie as a friend. We texted each other all the time, swapping advice about the kids, mocking the WhatsApp thread for the FOMHS, or Friends of Muswell Hill Primary School, in which type-A creative professionals—film directors and West End set designers—competitively volunteered.

Cherie was the only mom I knew well enough to have a running joke with. When Cherie was stressed about Zach, Cherie's husband, Benjamin, had once said, "You need to take some time for yourself—get your hair done and get your eyebrows shaped." Ever since then, when one of us felt overwhelmed, the other would humorously suggest, "Maybe you need a visit to the brow specialist." A text wasn't going to cut it now. I'd have to apologize properly, even if it *was* an accident.

Maybe I should try to be more active in FOMHS. It could help Stella socially if I knew the other kids' parents better. In fact, the first meeting of the school year was this coming Sunday afternoon—pizza and prosecco at Emmy's house. Emmy would, I hoped, be over the bird incident.

Meanwhile, tomorrow was the first day of school. It was a Thursday at least, so the school calendar this year meant Stella didn't have to struggle through a full week right off the bat. But I couldn't let her start the term with a weird haircut. I went up to her room. "Let's even out your hair, darling."

To my surprise, she let me brush it out and trim it. But I didn't feel pleased that for once she was letting me touch her. I felt unsettled. Something about her smelled slightly off. It was a subtle difference, like a different laundry soap had been used to wash her clothes, even though I'd washed them myself. She smelled like someone else's child.

NOW

7.

Y ou sound almost disappointed that Stella didn't go into freak-out mode," says Dr. Beaufort.

I'm dumbfounded. "Freak-out mode," I say carefully, "feels like having a cattle prod applied directly to your brain stem."

She winces. "What strikes me about your story—"

"It's not a story, it's the truth." I've got a bitter taste in my mouth from the turmeric-ginger-carrot juice I forced myself to chug for breakfast, brought on a tray to my room. There was a vegan chickpea frittata too, which I took a photo of before I wrapped it in toilet paper and hid it in the bathroom bin. For all I knew, they kept tabs on what I ate. I sent Pete the pic with a text: **Slept well and had yummy frittata and juice.** Pete texted back: **Girls doing great.** I asked if I could FaceTime with Stella. No reply, and now I try not to panic. Pete loves her. I must trust that he can keep her safe. My job is to get out of here, which means winning over Dr. Beaufort. I swallow down the bitter taste. "I apologize for interrupting. Please continue."

"When *you* got upset—at your friend Cherie—Stella recovered. She no longer had to go into freak-out mode. You got the emotional release that you both needed."

This woman has got it all wrong. "In freak-out mode, it's Stella's emotions that boil over, not mine," I explain.

Dr. Beaufort studies me. "I notice that you scratch your arms a lot. What would happen if you sat with the urge to scratch? What if you just let yourself feel the discomfort?"

That painting on the wall of the woman in the river catches my eye, and I see that she's not about to get swept away by the current. She's steeling herself to plunge in and swim. It's so easy to miss the truth, unless you study a situation closely, which Dr. Beaufort clearly isn't. "You think I caused freak-out mode?" I ask. "Because I'm so tightly wound? You know, they used to blame autism on the mothers. Schizophrenia too. Not that Stella is either of those."

Dr. Beaufort nods. "What about your mother? We haven't really talked about her."

I snort. "You want me to talk about how my mother shaped me. But she didn't. We were very different people."

"You didn't have anything in common?"

"We used to look for birds." I hadn't thought about this in years. Until I was thirteen, my mother took me on a birdwatching trip a couple of times a year. We visited woodlands, heaths, and marshes—she never considered I might like to be near a beach or playground. In truth, I loved the ritual of rising before dawn and assembling our kit: binoculars, notebooks, and thermoses. I loved driving past dark farms on our way to the birding spot, the only ones awake.

Edith always grew calmer after a few hours in the woods. If I fumbled my binoculars or misidentified a bird, she didn't mind. I still tried my best, desperate to please her. Once, I caught the drill of the rare lesser spotted woodpecker, and Edith raised a finger to her lips and crept to the source of the sound. Suddenly, there it was, right in front of us, perched in a hollow tree. I was disappointed. Apart from its crimson crown, it was just a stumpy brown bird, no bigger than a box of matches. But then I realized that Edith was trembling a little, mouth open in wonder, and I dared to slip my fingers into hers.

The year I turned thirteen, on a trip to the Forest of Dean, I woke up with a stomachache. I trailed behind Edith as she crept through the early morning woods, squinting through her binoculars. The ache tugged at my lower belly, and when my breasts started hurting too, I got an idea of what was happening to me. I looked at Edith's narrow back and wished I could ask questions. When did your period start and how did you know it was starting?

But I didn't say anything, because Edith was very particular about using the "right" words. These weren't the ones she'd grown up with, in a Lancashire mining village. Once she made it to Oxford on a scholarship, she smoothed out her Northern vowels and never again referred to the evening meal as tea. I had no idea what she would call a period, and didn't want her to think me déclassé.

Suddenly, Edith rounded on me and whispered, "Stop trampling like that. You're frightening every bird away."

"I don't feel well."

Edith rarely looked me in the eye, her gaze traveling over my shoulder as if expecting somebody more interesting to show up. She sighed. "What's the matter?"

I always tried to stay calm around my mother, for fear of triggering her temper. But I had an irritable feeling, like tiny legs walking on my skin, and this made it impossible to think straight. "I've had enough. This is boring."

Edith had my fair complexion, flushing easily. "Then go back to the cottage."

I shivered. "By myself?"

"Go on. Shoo!" she hissed, flapping her hand at me, and I ran.

It was several miles by road back to the cottage, and I took a wrong turn and made the way longer. When I finally got back and went to the toilet, my knickers were bloody. I hid them in my suitcase, found a new pair. When she got back, Edith acted as if nothing had happened, but I couldn't bring myself to tell her about my period. Maybe she wouldn't have been annoyed, but she'd be unbearably brisk. So I improvised pads out of toilet paper until we got back to Oxford and I could help myself to her stash of sanitary towels under the sink.

The next month, my period pain was so bad I stayed home from school. By then, Maureen only came in one day a week, but it happened to be her day. She found me curled on my bed, clutching my stomach. "Is it your monthlies?" she asked, nodding sympathetically. She brought me a glass of water and a wet flannel and wiped my face. Then she opened the window and told me to stick my head outside, even though it was raining. I filled my lungs with fresh air, and I felt a little better. But I still had a heaviness inside, because if that was all it took to help, why couldn't my mother do it?

"My mother and I really had nothing in common," I tell Dr. Beaufort now, folding my arms over my chest.

She blinks. "Maybe we'll come back to her later. Tell me, did Stella have these 'freak-out' episodes with Blanka?"

"She had no reason. Blanka gave Stella everything she wanted," I tell her. But I give Stella everything she wants too. Is it possible that being with me—her own mother—makes Stella so anxious she simply has to erupt? I rake my nails over my skin.

Dr. Beaufort hands me a bottle from a side table: lotion. "For your arms. Your mother's temper terrified you and you vowed not to subject Stella to the same treatment. But it can also be frightening when an adult *never* loses their temper. A child, especially a sensitive one, always knows when there's anger and grief simmering beneath the surface."

"This is all backwards," I say. I must have broken my skin when I scratched, because the lotion stings. "Let me tell you about the last time Stella went into freak-out mode, and you'll see there's *no way* any parent could want that."

But now that I think about it, the last time it happened, it brought us all closer together.

8.

The day I pushed Cherie, Pete didn't come home until after I was in bed. I didn't get a chance to tell him about it until the following morning. It was the first day of school, so I delivered breakfast to Stella's room bright and early. While she was getting ready, I found Pete in our bathroom, shaving, and gave him the bare outline of what happened. He wiped the foam off his face. "It's not like you attacked her. Just explain it was an accident."

"It's going to take more than that," I said. "Maybe I'll get her some flowers."

"This is the last thing you need when you're feeling so unwell." Pete dried his face and moved towards me. He knew instinctively when to stop problem-solving and just give me a hug. But the urge to throw up came on suddenly, and I pushed him aside and dropped to my knees in front of the toilet.

Pete rubbed my back as I retched. "It sucks that you're the one who has to go through this. I wish I could take the pregnancy. Give you a break."

"Like a seahorse," I murmured. The female puts her eggs in the male's pouch. The three of us had seen an exhibit at the London Aquarium when Stella was four, just after we'd moved back to the UK.

"That was a good day, wasn't it?" Pete said. Stella melted down because the aquarium was too crowded, but outside, we bought fries and ate them as we walked along the Thames, making plans for when parenting got easier. We'd heard that between five and ten were the golden years.

I couldn't throw up. I flopped back against the tub, and Pete said, "Go back to bed. I'll take Stella to school." He paused. "You need to let me do more, when I'm around."

I took his hand. "Will you check in with Mr. McNaughton? Make sure he's ready for her." I'd written Stella's teacher several panicked emails over the summer, explaining that school was challenging for her. In year two, Stella showed kids how to fashion an ultrafast paper airplane called "the Hammer," and one of them hit the teacher in the eye. In year three, Stella had told the other kids that when slugs mated, the male's penis sometimes got stuck, and the female consumed it because it was high in protein. After that, the kids had follow-up questions for the teacher, and the teacher had a talk with me about how very bright children could turn to manipulation if they were bored.

I asked the teachers in years two and three to provide extra work for Stella, but they said they had to focus on the less-high-achieving students. Fair enough. Stella had to be content with reading furiously during breaks and when she got home. She would have been happier at home, but she needed social skills as well as academic ones, so she went to school with other eight-year-olds, normal kids who weren't sure if the Earth circled the sun or the other way around.

I went back to bed, but I was too worried to sleep. I wished I could at least make Stella look like the other girls, but with her issues, it was impossible. By pickup time, her hair looked like a troll doll's, and her nonchafing elastic-waist trousers were slipping down her narrow waist. Her school polo shirt was three sizes too big (she hated anything that clung around her neck). I had to pick my battles, and the battle I had to win was getting her to school. If she insisted on looking like an orphan from *Annie*, there was nothing I could do about it.

Finally, I dragged myself out of bed and, hand under my nose, went to another Muswell Hill boutique and bought a decorative crystal diffuser and some Diptyque Fleur D'Oranger room fragrance, an impersonal gift, but I didn't care. I sat on a bench to write a proper apology note. But then I remembered how Cherie had told me to let Stella go into freak-out mode to "release tension," like she knew what Stella needed better than me. In the end, I just scrawled, *Sorry about yesterday.* That would have to cover everything. I left the gold gift bag and card on her doorstep, along with her special scissors, and scuttled away.

I thought I might get a quick text from Cherie before school pickup, but nothing. The year five classroom had a different entrance, so I didn't have a chance to run into her and confirm she'd received the gift. Then, to my surprise, Stella emerged from the classroom talking to Lulu. That was a change. Even more surprising, Mr. Mc-Naughton gave me a covert thumbs-up. I wanted to debrief with him, but Stella tugged on my hand, eager to get moving.

Around six, Pete surprised us by coming home early again. "Look what I got for Stella." He grinned and held up a child-sized boogie board designed to look like a blue fish with yellow stripes. "What's a way to get rid of fear of the sea and for Stella and I to spend time together?"

"It's a nice idea," I said. "But Stella can barely swim."

Pete looked crushed, and I felt bad. Pete's dad had taken him backpacking in the wilderness from the age of six. His vision of fatherhood included lots of outdoor activity, and he was stuck with a child who couldn't stand the feel of grass under her bare feet.

Pete's phone dinged. "Sorry, baby," he said. Nathan, the needy CEO, bombarded him with Slack messages. He'd said Pete didn't have to answer them instantly, but it was easier to deal with them as they came in; otherwise Nathan spiraled. Pete tapped out a response and sighed. "I have to run back into work later," he said. "I thought this boogie board would be a nice surprise."

"I'm sorry. Just—one step at a time, OK? She had a good day at school."

"That's great news." But Pete's gaze went to the pale patch on the floor he'd made when cleaning up after Stella's birthday party. I could have told him not to use bleach on the old wood, but he didn't stop to consult me.

With a start I realized that Stella was standing in the kitchen doorway, wearing one of Pete's white button-down shirts, with only two buttons done up. How long had she been there? "Hey, Stella Bella," Pete said. "Congratulations on getting through your first day of year four. Did you miss me? Is that why you're wearing my shirt?"

"It's my science outfit," Stella said. She began pushing a chair to the freezer, legs scraping the floor. "I need my bird."

"Um, sweetheart? I might have thrown it away," said Pete. Stella froze. I glared at Pete, and he muttered, "I thought she'd forget about it."

The color drained from Stella's face. She looked small and helpless suddenly, swallowed up by Pete's shirt. "But it was *my* bird. I found it." She turned to me. "Mommy, could you please get it out of the bin?" I jumped up, but Pete laid a hand on my arm.

"It's in the green bin outside," he said.

"I can get it back then," I twittered. I went to the sink for my rubber gloves.

"It's under two days' worth of kitchen compost now. Leave it."

I tried to take a deep breath, but felt like my lungs wouldn't inflate. Pete had no idea what he was in for. I knelt down to get my rubber gloves from their hook. "Stella, stay calm, I'll get your bird," I panted.

"Sweetheart," Pete said. I turned around. He was holding the gloves: I must have left them beside the sink. "This has got to stop." He balled the gloves up and stuffed them in his pocket.

Stella began to scream.

Pete had once suggested I try a mantra on Stella: "Screaming doesn't get you what you want." That was the time she screamed so hard I took her to the emergency room. I'd seen other kids have tantrums: they jumped up and down, emitted high shrieks, then melted themselves onto the floor. Stella wrung her hands and keened like she was a mother whose only child had just been blown to bits.

Inside thirty seconds, I felt I'd do anything to make her stop. I'd comb the beach for another dead bird. I'd do it right now.

Pete said something, possibly, "Screaming doesn't get what you want." But her screaming was so loud I couldn't hear. I stood on tiptoe and spoke directly into his ear: "She's going to make herself ill. She's going to damage her vocal cords. Give me the gloves. I'm going outside to the bin."

Pete backed away from me. I had no chance of getting the gloves off him if he didn't want me to have them. I grabbed my phone and started googling to see if I could get a dead bird online, but it was illegal to sell wild birds in the UK. I could drive to the beach, though. If necessary, I would catch a bird and wring its neck with my bare hands.

Pete kept repeating the mantra. When I tried the mantra, I maxed out around thirty or forty times. I swear Pete only got to about fifteen before he was on his knees, crooning her name and trying to take her in his arms. "Stella, honey, it's OK, baby, it's OK."

Stella screamed louder and flailed her arms about.

I began to shake, and Stella shook too, her eyes black hollows, mouth twisted out of shape. Her grief seemed existential and entirely justified. She knew the truth: we're all trapped in our own heads, incapable of communicating, alone.

Pete gave up trying to hug Stella and started to pace. It had taken me so long to accept that Stella did not like to be physically comforted. I told myself that it was merely a personal preference, like disliking raw tomatoes. It didn't mean anything. But whenever she began screaming, I was afraid this said something deeper about her. If a child didn't like to be nuzzled, did that mean she didn't like being loved? If she didn't want to nestle in my arms, did that mean she wasn't capable of giving love? Maybe she had inherited that gene from my mother.

Stella was now crouched on the floor, rocking, and I sank to the floor too. I could bear it if Stella didn't love me. But I couldn't bear what it meant for her. She had something essential missing. She'd always be alone, never have—

"Shut up!" Pete yelled. "You shut up right now!" He bent down and grabbed Stella's shoulders. Her little arm flew up and whacked him in the face, knocking his glasses to the floor. He snatched them up: one of the lenses was shattered. "I don't have a spare pair. How am I supposed to go back to work tonight? Fuck. Fuck!" He punched the fridge so that a carelessly sealed bag of muesli fell off the top and spilled all over the floor. Then he stormed out of the room, and the front door slammed.

Stella took great, ragged breaths. She wasn't screaming anymore, at least. I was having trouble catching my breath too. I was shocked that Pete had lost his temper like that. He almost never lost control. I ached to cradle Stella in my arms, but all I could offer was some pretzels, which she refused. She let me dab her swollen eyes with a cool washcloth.

Now that she wasn't screaming, I felt shaky, as if I'd had the flu for a week. I started to make some jacket potatoes with cheese for dinner. The storm had retreated as suddenly as it came. Stella now seemed perfectly fine. Pete texted, I feel awful. Walking about trying to get my head together. You guys OK?

Much better, I type, feeling sorry for him. Hope you can see OK with only one lens.

When the potatoes were ready, she asked if she could eat in her room, and when I checked on her, she was forking up mouthfuls of food. She didn't say anything more about her bird.

After Stella was in bed, I sat alone at the dining table with a glass of water. Overhead hung the light fixture Pete had made after we moved in together in San Francisco, an old California railroad tie suspended from the ceiling on chains, with pendant lights, the effect both delicate and imposing. I would never have imagined I could make my own light fixture, but Pete took a class in metalworking and figured out how to do it. I felt bad now, thinking of that hopeful Pete, who'd had the time and imagination for such projects.

But Stella wasn't a project. There was no class that could teach you how to deal with freak-out mode. Now, at least, he understood that it wasn't merely a tantrum. I didn't know what to do about it, but I did know that until we understood it better, the only thing you could really do was be there by her side. She didn't need professional help. She needed two parents who would let her be her weird, unique self and try their best to understand her.

Pete came back about half an hour after Stella had gone to sleep. When had those grooves appeared, going from his nose to the corners of his mouth? He pulled me into his arms. "I'm so sorry. I don't know what happened. I snapped. I understand now why you took her to the emergency room. You didn't know what else to do."

I led him to the sofa. "Freak-out mode fries your brain."

Pete nodded. "I should be able to comfort my own daughter. We don't spend enough time together. I've put way too much into Mycoship. You and Stella are what really matter."

I stroked his hair, feeling generous, because at last, someone else understood the terror of freak-out mode. "Stella knows you love her." When Stella was born, Pete held her skin to skin under his shirt, her bud mouth suctioned around his little finger. The day she lost Sunny, the plush sunfish she'd had since she was a baby, he'd combed the Internet until he found an identical replacement (not that Stella was fooled). When we had friends or family over and she felt overwhelmed, Stella liked to hide on the bottom shelf of our pantry, which she called her alone-time cupboard. Pete never insisted she come out. He installed a light in there, as well as a handle on the inside of the door.

It was only when school started and she still shrank from playdates that he balked at how much time she spent in there. And then he insisted that she have a party for her eighth birthday.

I'd wanted to take Stella to the science museum or the aquarium. But Pete said that his friends had invited her to their kids' birthday parties, and now it was time for us to reciprocate. He booked an animal entertainer, who brought along a pile of cages. Stella kept shooting desperate looks at me as the man brought out one panicky ball of fur after another. The pièce de résistance was an enormous snake the thickness of a fire hose and the color of a rotten banana. After some encouragement, the other kids had groped the snake while Stella covered her eyes, the only one to empathize with the reptile.

"I should never have organized that birthday party," Pete said now. "I feel like it was all my fault. I could see she didn't like the animal entertainer. I should have put a stop to it. Then maybe she wouldn't have—"

"I'm sorry too," I interrupted. I wasn't apologizing for anything in particular, but there was no need to rehash what happened next.

I laid my head on his chest. It took guts to apologize and even more to delve into why you'd erred. In my etiquette column, I'd talked about a shallow versus a deep apology. In a shallow apology, you enumerated what you'd done wrong and apologized. In a deep apology, you talked about *why* you had done something. A shallow apology was fine if you didn't know the other person and the wrong done was small. But if it was someone you cared about, someone you loved, and the wrong was tremendous, only a deep apology would suffice.

"You've been under a lot of stress," I said. "It's not easy being responsible for all these other people." The employees at Mycoship were making token salaries, gambling on it being successful. In California, Pete had worked for CannaGauge, his parents' cannabis-testing equipment company, and he'd grown it until it was big enough to support us comfortably, as well as his parents. He could afford to pour his soul into Mycoship. But it was stressful for the others who worked there, unable to put anything into retirement or savings. Pete felt he owed it to them to make Mycoship succeed.

Still, maybe he was overdoing it. I saw my opportunity. "Maybe you could establish some boundaries with Nathan, like it's OK to contact you on weeknights, but weekends are for family."

Pete tensed: I could feel it in his chest, in his arms around me. "We're so close to making it, you know? I feel like we're right on the verge of all our hard work paying off. If we could just get one or two big-box retailers to take a gamble on us." At the moment, Mycoship's clients were small luxury businesses with an ecological bent, companies that made artisanal gin or beeswax candles. Pete wanted mycelium packaging—which actually enriched the soil when discarded—to be as commonplace as Styrofoam. "Tell you what, we'll have one family day every weekend. Will that work?"

"It's a good start." As I hugged him, I kneaded his back with my knuckles, smelling his familiar, comforting smell of citrus zest and freshly sharpened pencils. "Maybe you *can* teach Stella to surf," I murmured, catching sight of the new boogie board. "You managed to teach me."

Pete chuckled. "You weren't that bad."

Pete had persuaded me to try surfing after we'd been dating for a month. "Catching a wave is like flying. You're going to love it."

But no matter how many times I got it right on land, I couldn't "pop up"—move from lying on the board to standing—in the water. I fell off my board again and again.

One afternoon, when we were in the ocean, paddling back out to the lineup after I'd wiped out yet again, Pete said, "You've just got to believe in yourself," and I snapped.

"Could you sound any more Californian? You also have to know when to give up. This just isn't for me."

I braced for Pete to lose his temper. But he just nodded. "You're right. It doesn't matter if you never catch a wave. I'm happy just being in the ocean with you." He reached out for my hand, and my whole body relaxed. We lay on our boards, feeling the ocean's rise and fall. A pelican skimmed low over the water. Then a wave moved towards us, and I knew I could catch it. I leaped to my feet in one fluid motion and rode nearly to the shore. Pete leaped off his board beside me, his face alight, and at our knees, the surf fizzed like champagne.

9.

In the morning, Pete didn't rush off to work. He took his time apologizing to Stella, a version of the deep apology he'd given me last night: He'd reacted badly because he hated to see her so upset; he was tired and overworked. He wanted to spend more time with her. "So can you forgive me, sweetie?" he finished.

"Oh yes," Stella said. Pete squeezed my hand, and Stella, her face inscrutable, studied our linked fingers. I felt sick but also ravenous. I ate two pieces of buttered toast, but was still hungry. The troika tin caught my eye, and I had a sudden craving for sweet pastry, something rich and heavy to take the place of the ache inside. But when I opened the tin, it was empty. "Pete, did you eat these?" I asked.

Pete raised his eyebrows. "I was in bed with you all night."

I turned to Stella. "Did you eat the pastries, darling?"

"Someone else creeped in and ate them," she announced. I couldn't help smiling at that "creeped." Stella was so precocious that I savored any childish solecism.

"Well, I hope whoever it was brushed her teeth afterwards," I said, deciding to let it go.

"Didn't you have enough to eat at dinner?" Pete said. "Is that why you had a midnight feast?"

Stella shook her head. "*I* didn't have a midnight feast."

I frowned. If Stella did something wrong, she usually defended her actions. An outright lie wasn't her style at all. But maybe she was asserting her independence.

Something was going right because she got ready for school in half the usual time. To my amazement, she put on her school dress of her own accord. Previously she'd refused to even try it on. Something else was different too. Usually in the morning her wild hair seemed to grow straight out from her head, as if it were alive. Today it lay flat and limp. "What happened to your hair?" I said.

"I brushed it!" Stella was outraged. Pete and I exchanged stunned looks. She had such a sensitive scalp that usually I could only brush a few strands at a time, and I had to hold them near the top to avoid the slightest tug on her head. I couldn't deny she looked much neater. Still, I felt a pang: she'd robbed me of one of my few excuses to touch her.

After I dropped Stella off, I double-checked that I hadn't received a message from Cherie: nothing. I figured that Zach was refusing school again, and she was too overwrought even to shoot me a text. But at pickup, I saw her in the distance, double-parked, hustling Zach into her minivan with his ukulele. I raised my hand, but she didn't appear to see me. Bile rose in my throat. She deserved more than a scribbled card. I should have gone to see her.

I swallowed and forced myself to focus on what mattered: Stella had got through the second day of school without the teacher keeping me behind to talk, without Stella's face looking like thunder at pickup time. Stella even waved a timid goodbye to Lulu.

I was so pleased with Stella that I walked to our favorite café on Muswell Hill Broadway for a treat, but when we got there, she said she wasn't hungry. I hadn't realized that the way home from the café led past Irina's house until I saw her sitting in her front window, staring into the street. I wondered if I could get away with turning around and going home by a different route. But Stella waved, and Irina beckoned us up her front path.

When she opened the front door, she didn't look good. Her bare legs were blotchy, her feet in dirty sheepskin slippers, and it looked like she had put liner and eye shadow on only one eye. I felt terrible for her. Still, I didn't want to linger. I could smell the rubbish in her wheelie bins, but I could also smell the hard plastic the bins were made of, and that was worse.

But Irina produced yet another biscuit tin, apparently from behind the door, like she'd had it ready. "Do you know any hungry little wolves?" she asked Stella.

"Owooo! Ow-owooo!" said Stella, making me start. It wasn't like her to be so playful with strangers. But Irina wasn't a stranger, I remembered: Blanka had brought Stella here. "Mommy, let's have some snacks," she said, trying to tug me over the threshold.

"You said you weren't hungry," I told Stella. Then I addressed Irina. "Thank you, but we should be getting back," I said. Who knew what inappropriate thing Irina might say about Blanka? But Irina sagged, and I felt guilty.

"Why don't you come over to our place for a cup of tea?" I offered. "Then I could do Stella's dinner at the same time."

"That is very nice," said Irina, and even though I felt I'd done the right thing, my heart sank while we waited for her to get her purse. Now I had to warn her not to mention Blanka, but I didn't want to sound callous: "Sorry about your child's tragic death, but I don't want it to upset my child, who is very much alive. So could you play along with our charade?"

On the threshold of our house, Irina hesitated, and a shadow passed over her face. The poor woman must be thinking about Blanka, who had spent so much time here. I put a hand on her sleeve. "Come in," I said. "I'll get you some tea."

Inside, Irina looked around and blinked. We had a pared-down style anyway, but as it happened, our bookshelves were completely empty at that moment. Before I got pregnant, I'd spent hours refinishing them, and once I started feeling sick, I'd lacked the energy to arrange our books and ornaments. Actually, I found I quite liked to rest my eyes on empty shelves.

In the kitchen, Stella surprised me by asking Irina to read to her from our latest library book, *Shipwreck: A History of Disasters at Sea.* Despite her poor English, Irina gamely ploughed ahead. I served Stella separate bowls of penne, kale chips, and blueberries, and to my relief, she ate. I made a mental note to try reading to her at meals. Pete texted to say he'd be home late—because he'd left early the previous night, he had a lot to catch up on. The pantry burped up the smell of stale pretzels, and my stomach lurched.

"Thank you so much for coming," I twittered to Irina. "I need to give Stella her bath now." I was pretty sure that once again she'd veto the bath, and I'd have to wash her with a damp cloth while she stood on the bathmat. But there was no need to explain that.

Irina didn't get up. I clamped my hand over my mouth. I'd never even allowed Pete to see me throwing up. Sweat broke out on my forehead. Irina stared at me for a moment. Then she stood up. "I do bath."

"That's so nice," I said, "but—" I tried to think how to explain that Stella would undoubtedly not want a near-stranger helping her with her bath.

She turned to Stella: "We can make ship, *Titanic*."

Stella jumped up and down. "I can be a giant squid! I'll eat everyone on board!"

Was it possible Stella had had baths at Irina's? Her gaze flickered over my torso. "Rest." She put her hand on my shoulder.

"She likes the water no more than lukewarm," I began, swallowing back saliva. "You have to—"

"I understand." Irina nodded towards my belly. "You can rest."

I was about to explain that Stella also needed the door closed while the water ran. Then a wave of dizziness washed over me, and I sank onto the sofa. Irina followed Stella up the stairs. My urge to be sick passed. Edith would never have offered to give Stella a bath. When Stella was a toddler, she went through a phase of refusing to wear nappies—tight waistbands were torture—so I had to watch her like a hawk and whisk her to the potty any time she looked like she needed to go. I hadn't had a shower or eaten a meal sitting at a table for two days. While I knelt on the floor, awaiting a telltale grimace from Stella, my mother watched from the sofa with her weak Earl Grey ("Barely let the tea bag *touch* the water."), making me feel even more flustered. Her idea of reassurance was to tell me, "It seems hard at the moment, but motherhood is only one phase of your life."

But now someone else was in charge, and for a minute, I would enjoy it. I picked up my phone and started watching an old episode of *Neighbours*, the Australian soap I'd watched after school with Maureen, our cleaner. Even when I grew too old to need a babysitter and Maureen only came once a week to clean, she still stuck around after work to catch the show.

After school on other days, I found myself borrowing cookbooks from the library, imagining meals meant to be shared. Edith only liked plain food, but one day, to accompany a special episode when two characters got married, I made a pavlova for Maureen. She had three helpings.

The following week, she brought the ingredients for shepherd's pie and asked if I wanted to learn how to make it. We peeled and chopped, side by side. I dared ask if we could add a little Dijon mustard, and Maureen was intrigued. When the pie was done, she set it on the table with a flourish: "Madam, dinner is served!"

After a few mouthfuls, she said, "The mustard makes it"—she kissed her fingers. "We should open a restaurant and make this our signature dish."

I felt warm inside. I stood up, did a silly bow, and picked up the salad servers: "Would madam like some *salade verte*?"

"Ooh la la!" She held out her plate.

As we ate the salad, I said, "What would we call it? This restaurant."

Maureen's eyes sparkled. "Something French, because that's fancy. Only I don't know a single word of French."

"You know *ooh la la*," I pointed out. "And maybe *bonjour*?"

Maureen giggled. "We'll call it the Ooh La La Bonjour restaurant."

After that, we made dinner most Thursdays, and when Maureen wiped a smear of sauce from a dish rim or scattered parsley over the top, she said, "Nothing's too good for the Ooh La La Bonjour restaurant."

Edith wasn't home until seven, so if we ate early, we had the kitchen to ourselves. When Edith eventually got home, I told her I'd already had supper, and didn't mention that I'd eaten with Maureen. Somehow, I knew she wouldn't approve.

Then one night, I pretended to be a snobby French waiter, pouring a splash of water into Maureen's glass and making her sample it as if it were wine. "Does it have zee delicious tang of London pipes? Nothing but zee best for madam!"

Suddenly, Edith stood over us—we were laughing so much we didn't hear her come in. Maybe it was the cold that made her look so drawn, her cheekbones sharp, a bright spot of pink on each one. She turned to Maureen. "What are you still doing here? I thought we agreed nine to four."

"I was keeping Charlotte company while she has her tea."

"I can't pay for extra hours."

"I wasn't expecting any pay." Maureen stood up and carried her dish to the sink. Her posture was queenly as she squirted soap onto a sponge.

"Charlotte will clear up the *supper* things," Edith said. "I'm sure you'd rather be at home with your family."

The boeuf bourguignon we'd made roiled in my stomach. Edith might as well have said, "Your real family." As Maureen left, I wanted to run after her and fling my arms around her, promise I'd call the evening meal "tea" for the rest of my life.

After that, although Maureen and I still managed a chat at the end of her workday, she didn't stay long. When I left home, we had a few stilted phone conversations, but soon our only contact was Christmas cards. One year hers had my name on the envelope but nothing written inside. I felt hurt that she didn't care enough to scrawl something, but then, during one of my monthly calls with Edith, she told me Maureen had early onset Alzheimer's and was now living in a care home. The next time I was in the UK, I visited her, but she didn't remember my name.

I stopped the episode and swiped at my eyes. Then the sound of splashing and Stella chattering came from the bathroom. She was in the bath, and she sounded *happy*. I was stunned. How had Irina managed that?

Stella was lying full-length on her stomach in the bath. Irina sat on the toilet lid, smiling. I perched on the edge of the tub and dipped my hand in. I jerked it back. The water was *hot*, or rather, the temperature of a normal bath. When Pete had run a bath of this temperature, Stella had acted as if he were trying to boil her alive. But now she wriggled about, making little waves. I found myself grinning at Irina, and she smiled back. Stella rolled onto her back, her skin as pink as a newborn's. I felt a surge of joy. This was a glimpse of another realm. It was the same way I'd felt once, when while out surfing, I'd seen dolphins riding the waves.

10.

The next morning, a Saturday, Stella put her clothes on before emerging from her room—a first—although she chose a shapeless dress that came almost to her feet. I checked the label: it was ten-year-old size, much too big. Pete's cousin had sent it along with some other hand-me-downs. It was black, and I'd bundled it into a drawer because I didn't think little girls should wear black.

"I made waffles, your favorite," I said. "It's family day today. Daddy's spending the day with us."

Pete was already at the table, halfway through his second waffle.

"Can I eat in my room?" Stella asked.

"If you eat here, I could read to you," I said. This had worked for Irina, and I had *Shipwreck: A History of Disasters at Sea* at the ready. But Stella shook her head.

"Fine," I said. A family should eat together at the table. But I wasn't about to rock the boat when things were going well. I totted up the successes: two days of school without incident, a proper bath, and brushing her own hair. I dared to hope that her extreme sensitivity was a phase.

"We're going to visit a wildlife refuge today," I said. "They have peregrine falcons." Stella hated the sight of wild things in captivity, but this place was OK because most residents were temporary, being taken care of in the wildlife hospital before they were given their freedom again. The ones who stayed were only the ones who wouldn't survive in nature. I'd called them that morning to confirm there were no actual cages.

"Yay!" Stella caroled. Pete grabbed her hands and spun her round. My heart swelled.

But when we got there, the air was a palimpsest of awful smells: bleach and cat litter and, on top of that, the visitors' smells of hair products, skin lotion, fabric softener. People had no idea how much they stank. Life must be terrible for dogs. My phone pinged, and when I saw it was from Cherie, my heart lifted. But all she said was, Thanks for the card and gift!

You're welcome, I wrote. We OK then?

Her only response was a thumbs-up. I stared at the screen, willing something else to appear. In this context, just a thumbs-up—by itself—seemed tantamount to a thumbs-down. It was clear that she didn't want to communicate further, at least for now.

The glass bird enclosures were open at the top, and the kestrels and falcons could fly up to perches there and survey the visitors. Stella stared up at them, captivated. I was glad the birds seemed content, but I regretted the loss of their wildness. Part of me wanted them to swoop back and forth around the museum, strafing the visitors until they found an open window.

"Do you think you're going to throw up?" Pete murmured to me, and I realized I had my hand across my mouth. I shook my head. The Sisyphean punishment of morning sickness was that I constantly felt as if I were about to do so, but never actually did.

"I'm fine," I said. "I'm totally fine." I twined my fingers in his. I was happy because he'd barely taken his phone out of his pocket.

While Stella studied a cormorant, I seized my chance to speak to Pete out of her earshot, and told him how Stella had had a bath, with Irina presiding, the previous evening.

"Wow," he said. "Seems like it's good for Stella to spend time with another adult. You two have such an intense relationship."

I bristled. What was that supposed to mean? Then I forced myself to take a deep breath. Maybe Pete wasn't criticizing my relationship with Stella, just making an accurate observation. "She did enjoy her time with Irina," I said.

"It's good for you to get a break." He glanced at Stella to make sure she was out of earshot. She didn't know about the miscarriages. "After what you've been through with the other pregnancies, you should be relaxing now. That's why you gave up your job, isn't it?"

I frowned. The thought of a few hours on my own, without Stella, without even Stella-related tasks, filled me with panic. I hated being alone. When I was seven years old and the doctors discovered the tumor in my thyroid gland, the next step after the surgery to remove it was radioactive iodine, which came in a drink.

The doctor said that after I swallowed this at the hospital, I would be radioactive and should stay six feet away from other people for five days.

My mother didn't explain what a thyroid was, or how the medicine worked. Her vagueness made me feel like she was hiding the truth: there was something terribly wrong with me. That was why I had to be kept away from others.

Maureen checked on me during the day, and my mother said good night. Otherwise, I stood at the window. The mother across the street walked her children to school in the morning and went to pick them up in the afternoon. Then they all appeared in their lit front room, eating buttered crumpets in front of the TV. Snuggling. My mouth was dry, yet tears leaked incessantly from my eyes.

After two days of solitude, I realized there were people watching me from inside my dollhouse. The clicking of the radiator took on a pattern, repeating an urgent message. The walls billowed, like panels of fabric. My own life, my own animation, was leaking out into everything around me.

By the fifth day, I couldn't speak.

I returned to normal after a week or so, but I learned that although you think your personality is something essential and unchangeable, really it relies on the pressure of other personalities holding its shape. Without other people, your edges dissolve. You don't become more yourself when you're completely alone. You become less so.

So now I said quickly, "I want to be with Stella. That's what makes me happy."

At lunch in the café, Stella refused to touch her meal, even though it was her favorite, a veggie burger (which I hastily deconstructed) and chips. Not wanting to make a fuss on our day out, I persuaded the server to pile it all into a cardboard to-go container and squashed it into my handbag. As we were leaving the café, Pete exclaimed, "Hey!" It was Emmy's husband, Nick. He'd been at Stella's birthday party, and greeted us with what felt like overcompensatory warmth. He nodded down at Lulu, sucking a juice box. "It's Dad-urday," he explained. "Every Saturday morning, I take Lulu so Emmy can have some downtime with the baby."

"Downtime with the baby," I said. "I'm sure she appreciates that."

To my surprise, Stella sauntered over without being summoned, even raised her hand in greeting. Lulu merely fluttered her fingers, but Nick shooed his daughter away. "Go play with Stella."

Lulu trailed after her apprehensively, but Stella found a lever that made the jaws of a mountain lion's skull clack shut. Then she watched while Lulu made the jaws of the skull clack again and again.

Nick and Pete chatted and were soon involved in a deep conversation about whether Nick thought Pete should grow a beard. I went to the bathroom and dry-heaved over the toilet. When I returned, Lulu was holding Stella's hand, and Stella, to my surprise, was allowing this. "Can we go to the playground, please, please, please?" clamored Lulu.

I began formulating an excuse, but Pete spoke first. "Great!" he said. On the way there, he murmured, "She needs more physical activity. When I was her age, I rode my bike all over the neighborhood."

In the playground, Pete and Nick chased the girls around. Several other kids joined in, overjoyed to find an adult not glued to a phone. The one bench was full, so I had to perch on a fiberglass rock, unable to get comfortable. Usually, Stella hated playgrounds, but now when the dads raised their arms and did monster roars, Stella trotted after the other shrieking kids.

Then Pete went to grab coffee, and Stella gave up playing and just stood and watched. Blanka used to watch Stella with the same impassive expression. For some reason, she rarely sat down at our house, and almost always stood. Also, she never looked at her phone. She wasn't the type to sit on the floor and do craft projects, but she was never distracted. She had a special kind of total presence, one that somehow also felt like absence.

I didn't like seeing that expression on Stella's face. I went to stand by her side. On a car journey, just the two of us, Stella had once asked, "When do cows say meow?" When I didn't know the answer, she explained, "When they think they're cats." This led to us imagining a series of books about animals that think they're other animals.

Meow, I'm a Cow
Woof, Where's My Hoof
Neigh, I've Got Eggs to Lay

From time to time, one of us would start the game again.

"Meow, I'm a cow," I said now. Stella said nothing. She must not have heard me. "Meow, I'm a cow," I said.

Usually, she shot back an answer without thinking. Today, nothing. How could she have forgotten our game?

"Stella?" I said, and she didn't even react to the sound of her name. "Meow, I'm a cow!" I said, my voice sharp.

Stella blinked. She shook herself as if she were waking from a nap. "Ribbit, I'm a rabbit," she finally said.

11.

"You didn't like how Stella was changing," says Dr. Beaufort.

It's only half past two, but outside the window, light leaches from the winter sky. After this morning's session, Rosemary, the director here, showed up to tell me about all the therapeutic activities available for the afternoon. But I'm not going to waste time doing restorative yoga or basket weaving when I need to convince Dr. Beaufort of the truth. So far, I fear I haven't been doing very well, so I asked for this second session.

"I'm fine with Stella changing," I explain. "But this change didn't feel like her."

Dr. Beaufort puts her head on one side. "Stella was starting to fit in." She pauses. "But that was difficult for you."

"I *longed* for her to fit in. I was terrified of her being alone. I dreamed of watching her turn a cartwheel on the beach, of plaiting her hair." I press my good hand to my mouth. I've never admitted this before. "I just don't want her to fit in at the expense of losing herself."

Dr. Beaufort shrugs. "Children are always changing, no? When we're talking about a child, a person still in the process of becoming, it's hard to say definitively what their essential nature is."

My bad hand throbs. I get what she's saying. Common sense says that this new Stella *is* the real Stella. The girl who burned so brightly, my curious, playful, brilliant girl—*that* girl was merely a phase, and this dull, stolid person is her true self.

On the night of Stella's birth, I smelled the secret sweetness at the heart of everything and thought then that even if she became a serial killer, I would love her. I can't let my love waver now simply because her spark has gone out.

I cradle the hand in my lap. Maybe it is infected, and if so, I deserve it. I need to do better. But I feel so weary. I slump back against Dr. Beaufort's sofa cushions and pull her nubbly throw over myself. I made a promise that I would do anything for Stella. I would fling myself under a train. But that sacrifice, over in a moment, would be so much easier than having my child turn into someone I don't recognize.

12.

In the car on the way home from the wildlife center, Pete was jazzed. "Nick said he'll tell Emmy to set up a playdate for the girls," he said, clearly thinking we could put the birthday party behind us after all. As he drove, he felt the stubble on his chin. "You know, I think I will grow a beard."

At home, Pete said he would take charge of dinner. "There's some broccoli that needs using," I began. "Stella needs to eat as soon as possible."

"Uh-uh," said Pete, shaking his finger at me. "You have to learn to let people look after you, Charlotte. Go lie down."

"Thank you, baby," I said. Nick pretending to be a monster in the playground was probably his parenting contribution for the entire week. He retweeted men's rights activists. I doubted whether he cooked or did the dishes, and definitely not both on the same night. I was lucky that Pete did his share and more when he was home.

I lay on the living room sofa while Stella sat at the coffee table with a notebook that Pete's mother, Dianne, had given her, stamped with the humorous title, *World Domination Plans*. She was scribbling in the notebook.

"What are you writing, darling?" I asked.

"It's secret."

I felt uncomfortable. If it was secret, did that mean it was something she thought I wouldn't like? Perhaps she was writing her thoughts about Pete and me. Pete announced that dinner was ready: burritos.

Stella said she wasn't hungry, and Pete gave her permission to go to her room. I was too tired to protest.

"I think Stella would do better socially if we give her more space," Pete said as I picked at my burrito.

"What do you mean?"

"Well, take today. You were in the bathroom feeling sick. I was chatting with Nick. We kind of just left the girls to themselves. Stella got on great with Lulu."

The burrito smelled like cat food. I couldn't eat any more. "A few days ago, you were so worried that you wanted to take Stella to the doctor. Now, on the evidence of one day with her, you think all she needs is more space?"

Pete looked at me, concerned. "I wasn't criticizing your parenting."

Stella appeared in the kitchen doorway. "Can I please have my bath, Mommy?"

"But you had one last night," I said. Because of Stella's aversion to hot water, we'd never had a daily bath routine.

Pete sent a message to me with his eyes: "Let's give her more space."

"I'll do the dishes if you'll get her bath started," he said.

In Stella's bathroom, I shut the door and turned the water on. I always ran only hot water first, because when we first moved in, our hot water was liable to run out. We'd replaced the boiler since then, but the habit of running hot only first had stuck. Closing the door behind me, I went to her bedroom for a nightdress, then realized the clean laundry was still in a pile on our bed.

When I went back to the bathroom, the door was open. Pete must have gone in to check on the bath. Maybe he'd decided she was ready to handle the sound of running water. But when I went in, I was stunned to see Stella already in the bath, with the tap still on. I gasped—that water was scalding. I turned it off and knelt down. "Sweetheart, are you OK?"

Stella seemed not to hear. She lay with her ears underwater, only her face sticking out. I put my hand in, and the water was hot enough to make my skin itch. But it wasn't hot enough to burn. She was fine. "This is nice bath," she said dreamily.

"What?" When Stella began to talk, it was in full sentences. I'd never heard her drop an indefinite article. I plucked at her arm to make her sit up. "What did you say?"

Stella sat up, hair dripping. "This is a nice bath. Thank you for running it." She studied her reflection in the tap while I washed her hair. She even let me rinse out the shampoo without complaint. Maybe Pete was right and she did do better when her parents weren't breathing down her neck. Something twisted in my heart: "You two have such an intense relationship."

When I went into the kitchen, Pete had done the dishes and wiped the counters and now was removing the stove grates in order to get at the crud beneath them. "Thanks for doing that," I said. "Did you know that Stella's keeping a secret diary? She's like Harriet the Spy."

"Who?"

"A girl in a children's book who's always writing in her diary. She wrote a lot of things about the people around her, and not all of them were very nice. Are you not curious to know what Stella's writing? I'm tempted to take a peek."

"No way," Pete said. "She could leave the diary wide open on the coffee table, and I still wouldn't read it. You're not planning to read it, are you?"

"I was joking! Of course I won't read it."

He nodded. "By the way, were you not able to remove that mark?"

I was stunned to see that the cross was back. It looked like felt-tip this time. It had started out at child's-nose level and was nearly at the level of my nose now.

"We need to talk to her about this," Pete said.

"She knows not to draw on the wall," I said. I went to the sink and squirted soap onto the sponge. Pete gently took the sponge away.

"We have to make *her* clean it off," he said. "She has to learn to handle her own problems."

I couldn't think of a good reason to disagree, in this particular instance, even though I felt uneasy about leaving the cross there all night. It was ridiculous, but I felt like the only way I could be sure it wouldn't move any higher was to sit in the kitchen and watch it.

Pete's phone rang, and he groaned. "Nathan," he said. "Dude

doesn't understand what it's like to have a family." He declined the call. At once, his phone rang again.

"Take the call," I told him. "It's fine. We had the whole day together."

I remembered that Stella's rejected lunch was still sitting in its box in my handbag. It was squashed and unappetizing, and I was about to toss it in the compost. Then, on impulse, I went up to her room and knocked. "Stella? I'm leaving some food outside your door." I stood there for a moment, wondering if I should bring it in, but then I reminded myself what Pete had said: "She'll eat when she's hungry."

I went into the living room and got out *50 Stress-Relieving Designs* and began to color a wise owl perched on a branch, its body an intricate network of paisleys. My mother thought coloring books stifled the intellect. But the day after her death, I'd felt an uncontrollable urge to grab an adult coloring book off the rack at WHSmith and hadn't looked back since.

Pete joined me on the sofa. He was bursting with news. "Nathan got us a meeting in Atlanta with Home Depot."

I hugged him. "That's amazing, my love." Nathan had been trying to get a meeting with Home Depot for months. Mycoship's first big-box retailer. At last.

"The catch is we have to leave now so we can catch the red-eye. They want to see us Monday first thing."

"Now?" My heart sank. I'd have no relief from childcare for the rest of the weekend. If I felt ill, there was no one I could call. "If the meeting is Monday, why can't you fly out Sunday night?"

"I'm so sorry, baby. I hate to leave you when you're not feeling great, but we need tomorrow to whip our presentation into shape."

I wanted to ask him not to go. But if major retailers started using biodegradable packing materials, it would be a giant win for Mycoship and for the oceans, choked by single-use plastic. Pete still talked about the time when, out surfing, he found a dead baby otter with a six-pack ring cutting into its neck.

While Pete threw things in a case and called an Uber, I went to check on Stella: the cardboard box of leftovers was gone. Her bedroom door was ajar. Wet snuffling noises came from within. I peeked in. Stella was sitting on her bed, cramming her mouth with limp chips and cold veggie burger.

She was so absorbed that it took her a minute to realize I was there. When she did, it was like she didn't recognize me. She stared at me with such suspicion, clutching the greasy box to her chest as if I'd try to take it away. I backed out of the room. Bits of food fell onto the bedclothes as she shoveled it in. "Little Wolf," Irina had called her.

13.

The next morning, I dragged myself out of bed, I toasted a leftover waffle and knocked on Stella's door. "Room service." For now, I'd accept her need to eat in private, even if I didn't like it. She was eating, that was the important thing. Stella opened the door, wearing yesterday's dress, her hair hanging down, as if it were wet. "Thank you, Mommy." Then she closed the door in my face.

I fretted about what to do about the FOMHS meeting, which was at five that afternoon. Charlotte Says: Flakiness is the plague of modern times. Never cancel, except in an emergency. But now I had no childcare. I couldn't take Stella to the meeting, which was about prosecco and gossip as much as fundraising plans, and I couldn't miss the meeting either, because I needed a regular connection with the other moms in order to organize playdates. I wished I had someone I could leave Stella with, but the only person I could ever have asked that favor of was Cherie.

The cross on the wall caught my eye. Could it be connected with Stella's insistence on taking her meals alone? When Stella emerged from her room, I pointed to the cross and said, "That wasn't me or Daddy. Any idea who it was? Tell me the truth."

"People should always tell the truth," Stella said piously.

I exhaled sharply. "What *is* the truth? Why won't you eat when I'm around? Why does that thing keep appearing on the wall?"

Stella was silent, as if my questions were simply unanswerable, like so many of hers were: "Do trees care about each other?" "Where did the ocean come from?" "Is planet Earth going to get hotter and hotter until it's four hundred and sixty-four degrees like on Venus?"

"May I go back to my room?" Stella said, and I nodded, defeated. Pete had said she had to clean it off, but I didn't have the heart to insist if she thought she didn't do it.

The doorbell startled me. On the doorstep was Emmy, her striped dress paired with tan ankle boots, her fringe looking as if she'd measured every strand of hair with a ruler. By her side was another school mom who always wore lurid yoga leggings. Her name escaped me.

Emmy was clearly not here to organize the playdate with Lulu that Nick had suggested yesterday. Her face was grimly self-important, and my stomach sank.

"We've come to tell you that you're disinvited from the FOMHS meetings, starting with this afternoon," Emmy said. Her breath was swampy with green smoothie. "I just heard what you did to Cherie."

"Cherie told you?" I whispered. "But she already accepted my apology."

"This didn't come from her." Emmy pulled up a video on her phone: the freeze-frame was of me, standing legs wide apart, brandishing scissors, while Cherie lay crumpled at my feet.

"Where did you get this?"

"I live right next door?" said Lurid Leggings. Emmy hit play. The video had been edited. I heard myself shouting, "Stella isn't like Zach! She's absolutely nothing like Zach." Oh no. Then I shoved Cherie, or it looked that way. Cherie gave a little scream, which I didn't remember, sat down hard on her front path.

"You physically assaulted her," said Emmy.

"It was an accident," I protested.

"And you denigrated her special-needs child."

I turned to Lurid Leggings. "You've edited the video."

She looked self-righteous. "People have short attention spans."

"Emmy, please," I said. "I did say those things about Zach, but there was a larger context."

"So, you admit it," Emmy said. She was so sure she was in the right. In her downstairs toilet, she had a framed copy of "Desiderata," and I thought of the line "No doubt the universe is unfolding as it should." Emmy certainly seemed to think so, and it was easy to believe that if you never really had any problems.

"I saw it," Stella announced, appearing beside me. "Zach's mommy was being mean to my mommy." I loved her so fiercely. But then she continued. "If someone invades your personal space, you should punch that bastard right in the face."

I gaped. "Stella! That is not how we talk. Go to your room."

She retreated, and I closed my eyes, feeling hot and prickly all over. "OK, OK," I said. "I get the message." I felt so ashamed, desperate for them to go away. As I shut the front door, I distinctly heard Emmy saying, "Cray-cray."

I certainly looked cray-cray in the video. I thought of all those videos I'd watched of little kids freaking out. Now other people had watched this video of me. But those videos of kids were anonymous, taken by their parents to help other parents. This video was taken to warn the other moms about me, a menace who had to be disinvited from FOMHS.

I called Pete, even though it was still early in Atlanta, and did my best to make this into a funny story.

"Those moms are the crazy ones," he said. "They're treating you like you're some kind of psycho."

I tried to laugh. "I know! But they know I'm not. I've been out for margaritas with them." On one occasion, we'd laughed ourselves silly at the thought of the nit-removal party we were going to invite people to: "The pleasure of your company is requested/For an evening of cocktails and nit-picking . . ." For some reason, the phrase BYONC (bring your own nit comb) was especially hilarious.

But now that I thought about it, the way the nit party came up was that I'd been talking about hosting a get-together at my place, musing about what type of event I could have. "A drawer-organizing party," someone had joked. I'd laughed along. Then Emmy had suggested the nit-removal party. I thought they were laughing with me, but now I realized they were laughing *at* me.

I sat down on the sofa and cradled a cushion to my chest. "I don't think they ever actually liked me. They thought I was uptight."

"They only know one tiny part of you. In San Francisco, they would have killed to be invited to one of your parties."

"Do you ever wonder about that time?" I asked.

"What about it?"

"Were we really friends with all those people? I've lost touch with pretty much all of them."

"Long-distance friendships are tough," Pete said.

But after I got off the phone with him, I reflected that he was always texting and calling old friends. I was the one whose friendships were so flimsy they had melted away. My time in San Francisco had been my proof that I *could* make friends. But now I looked back on all those parties and dinners, I realized I was always too busy to sit down and talk with anyone. I couldn't remember a single conversation.

Maybe I didn't know how to get along with others, and the FOMHS mothers saw the truth.

I got the rubbing alcohol from the cleaning supplies cupboard and poured it onto a clean cloth. Then I went at the cross. It didn't work, and I tried nail polish remover, and then toothpaste. Finally, I got a paring knife and scraped off the paint. I would need to paint over the ruined spot. But for now, it felt good, so good, like scratching a mosquito bite until it bled.

14.

By the time I'd finished gouging the wall, it was lunchtime, so I forced myself to make something for Stella. Sometimes when I cooked, I felt as if my mother were standing in the kitchen watching me. She did this when I was growing up, and later, on the rare occasions she visited us or we stayed with her. Sometimes she said, "Is that how you chop an onion?" or "Will Stella eat that?" Someone else might not even have recognized these comments as criticisms. Mostly she just watched, her eyes following me as I chose a knife, as I chopped, as I heated oil in a pan or grated cheese. If you have something to say, say it, I thought now, and then gave one of those small starts as my brain realized that this particular thought groove had expired. Pete said that for months after his dad died, he thought of funny or interesting things to tell his dad, then remembered with a jolt that he was dead. I thought of Edith telling me I was using the wrong spatula.

I tried to perk up, but everything reeked. The sponge smelled moldy, even though it was a new one I'd unwrapped yesterday, and its smell fought with that of biodegradable peppermint dish soap. I texted Cherie and told her about Lurid Leggings' video. **Emmy threw me out of FOMHS. I'm a pariah!** Confused face, melting face.

The old Cherie would have responded with a tears-of-laughter face and **OMG I wish she'd banish me too. Btw did you see what she was wearing yesterday? She looked like a walking zebra crossing.**

Nothing.

Cherie could have offered to text Emmy and set her straight about what had happened. But I wasn't surprised that she didn't. That thumbs-up the previous day had clearly meant what I thought: she didn't really forgive me after all.

I was starting to regret apologizing to her. Normally I apologized for everything, including things I hadn't done. I apologized when someone stepped in front of me to grab the last shopping basket at the supermarket. I apologized to Pete when he came home late. I apologized to Stella when the bath temperature wasn't to her liking. Charlotte Says: If in doubt, apologize. It doesn't cost you anything.

I felt that this apology had cost me something: I'd put myself in the wrong. Cherie could stand to apologize too.

I finished making Stella's lunch and delivered it to her room. Then I flopped on my bed. If my friendship with Cherie was still intact, I could return to our running joke and text: "Never mind, a spot of eyebrow reshaping will cheer me up." Instead, I scrolled through home-organization photos, my eyes stinging. I aspired to cupboards and drawers where the entire contents were visible at first glance. I hated losing things that I knew were somewhere inside my house.

My bedroom door banged as a breeze blew through the hall. How long had I been lying here? "Stella!" I went to her room. Everything was as usual: the birds of California poster, her collection of mussel shells that looked identical but weren't (she noticed when I tried to throw a couple away), the stuffed owl we'd sewn together, made from some fluffy fabric that molted everywhere. But no Stella. A trickle of cold in my chest.

Was she in the alone-time cupboard? No. Back to the living room. Could she have crept behind the curtains when I was sleeping?

The front door was wide open. Hence the breeze.

I had the strange sensation that what was happening was preordained. This was always going to happen. From the first night of her life, I'd wondered how I could deserve such glorious riches. When I got to take her home from the hospital, I could hardly believe it. It was like a mythical creature had come to live with us, a phoenix. Now she had flown.

I ran out the front gate. There was no one on the street. "Stella!" No sign of her. Which way should I go? Could she have walked somewhere on her own? But she was eight years old and had never gone anywhere alone. She'd never even walked to the toilet in a restaurant by herself.

"Stella!" I screamed. All the houses seemed to contain people who were watching and thinking, Cray-cray bitch. There was no one I could even ask for help. I felt as if cold water poured down my throat and into my belly, at such a tremendous speed I would burst.

Two blocks up, an older woman with Russian-doll hair and a

dark-brown skirt turned onto our street. "Help!" I screamed. The woman waved. It was Irina.

Then there was Stella, dancing around the corner. I charged up the street and threw myself upon her, pressed my face into her hair, wanting to press her back into my body, into my flesh, where she would be safe. She actually let me hold her, though she didn't hug me back.

I fought to catch my breath. "Where were you going, darling?"

"To my swimming class. But Irina said I should go home."

I'd forgotten about the private swim lesson I'd scheduled on Sunday afternoons. Usually, I had to drag her to the pool. But never mind. "You can't go by yourself. You know that," I said. I couldn't get my heart to stop thumping: What if she'd tried to cross a busy road?

Stella said calmly, "I've gone out by myself lots and lots of times."

This was patently untrue—her first barefaced lie. I didn't know what to do. Should I punish her? I didn't have the parenting techniques for this. Putting Stella in a time-out would be no hardship for her. Was she openly defying me, trying to get a rise out of me? Was that what the cross was? Her refusing to eat at the table?

I looked at Irina hopelessly. She seemed to understand what was needed. She crouched down so her face was at the same height as Stella's, and she took her firmly by the shoulders. "Now you listen," she said, her voice fierce. I stared. I had never once spoken to Stella in a voice like that. I was about to intervene: How dare this woman talk to Stella like that? But something stopped me. Irina made sure she had Stella's full attention. Then she barked, "In this country, child cannot walk alone. Understand?"

I waited for Stella to lash out, but she nodded solemnly. I was stunned. Is this what I should have been doing all along? When Stella displeased Pete's mother, Dianne, she suggested CBD oil, convinced this was the balm for all ills. When Stella displeased my mother, she turned to me and said things like, "She certainly talks a lot," and "Is that all she's going to eat?" Stella turned up her nose at Dianne's CBD gummies, and my mother's little comments made her worse. But she seemed to take Irina's words to heart.

"OK," she said.

Irina stood up and laid a hand on my shoulder. Her hand felt warm and heavy. My eyes pricked, but I pulled myself together. "Thank you," I said. "Are you going out somewhere?"

She looked a lot better than the last time I'd seen her. Her hair was darker, carefully dyed and neatly pinned back. She wore a white blouse and dark skirt, tan tights and what looked like men's business shoes. She had the same blue eye shadow as when I'd seen her on Friday, but on both eyelids this time.

"I come to see you," Irina said. She held up something mummified in cheesecloth. She nodded at Stella. "And Little Wolf, of course."

Stella howled obligingly. "What's that you're holding?"

"Sorry, this is not nazook. This I make for your mother," Irina said. "This is"—and then she said something that sounded as if she were trying to get a hair off her tongue. Stella and I stared at her, and she said, "In English, I translate as oily bread."

"I like nazook," Stella said.

Irina smiled. "Next time, maybe. Today I bring oily bread. My husband's recipe. Makes mothers feel better."

It did not sound at all appetizing, but I was touched. "Thank you so much, that's very kind of you," I said, meaning it. "I can't wait to try it." I reached out for the bread, but she held on to it.

"Blanka's father has bakery. Long time ago. He teach me many breads. This is how I make oily bread: I roll dough to size of table, very, very, very thin. Then I roll it up and make . . ." She shook her head. "Shape like snail?"

"A spiral!" Stella said.

She nodded. "And then I roll out to size of table again and again roll up like snail." She cradled the bread. "This I do seven times."

"Seven," I said. "Gosh." Of course she wanted to watch me sample something she had worked so hard on. It was the least I could do after she had helped find Stella. And now that she had mentioned Blanka, I couldn't send her away, a grieving mother who nonetheless had found the energy to make bread for me.

"Stella, will you draw me picture?" Irina asked once we got back to our house. "Maybe nice picture I can take home?" Stella beamed and trotted off to get her drawing supplies. Irina sat down on the sofa and unwound the bread from its wrappings. It looked like greasy, greyish pita. I'd written an etiquette column on how to politely choke down foods you don't like. Charlotte Says: Take a tiny bite, so you can swallow it without tasting it, like a pill.

Then I smelled it, and for the first time in days, my stomach growled. It smelled like funnel cakes at a fair on a summer evening or french fries when you're drunk. I picked it up in both hands and tore into it. It was rich and flaky and unbelievably delicious.

"This is amazing," I said with my mouth full. I ate until the bread was gone.

Finally, I sank back into the sofa. I didn't feel sick. I felt like a scurvy-ridden sailor who had eaten an orange. I was weak with gratitude.

"Where I come from, bread is holy," Irina said.

"It's the opposite of here," I murmured dreamily. Emmy said gluten was bad for you, regardless of whether you had celiac, and Lulu had to bring her own personal "cake" to other kids' birthday parties: a puck of sunflower seeds and psyllium that was like some nutrient-dense substance you would take on a trek across Antarctica.

"When you marry, you put bread on shoulders of man and woman like cape. For luck," Irina said.

"Did you wear a bread cape when you married?" Stella had come down the stairs so quietly we hadn't heard her.

"Of course," said Irina. "My husband and I are very happy. We live in little house in forest." I was puzzled. A little house in the forest? It sounded like the beginning of a fairy tale.

Sure enough, Stella said, "What happened next? Did something bad happen? Was there story trouble?" Story trouble was an idea they'd taught her in writing class at school.

"Sweetie, Irina was telling us about her life, it's not a story." Though I reflected that because the husband was no longer with us and Irina had left her country, something bad obviously did happen. I felt uncomfortable. I didn't want to ignore her suffering. But I also didn't want to revive her trauma. Or worse, betray an appetite for it.

I would let her choose how much she wanted to tell me. And apparently, she'd told me enough.

"You rest now." She turned to Stella: "Little Wolf, you want to make doll?" I tensed. Stella loathed dolls. But she bounced up and down, almost shrieking. "Yes, yes, yes!"

"Really?" I said. Irina picked up *50 Stress-Relieving Designs* from the coffee table and opened it to a mandala I had completed.

"You do this? Beautiful. Like window in church." She nodded approvingly, handed the book to me, and followed Stella back to her room. I could hear Stella chirping and Irina murmuring back. My mother had never played with Stella like that. I still had to tell Irina not to mention Blanka's death, but surely it wouldn't come up. I didn't want to bring her down by talking about Blanka, not when she was clearly enjoying the distraction. I decided to spoil myself by taking *50 Stress-Relieving Designs* to work on in bed.

Usually, I was on high alert for any sign that Stella needed me. But with Irina in charge, I lost myself in a swirl of goldenrod and magenta.

A knock on the door roused me from my trance. Just over an hour had passed. "Stella wants to show you something," Irina said. I followed her to Stella's room, where Stella held something aloft, like a trophy. "We got stuff from outside, and look what I made!" It looked like a bundle of twigs tied together with dried grass. I was perplexed: Why not use her craft supplies? She handed it to me, and as I examined it, crude arms and legs emerged. If you looked at it right, you could see that it had a dead leaf for a dress, an acorn for a head, hair of moss glued on with sap. I smiled as I gave it back to her. "What are you going to call it? Is it a boy or a girl?"

"Stick Thing," Stella said.

Irina smiled. "Is good to make doll when baby comes."

Stella laid out her softest hoodie on the bed and began to swaddle Stick Thing. It was a little odd to see her playing with that poky dark bundle. But I told myself it was only my cultural blinkers that made me think dolls had to be cheerful and lifelike. Maybe it was a folk tradition from Irina's homeland for a soon-to-be older sibling to make a doll.

I'd told Stella about the baby when I reached the end of the first trimester. She didn't ask what the baby's name would be or if it would share her room. She asked what would happen if the baby came out too soon. She'd focused on the possibility of something bad happening. Irina was teaching her that a new baby was something to look forward to.

Not to mention the fact that it was pretty amazing to see Stella playing with a doll. She spent so much time reading, and maybe Pete was right, maybe she didn't play enough. Maybe if she learned to play, she would connect better with other kids.

Irina said she had to go, and I suddenly realized it was time to make Stella's dinner. The afternoon had flown by with Irina here. I walked her to the door. "I can't thank you enough." For the bread, for getting Stella to act like a kid for once, for the hour in which I was free from anxiety about her.

Irina paused on the threshold. "In my country, if mother is sick, she is not alone. She has mother, aunts, grandmother." She was close enough for me to smell her, and she didn't smell bad: sensible soap, stewed tea, something vaguely spicy underneath. She reached up and touched my cheek. Out of nowhere, I remembered that my mother once gave me two jars of mustard as a combined Christmas and birthday gift. It was gourmet mustard, but still, clearly a regift. She couldn't even shop for a present for me, let alone make one. I swiped my eyes with the back of my hand. "When can you come back?" I asked. "Tomorrow?"

15.

On Monday morning, I woke up longing for the oily bread. The thought of any other food nauseated me, but I was pierced by hunger for this one specific thing. Irina said she'd return today, but we didn't settle on a time. I'd felt so sated when I said goodbye I hadn't thought to ask her for more bread.

But you couldn't *ask* for a gift, especially not one like that. Surely, she'd understand I needed more. I wanted to google the recipe, but I couldn't remember the name.

I dropped Stella off at the school gate, and for once, she let me drop a kiss on her head. As she walked in, I noticed that, even though she'd finally worn the school dress and brushed her hair, she still looked out of place. Her hair seemed greasy, and she walked with shuffling steps.

I walked home quickly, reminding myself of how hard mornings used to be. I should be rejoicing at this change. But at home, I couldn't settle to any activity. All I wanted was the bread. I called Irina, but it went to her voicemail. I wanted to growl, "Bring more bread now." I forced myself to take a breath. "When you come over later, I mean, if you are coming, I would love some more of that bread, if you have any."

To distract myself, I folded laundry. I used the duvet case as an envelope for the pillowcases and fitted sheet, so each sheet set formed its own neat little package. I kept checking my phone: nothing from Irina. In my column, I'd railed against people who say when parting, "Let's have coffee sometime," or "We should go for a drink." Charlotte Says: If you're not intending to follow through on plans, then don't make them. Bite your tongue. Had Irina simply said she'd come over out of fake politeness?

I left another message with Irina. "Not sure if you got my first message, but I thought you said you'd come over today? With more bread, if you have any." The nausea had become so intense that the room seemed to tip sideways. Before I staggered off to pick Stella up from school, I left a third message: "Can you please, please come over and bring some bread?"

She came at 5:00 p.m., when I was in despair. I practically snatched the muslin-wrapped bundle from her arms. "Irina!" Stella ran to the door. "More nazook!" she sang, having noticed the troika tin at the top of Irina's bag. In the kitchen, Irina set some nazook on a plate for Stella without asking me if this was OK, but I liked it. I liked that she made herself at home and fed my child. School moms asked if we had special dietary requirements before offering us any food. When Pete's mom, Dianne, visited, she always asked, "Is this OK?" and "Would it be OK if?" before giving Stella anything. And then there was my own mother, who honestly would never have thought to prepare a snack for Stella.

The bread was still warm, even more delicious than before. Irina watched me finish the bread and Stella inhale the nazook. She glowed, as if she were a mom watching her kid guzzle kale. Today her hair had an impressively luxuriant chignon, and I thought it was probably a hairpiece. Where could you even buy such things? She had on full makeup, a black cardigan and white blouse and elastic-waist black skirt. Her eyebrows were carefully penciled.

After I finished the bread, I felt self-conscious, grease on my face. I brushed the crumbs on the table into the palm of my hand. I'd been so desperate for the bread that I hadn't even bothered with a plate. I shook out the square of muslin she'd used to wrap the bread. It was like the swaddling wraps I'd used on Stella when she was a baby, although this square was as fine as a cobweb from being washed many times. I realized suddenly what it meant that the bread was warm: Irina had made the oily bread again. For me, she had again rolled the bread out seven times. That was why it had taken her so long to come over. My eyes watered, and Irina patted my hand.

After the bread, I couldn't stop yawning as we sat at the kitchen table. Irina pulled out her tapestry bag, which she had stowed under the table. She opened it to show me that it was full of bright yarn. "I teach Stella to crochet," she announced. "In my family, girls learn at three, four years old. Already is very late to start."

"That's so nice of you, but I'm not sure if it's really her kind of thing," I began. She didn't like instruction; she liked to do things her own way. But Stella dusted the last flakes of nazook off her fingers and jumped off the chair to peer into the bag. "What are we going to make?"

"Whatever you want," Irina said, pulling out some crochet hooks, not the plastic kind. These looked like steel, antique. "Long ago, I learn with these same hooks," Irina said. "Belong to my mother's mother's mother." The two of them moved into the living room and settled onto the sofa. Stella seemed absorbed in Irina's instruction.

As Stella's needle found a rhythm, the phrase *mother's mother's mother* repeated in my head. The nausea was gone, and the most ordinary sensations felt luxurious. I went upstairs and got into bed, and the sheets had never felt so soft, as if they'd been hand-washed in a stream and dried in the sun.

When I woke up, it was 6:30 p.m. I panicked at the realization that I hadn't started dinner yet, but then I heard Irina and Stella murmuring in the kitchen. The sound of chopping followed, the click of the gas igniting on the stove. I dozed. Still later, a smell crept into the room: rich and savory, better than any scent that you could buy.

I followed the smell to the kitchen. Irina stirred something in my Le Creuset Dutch oven, a wedding gift I hadn't used in years. "Gomgush," she announced incomprehensibly, her cheeks pink from the heat. "Special banquet stew."

I knew then what that rich, savory smell was. "I'm so sorry," I said. "Stella should have told you. We don't eat—" Then I stopped. Stella was laying the table with cutlery and napkins. She folded each napkin into a careful triangle. I smelled mint, maybe, and paprika. Something about it was familiar, like it was the home cooking of my childhood, although in my actual childhood, Edith had merely opened tins and packets. The kitchen felt cozy, with steam-clouded windows. Would it hurt if Stella ate meat this once? This was better than scarfing cold french fries behind her closed door. On the table was Stella's crochet project, a cream-colored doily, already half-finished. Didn't she learn to crochet only a couple of hours ago? "That's amazing," I said.

"Beginner work," Irina corrected me. Stella appeared unbothered by this criticism, which was weird because she'd grown up having me say, "Good job," even if all she did was go down the slide.

"Irina says I won't win the contest of the seven beauties," Stella said as Irina carried the pot to the table.

I was confused. "A beauty contest?"

"Crochet," Irina corrected. "Girls must try to crochet the best stockings in shortest time."

"Ah, that's . . ."

"Now eat," Irina said. Stella sat down, and I suddenly realized what governed whether she would sit at the table for a meal: Irina's presence. But I would puzzle this out later—for now I focused on the miracle of Stella eating stew. She was gobbling it up. I ate the carrots out of my serving as I looked on.

"Now she grow," said Irina with satisfaction. I smiled at her. I wasn't about to start eating meat, but maybe I could work a little harder to make home-cooked food and to make dinner special. We relied too much on readymade food from our favorite gourmet shop. It was decent quality, but it had no soul. Was that why Stella would no longer eat at the table when it was just the two of us?

I heard the front door opening, and then Pete came in, looking tired but handsome with a five o'clock shadow. For a moment I regretted making our downstairs into one huge room, because there was no hallway in which I could intercept him and explain what was going on.

"Baby, I can't believe you're back already!" I went to hug him. "This is Irina, Blanka's mother."

Irina stood, wiping her hands on the tea towel she had tucked into her waistband as an apron. She shook hands. Pete was about a foot taller than her. Irina had wiped her brow at some point and smudged her right eyebrow. I felt a pang for her.

"Hello, Stella Bella," Pete said, and Stella got up, wiping her mouth with the back of her hand, and stood in front of him as if expecting a hug. Pete stared at her for a minute and then put his arms around her. Our eyes met: This was a miracle, she never submitted to hugs. But also, what was Irina doing here? And why was our daughter eating meat? We'd always been lucky that we were a couple who could communicate everything with their eyes.

"Excuse us a minute," I said to Irina. I followed him upstairs into our bedroom, where he opened his suitcase and pulled out the various zippered pouches in which he kept his stuff organized when he traveled.

I sat on the bed. "I thought the meeting was this morning. How are you back already?"

"Nathan persuaded the key players to meet us for golf on Sunday instead."

"How was it?"

"Good," said Pete firmly. "It's great we touched base with them, but we need to circle back and confirm the key deliverables." When Pete took a work trip with Nathan, he always talked like this afterwards.

"Sounds like they want to do a deal! That's amazing."

"We're moving in the right direction," Pete said.

"Cautiously excited, I get it," I said.

Pete scratched at his beard. "Stella eating meat?"

"Irina made the stew," I said, "and Stella seems to love it, so I decided to let her have it this once. You know, she had that day where she didn't eat, so I really want her to eat."

"Fine," Pete said. "It's dead now, I guess. Do you think this visit is a little—well, odd? We don't know her, but all of a sudden, she's making dinner in our kitchen?"

"I felt sorry for her. Well, yesterday that was why she came over."

"She was here yesterday as well?" He emptied the dirty-laundry pouch into the hamper. "You're seeing quite a lot of her."

"Why not?" I said, even though I understood perfectly well what he was saying. I hadn't made any new friends for a while. Why would I choose to befriend an older woman who didn't speak English very well and had different values?

"Sorry, baby. You're right. I'm just tired," Pete said. "I was looking forward to having you guys to myself. I don't want to sound harsh, but maybe we could have her visit again another day. Can't you use that 'before you leave' thing from your column to get rid of her? 'Before you leave, I want to say thank you for this delicious stew.'"

In "Charlotte Says," I'd written: When guests outstay their welcome, a subtle hint is better than shoving them out the door. Simply drop the phrase "before you leave" into conversation.

But I didn't want to do that. Irina made Stella play with a doll and take a bath. She taught her to crochet. I wasn't going to ask her to leave, even obliquely.

Pete read my face. "You're right, we can't throw her out. It's just a little strange that she's so nice. I feel bad. Blanka was with us for such a long time, but we hardly knew her."

"Maybe Irina needs us." Also, I needed her. "She really cares about Stella."

It was rare to care that much about someone outside your family. I'd learned that the hard way when I visited Maureen at the care home, not long after I learned she was there. A nurse showed me to where Maureen sat in the lounge. Her hair was still dyed a harsh blond, just as she'd always had it, but she'd lost weight. I could see the ropy muscles in her neck. A middle-aged woman sat with her, round and comfortable-looking, like Maureen used to be: Maureen's daughter. "Sharon," she said, shaking my hand. I'd emailed to tell her I was coming.

I sat down in a chair next to Maureen. Like hers, it had a busy checked pattern that wouldn't show stains. Maureen's hands fluttered, plucking the air.

"Charlotte's here, Mum!" Sharon said. "Remember Charlotte? Edith's daughter."

Maureen jutted her chin in what was either a nod or an involuntary movement. "I'll get us some tea," Sharon said. "Leave you two to catch up."

Maureen's hands used to be so deft: she could chiffonade parsley twice as fast as I could. I wished I could make her hands rest. I pulled out the beribboned box of macarons I'd brought and showed them to Maureen. "Fancy enough for the Ooh La La Bonjour restaurant, don't you think?"

Nothing. Maureen blinked and tried to get up. "Better finish the ironing," she muttered. "Can't stay past four."

I put my hand on hers. Did she think I was Edith? "Sit down. The ironing's all done."

Maureen sat, but her hands still fussed.

"Sharon seems nice," I said hopelessly.

Maureen blinked. "When you're not sleeping, you can go right off the rails. Sharon's got the baby blues. Just like you, she's on her own."

She did think I was Edith. "I'm managing just fine," I said. "Sharon will be OK too." If Sharon had had the baby blues, she was long recovered: she'd mentioned her teenagers when we emailed.

Sharon returned with a tray of tea. She poured it, and asked me, "What are your other plans while you're visiting from California?"

"I just came over for this." Edith was in Yorkshire, delving into the Brontë archives, and had said we'd have to catch each other next time.

"Just for this," Sharon marveled. "That's very kind of you. Very kind indeed."

"I wanted to come."

"It's above and beyond. None of Mum's other clients have offered to visit, let alone their kids."

My insides twisted. Maureen had never told Sharon a thing about me. That time with her had meant so much to me, but to her, it wasn't worth a passing mention. I was just the daughter of someone whose house she cleaned. I didn't stay long after that, and when

I kissed Maureen's powdery cheek goodbye, she gave that little nod again, as if I were merely a stranger who'd let her pass through a door first. That was the last time I saw her. She died of pneumonia, just before Stella was born, and I spent three days watching *Neighbours,* imagining she was by my side.

"Earth to Charlotte?" Pete sat down next to me. "You OK?"

"I was just thinking how good Irina's stew smells," I said. Its rich, complex aroma penetrated even up to our bedroom. It didn't matter to Irina that we weren't her family.

Pete sniffed. "It does smell good. And you know what? I'm being a jerk. That poor woman just lost her daughter. I haven't even offered her my condolences."

"You sent those lilies," I said. "Anyway, you can't say anything right now—Stella still doesn't know about Blanka."

"Irina's on board with that?"

"It works out because she only uses the present tense when she talks about Blanka," I said.

Back in the kitchen, Pete declined stew but sat at the table with Stella while she ate a second helping and Irina looked on with approval. Stella usually picked at her food, but now she was cramming it in. Pete cooked bacon over the fire on our camping trips, cheating on his vegetarianism in homage to his dad, but otherwise, Stella had never tasted meat. Watching her, I wondered if she wasn't a picky eater at all. She was a carnivore. "Blanka loves this dish," Irina said.

There was silence while Stella ate. Pete rolled his neck, probably stiff after the long flight from Atlanta. It was understandable he wasn't thrilled to have to make conversation with a stranger when he was tired. Then I thought of something. I showed Pete the muslin cloth in which Irina had brought the bread. "Irina used this to wrap some bread she brought me. That's cool, isn't it? Her own reusable packaging."

"Plastic is waste of money," Irina said. "Cover bowl with plate, wrap bread in towel."

"Down with plastic," Pete agreed, relaxing. "Stella hasn't enjoyed her dinner so much in a long while. Thank you, Irina." He smiled at her, and I felt an unaccustomed ripple of pleasure. The four of us sitting around the table, Stella spooning up a proper meal without demanding we separate the components or taking minuscule bites.

"When can you come again?" I asked Irina, without planning to.

She smiled. "I decide. I come weekday afternoons until you feel better."

"That would be amazing. Are you sure?" My heart lifted. "I know this is a lot to ask, but would you be comfortable getting her from school?" If Irina did pickup, I wouldn't have to see Emmy and the other FOMHS moms.

Irina nodded. "I get her at school. I take break from hospice. I bring bread too."

I still couldn't quite believe it. "Really, every weekday?"

She touched my shoulder. "Is good for me. Child is hope. You know?"

"You can relax and gestate," Pete said to me. I nodded. I could nurture my body so I would have a healthy pregnancy, and this wonderful woman would look after my child, and not like a babysitter, but like a grandparent.

. . .

I'd told Irina I'd walk her out. On the porch, I paused. "Stella doesn't know Blanka passed away."

Irina peered at me. Maybe she didn't understand the euphemism. "Stella doesn't know Blanka's dead," I whispered, even though Stella was upstairs. "Would it be OK not to mention it to her?"

Irina looked almost savage for a moment. "I should say Blanka is fine, Blanka goes on holiday," she clarified.

"Don't lie," I said. "Just don't talk about it." I realized that my request was both completely reasonable and absurd. Or rather, it was too much. I could ask her to look after my child or I could ask her not to mention her dead daughter, but not both.

Irina set off down the porch steps. Halfway down, she turned. "Children need truth."

My skin prickled. Surely it was up to me to decide what truth my child needed and when. But Irina was already walking away. Because of the language barrier, she'd probably sounded harsher, more judgmental than she'd intended.

When I went back inside, Stella and Pete were playing Connect Four. I poured myself a glass of iced water and sipped it slowly. Before I had Stella, my friends with kids told me that going for a pedicure would become a rare luxury. With a child like Stella, pedicures were gone forever. Their kids might scream if they didn't feel like a bath, but they didn't thrash about on the floor until their head thwacked the base of the sink and bled.

It was a miracle that Stella was getting better, and I would do what it took to keep Irina on board. Maybe I needed to rethink my parenting. Plus, Irina had barely left and I was already feeling sick again. When Pete said, "Relax and gestate," he'd made it sound like the two verbs were equivalent. There was nothing relaxing about feeling sick 24-7. I was irked, but told myself to let it go. Pete only wanted to protect me, and our new baby.

When Pete came into the kitchen to make tea, I said very quietly, "You know, I think we should tell her the truth about Blanka. It might be good for her to experience something like this."

"I don't know," Pete said. "She's going to ask a lot of questions."

I took another sip of water and thought. When our koi suffocated because we didn't notice the pump got turned off, Stella cried until she vomited, and after that, the sight of the pond upset her so much we had to have it filled in. But that was a year ago, and though this might make Stella sad and even angry, if it meant Irina could keep coming, it was worth it. "Then we'll answer them."

We went into the living room, and Pete pulled Stella onto his lap. "Sweetie, we've got some bad news about Blanka." He paused. "She died."

Stella pressed her lips tightly together, and I felt the way I did when I saw her struggling through the water learning to doggy-paddle, her mouth and chin sometimes sinking below the surface, her little face set. I wanted to jump in and save her, but I knew I had to let her enter the deep end alone.

I blinked, and tears fell. But Stella didn't cry. "Are you sure?"

Pete nodded. "We're so sorry. I expect you have a lot of questions."

But she shook her head. She looked so expressionless that I said, "Do you understand, honey? Blanka's dead?"

She stared at me. "Oh yes."

Those two words again, Blanka's words. But now they didn't seem like a way of agreeing. They seemed like a way of silencing me.

Her reaction was so odd. How could she freak out about a slug or a koi carp but then take Blanka's death in stride? Maybe she cared so much about other living things because she didn't care about people. Maybe on some level she wasn't capable of truly feeling—but no, I wouldn't let myself finish the thought. "It's a big shock," I told Stella. "It must be a big shock."

She wriggled out of Pete's embrace and shrugged. "I'm not dead."

Pete and I looked at each other, flummoxed. "I guess she needs time to digest it," Pete said. I nodded, still parsing her previous words. "*I'm* not dead." Was she saying Blanka's death didn't matter, because she, Stella, was still alive? I thought she'd ask if I would die, if Pete would, if she would. Why had a child died before the parent? And what, exactly, had happened to Blanka? But she didn't ask any questions at all.

Stella had been so lively when Irina was here. But now, when it was just the three of us, there was something different about her, something I couldn't put my finger on—a vacant quality. An absence that was also a presence. Stella retrieved her half-finished doily from the dining table and moved to the sofa to work on it, barely glancing down as her needle nipped in and out. It really was remarkable she'd only learned that day.

16.

When Irina came over the following afternoon, Stella immediately begged to crochet. "Give us a minute, sweetie, I need to talk to Irina," I said. In the middle of the night, I'd realized that of course I had to offer to pay her. The gift of her weekday afternoons was too big to accept. But first, I let her know I'd told my child the truth. "By the way, Stella knows about Blanka now."

Irina nodded. "Good." If she was hoping that Stella would offer condolences, she was disappointed. This made me wonder: Did Stella actually get that Blanka was dead? But I had to get the money issue out of the way. "Listen, I've been thinking. I hope this isn't weird, but can I pay you?"

Irina looked confused. "For yarn?"

"For looking after Stella."

Irina smoothed her skirt. "This is not my job. I am nurse. I do not do this for money," she said.

Oh god, I'd made a colossal misstep. I had implied she needed a job. As if I thought every immigrant who spoke broken English must want money. "Of course not! I'm sorry," I gabbled. "I'm just so grateful. So grateful."

Irina nodded briskly. "Ah! I nearly forget." Irina pulled a small wooden icon out of her bag: an angel with clasped hands. "Blanka's guardian," she announced. "For Stella's room."

"Thank you," I said, and Irina's mouth twitched. She didn't like me thanking her.

"To watch over me," Stella said in wonder, and she traced a finger over the chipped gold-leaf background. I stared: no way did my scientific daughter believe in angels. But she was smiling at Irina, and Irina smiled back at her, like they shared a secret.

"Let's put it up over my bed right now!" clamored Stella.

Irina turned to me. "Where is nail and hammer?" I found Pete's toolkit, and she bustled up to Stella's room. What a difference from just a few days ago. When I first met her, Irina had moved as if the weight of the ocean pressed on her shoulders. She could have let that crush her. Instead, she decided to spend her afternoons with Stella. Now she had someone who needed her.

That Friday, after Stella was in bed, Pete came home with a bottle of champagne and announced that we were celebrating. "Sixteen weeks!" he crowed. My worst miscarriage had been at fifteen weeks. "We've made it further than ever before. I really think we're going to make it this time."

"Don't hex it," I said. "Anyway, I can't drink."

"The app says you can have one drink, and also, I got pomegranate juice to mix with it, which is full of antioxidants," Pete said. His beard was growing in nicely. It gave him a new authority. "Incidentally, we should also celebrate the fact that Stella's been at school for over a week without her or the teacher complaining."

He carried the drinks to the coffee table. "Red drink, white sofa?" I said.

Pete grabbed a crocheted afghan that Irina had brought and draped it protectively over the cushions. It was a generous gift, but it was the color of pond scum.

I sat down on the afghan. Pete clinked glasses with me and said, "To you and the baby."

"To you too, and to Stella."

"Yes, to Stella. She's doing great with Irina."

In the last couple of days, Irina had taken to ironing all our clothes, even our underwear. She also crocheted endless doilies with Stella and had continued to feed her meat. Stella had more color in her face, and I thought she had already gained a little weight. She now got herself ready for school without a murmur and bathed without complaint.

"It's early days, but maybe we won't even need that spreadsheet I made. Maybe you were right about not rushing to get her evaluated."

"She is doing great," I agreed. "But she's still eating in her room unless Irina's here. It would be nice if she ate at the table when it's just the three of us. Or just me and her."

Pete pushed a lock of hair behind my ear. "Much as I love Stella, I like the extra time with you."

I smiled and kissed his palm. Really, things were hunky-dory. I just wished I weren't so tired all the time. I longed for the second-trimester energy burst to kick in. The bread that Irina brought did wonders for my nausea. But I slept all day.

17.

One afternoon after a nap, I went into Stella's bedroom and sniffed the air. I liked to come into her room when she was at school, because even during the day, that honeysuckle odor lingered. It had grown less each year, and now, no matter how hard I sniffed, I couldn't smell it at all. Only lamb stew. It was mid-October now, and she'd been eating Irina's cooking every day after school for five weeks.

A book I'd bought for her, *Flight: The Complete History of Aviation*, was on her desk, where I'd left it at least a week ago. She hadn't cracked the spine. That was not like her. Her room was different too, unusually neat, the bedcover smooth. I ran my finger over her plumped-up pillow. For years, I'd nagged her to make her bed. She was hiding something.

I peeled back her duvet. A book stuck out from under the pillow. I tugged it out: the *World Domination Plans* notebook she'd been using as a diary. I hadn't seen her write in it for a while and realized she must be writing in it in her room.

Obviously, I would never read her diary.

But would it explain why she'd become so quiet, why her face lacked the play of expression it used to have, why she hadn't gone into freak-out mode for weeks? Or maybe she hadn't freaked out because she wanted to please Irina, because Irina was simply better at parenting. Maybe I just wasn't very good at connecting with my own daughter. My mother claimed I didn't recognize her until I was ten months old. Maybe there was something wrong with me.

A chair leg scraped, and I gave a start. When I looked round, Stella was under her desk with a container of leftover stew, spooning lumps of lamb into her mouth. Acid burned my throat, and I felt afraid. Normally Stella was so fastidious, insisting on a napkin for every single meal. And when I served her a dinner of leftovers, she looked at me as if I'd asked her to lick the bottom of the compost bin.

"Where's Irina? I thought you were out together." A muscle jumped under my eye, like a bubble in boiling porridge, and I placed my hand on my face to steady it.

"She went home."

"Sweetie, darling, come out of there. You should have found me if you were hungry. I would have got you a snack." Something more appetizing than cold fat and gristle. I knelt down and took the container of stew away. Stella stayed under the desk for a moment, wary, and then came out and stood before me, her shoulders hunched. She was so solid-looking these days, her tummy was even starting to stick out a bit. Her hair was losing its curl, and although I'd complained about her feral mane, I missed it.

"Why haven't you read the new book I got you?"

Stella shrugged. "It's too difficult."

I stared. This was the child who had taught herself to read at three and a half—I had nothing to do with it. Extraordinarily intelligent kids did sometimes grasp a new skill almost overnight, a phenomenon called sudden competence. But sudden *in*competence? I'd never heard of that.

Her face seemed rounder than usual, almost puffy. Then it hit me. She was ill. That was why she'd lost her spark, why she was finding reading difficult. In a strange way, I felt relief. If there was something physically wrong with her, then we'd fix it. Until she was well again, I wouldn't leave her bedside. I'd read aloud about historic shipwrecks, and we'd play Battleship for hours. And when she was better, she'd be herself again.

The next morning, I took Stella to her pediatrician, feeling grateful we could afford private healthcare and could therefore get a same-day appointment. Dr. Fleishman was a toothy woman about ten years older than me who wore loose dresses with Dr. Scholl's sandals. I wasn't comfortable around any doctor, but I could tolerate Fleishman. She always spent several minutes exclaiming at the beginning of the appointment about how precious Stella was and how marvelous it was that she was reading such grown-up books. Plus, she didn't tell me how to parent. When it came time to sleep-train Stella and to wean her, she told me what studies to read so I could draw my own conclusions. Once, Stella was sick of being offered stickers, so she told Dr. Fleishman that stickers were a waste of Earth's resources. Dr. Fleishman had laughed, but after that I didn't see any stickers in her office.

"Sit up here on the bed, honey." Stella climbed onto the bed, which was covered in clean paper. The nurse had already weighed and measured her. Fleishman looked at her notes. "She used to be in the second percentile for weight, and she's gone up—wow—she's gone up to the tenth. For height she was in the eleventh, and she's gone up to the sixteenth. She's really growing beautifully."

"That's actually why I'm here." I explained that I was concerned about her rapid weight gain.

"Since she's also gaining in height, I'm confident she's just growing," Fleishman said. She studied my face. "That's a good thing."

"Don't you think her face looks puffy?"

Fleishman felt Stella's neck glands. "All normal."

Stella stared into space, nct even looking at the brightly colored paper sea creatures dangling from the ceiling—a dolphin, a shark, a jellyfish. Last time we were here, a couple of months ago, Fleishman had said she liked jellyfish because they were so pretty. Did Stella like jellyfish?

Stella had said, "I like *Turritopsis dohrnii* because it can reverse its biotic cycle and turn itself into a polyp." Now she looked so vacant it was like she herself was turning into a polyp.

"As you can see, she's not her usual self," I said now. "She's not curious. She doesn't want to do her favorite things. Like reading. And her face looks different. It's rounder."

"Faces change as we grow." Fleishman studied Stella's face. "Do you feel OK, honey? You're sleeping OK? Got enough energy?"

"Oh yes," Stella said in that singsong voice that jangled my nerves.

"But her eating," I said. "She eats and eats. I'm concerned that such rapid weight gain isn't normal. Going from the second to the sixteenth—"

"Tenth for weight."

"Still, such a big jump."

"It's within the limits of what is normal."

"I'm thinking maybe you should test her thyroid gland. I really think her face is puffy. Her voice seems hoarse, even. Can't you hear it?"

Fleishman shook her head. "With hypothyroidism we would expect to see reduced growth. She wouldn't be shooting up like this."

I persuaded Fleishman to order a blood test for hormone levels nonetheless, even though Stella hated needles. "Could it be"—I mouthed the words—"a brain tumor?"

Fleishman shook her head. "There's absolutely no reason to think that."

"Or it could be Prader-Willi syndrome," I said. The previous night I'd read about a rare disorder that caused abnormal appetite in children.

Fleishman sighed. "I really advise parents not to google their child's symptoms." She smiled. "Your kid has puppy fat, but when you google it, it looks like kidney failure."

"You think it might be kidney failure?" I asked.

Fleishman shook her head. "Of course not. That was an example."

"You don't think I need to put a padlock on the fridge?"

Fleishman looked startled. "Absolutely not. At her age, you should not restrict her food intake. We'll see what the tests say, but really if anything, she seems exceptionally healthy." She made an extra note in Stella's file and then showed us out without her usual collegiality.

Stella didn't even flinch when the nurse inserted the needle at the lab. Maybe Dr. Fleishman was right and there was nothing wrong with her. But I couldn't help thinking about those birds in the wildlife center, the ones who sat on their perches instead of flying. They weren't the same birds they had once been: they'd lost their wildness.

18.

I told Irina that Pete and I would handle school pickup the next day. I made an urgent appointment for Pete and me to meet Mr. McNaughton, Stella's teacher. If Stella wasn't sick, maybe something was going on at school.

At three thirty, Stella emerged from the building with Lulu, her grubby socks and trainers contrasting with Lulu's frilled ankle socks and patent-leather Mary Janes. Lulu whispered something in another girl's ear, and they giggled. Stella smiled vaguely. My heart squeezed. A couple of months ago, she would have been cross-legged on the picnic table, bent over a thick book, her hair hanging forward and making a private cave.

"Pete, love the beard!" It was Emmy, in bodycon stripes today. I cringed. I'd been doing the morning drop-off as fast as possible, and because Irina did the pickups, I'd managed to avoid Emmy since she banned me from FOMHS. Now she jutted her chin at me in greeting, as if she'd never called me cray-cray.

OK, so that was how we were going to play it: pretend nothing had happened. I nodded back. Emmy stood closer to Pete than to me. "Lulu would love to do a joint costume with Stella for Halloween," she told him. She always swooned over Pete, who stood out from the other middle-aged dads, with his chiseled cheekbones and American congeniality, and he was only more adorable because he seemed not to realize it.

"Wow!" said Pete. "Great. Yes! What are they going to be?"

"You wouldn't have to do anything, Charlotte," Emmy said quickly, like she was being solicitous. Really, she was saying she didn't want me there. She turned back to Pete. "I *love* doing that kind of thing." As @LittleHiccups, she posted on Instagram about children's outings, parties, and, of course, the adorable costumes she crafted for Lulu and her baby sister.

"Can Stella come home with us for a few hours? I'll get her measurements, and then she and Lulu can play."

"We'll check with Stella," I said. I imagined Stella being forced to practice cartwheels and watch Japanese hair videos. Lulu had been acting like a teenager since she was about six. I pulled her out of earshot and murmured, "Do you want to go to Lulu's for a drop-off playdate?"

Before she answered, I knew what she was going to say.

"Oh yes."

As Emmy shepherded Stella and Lulu into her minivan, Pete swiped at his eyes. "Are you OK?" I murmured.

"Sorry." Pete blinked. "I can't believe she's going on a playdate, on her own. She's come so far socially."

I nodded, feeling hollow. *Oh yes.* Towards the end, Blanka kept on saying, "Oh yes," to everything I asked her to do, but she never did it.

Mr. McNaughton greeted us and showed us into the classroom. He was short and rotund with a bushy beard and black-rimmed spectacles and made me think of a Beatrix Potter character. He even wore a brown tweed jacket, and I liked to think that underneath he was covered in grey fur, that his home was a hole under the hedge with a tiny blue door.

We all sat on little chairs around a little table. Mr. McNaughton smiled. "Right up front, I want to put any concerns to rest. Stella is doing very well. I've prepared some of her work to show you." He laid out some long-division problems she could have solved two years ago, an indifferent drawing of a Viking longship, a writing exercise in which she had to put in the commas and then write her own sentence with commas. The writing didn't look like hers, which was big, loopy, and impatient. This writing was careful and tiny. *For dinner, they had roast beef, potatoes, peas, and cake.* "Her handwriting is excellent," he said. "As you know, handwriting is very important—"

"But people type everything nowadays," I interrupted. *Roast beef?* Where did that come from? Stella had never had beef for dinner in her life. And that Viking longship, different at each end. Stella knew perfectly well that longships were double-ended, enabling the Vikings to reverse easily if they encountered icebergs.

"Stella is really close to achieving her Pen License," McNaughton said.

"Great!" said Pete, because most of the kids had got their Pen Certificates in year three. But what did it matter if you had great handwriting if you were only copying out banal sentences?

"Is she not getting extra work?" I demanded. "I emailed you before the start of term. She's extremely bright. She needs to be challenged. If she's not challenged—"

McNaughton swept Stella's work into a pile. "She seems to find the work challenging enough." He pointed to the wall near the door, where he'd pinned a rectangle of card with colored paper pockets. He explained that each morning, the children took a lolly stick with their name on it and placed it in the pocket most closely corresponding to their mood: blue (sad/anxious), red (cross/grumpy), yellow (don't know what to do with myself), or green (happy and ready to learn). "Stella's always green," he said, smiling at us like the ultimate dream of any parent was to have a child who was always green.

I looked down at Stella's work, and suddenly I understood what was happening, understood the constipated handwriting and the roast beef, potatoes, peas, and cake. "Are you sure you're talking about the right kid? Look." I pulled up a photo of her on my phone: Stella, with her pale, thoughtful face, her blaze of hair.

"Hm," McNaughton said. "Yes, that's her."

"Why did you hesitate?" I said sharply.

"Has she changed her hair?"

"She brushed it," said Pete.

I was starting to feel very angry. "Well, if we're talking about the same kid, you haven't got to know Stella at all. She has a very high IQ. Off the charts."

McNaughton smiled, but he was obviously downgrading us from average parents to pushy nightmares. "She's had an IQ test?"

"No. We didn't feel like we needed to. But she reads at a very high level, you must have noticed that. Pete?" I tapped his knee. "She reads nonstop, doesn't she? History. Science. She's practically an expert on aerodynamics."

"I've had to push her to read in the classroom," McNaughton said.

"To be fair, we don't know that she was actually reading all those books," Pete said, scratching his head. "She could have been skimming. Maybe they were a security blanket, and now she's fitting in better, she doesn't need them."

"She *was* reading them," I said, astonished. "You were at work. I was there. She sat for hours holding the book, turning the pages. She talked about what she read."

McNaughton wanted to wrap this up. "She's really doing fine. Her reading is right where we'd expect it to be. You've got no reason to be worried. Her spelling, punctuation, vocabulary—all right on target."

"I'm telling you, she knows more words than many adults," I said. My voice shook. McNaughton no longer reminded me of a rotund and cuddly Beatrix Potter character. He reminded me of Mr. McGregor, the fat farmer who enjoyed killing rabbits.

"Honey," said Pete. He patted my knee, then spoke to McNaughton. "It really sounds like she's made a great start to the year." While the two men shook hands, I stared at the mood board, wanting to tear the whole thing off the wall. Who the heck only felt one color at a time? To be only one color, all the time, was to be numb. This wasn't Stella. She felt all the emotions, and she felt them all intensely. She was indigo, crimson, and gold. She was a whole sunset.

. . .

On the way home, I fumed. "He was basically saying Stella is middle-of-the-road. Stella isn't middle-of-the-road. He's made no effort to get to know her."

"It seems very important to you that Stella is gifted," Pete said.

"Her giftedness isn't *important* to me. It's a fact, like her red hair."

"She's a clever little thing, but maybe she isn't quite as bright as we thought. That would be good in a way. I've done research. Child prodigies are more likely to be unhappy. They don't even end up as high achievers. Wouldn't you rather have her be a happy nongenius?"

"It is not normal for a kid to change this much in a few weeks. You really want her to fit in, maybe so much that *you're* not seeing what's going on with her."

"That's not fair," said Pete. "I pay close attention to my daughter."

In fact, Pete's plan to keep Saturdays for the three of us had only lasted for one Saturday, because immediately after that, he got the promise of the Home Depot deal, which meant more work.

I assumed Pete would drop me off at home and then go back to work, but instead he hovered as I ate a piece of oily bread. "Do you eat anything at all apart from that bread?"

"It helps with my morning sickness," I told him impatiently. "The question is, why is Stella eating so much?"

"The doctor said she was fine. Look, let me make you something proper to eat, something with protein—"

I waved his offer away. "She's always writing in her diary. That could be hypergraphia, which can be a sign of—"

Pete shook his head. "It's like anxiety is your natural mode."

My phone pinged: a message from the doctor. "Stella's blood test is normal," I said. "No thyroid problem."

Pete didn't say anything; he didn't need to.

"OK," I said. "I'll try to—what was the phrase you used? I'll try to relax and gestate."

I went upstairs to rest, but instead of going to sleep, I went on Mumsnet, trawling posts about what caused sudden changes in behavior. Adrenarche—an increase in adrenal emotions that happened around the age of seven—could make kids rage and scream. Heavy-metals exposure could cause anxiety and defiance. But the more I read, the more alone I felt. There was nothing that makes your child calmer and better behaved. Because nobody else, not one other person on the entire Internet, had ever worried about that.

19.

After my second session with Dr. Beaufort, I don't want to be in my room, alone with my thoughts. I pump for Luna, dutifully, and produce a few drops of colostrum, which I give to reception. They have a special fridge for the mothers' pumped milk, everything carefully labeled. At least I don't have to feel guilty about not being there to breastfeed Luna: she's too premature to have developed the sucking reflex, and gets fed through a tube.

I go to the lounge, which has a tasteful Christmas tree with all-white fairy lights, silver ribbon, and delicate glass icicles. It is not a tree that any mother of young children would have—no foil-wrapped chocolate balls or pine cones daubed with glitter by little fingers. It honors the season without reminding us moms of what we are missing.

A woman with a severe ponytail has cornered another one by the fire—a high-end fake, judging by the lack of smell—and is murmuring to her in a low, intense voice. I sit in a chair by the window, but I can still hear everything she is saying. She's talking about how important it is to wash your hands thoroughly after you change a nappy. It's absolutely essential. Her husband doesn't understand this. He couldn't be bothered to wash his hands properly, so now she's stuck in here. She's terrified that in her absence, he's contaminating the house with the twins' fecal matter, which could make them very ill. Her hands are red and chapped, and she rubs them as she talks. The mom she's talking to is trying to read *Elle Decor*.

I stare at the darkening fields, feeling hollow inside. Have I become so consumed by my obsession that I'm impossible to live with?

I go to my room and call Pete. "How are you? How's Stella?" My voice cracks. I never have to ask this question, because I'm always with them. I've never spent a night away from Stella until now, and tonight will be my second.

Pete says Luna is gaining weight, and Stella is fine too. He's working from home so he can take care of her. "How are you?" he asks warily.

"I miss you," I tell him.

He takes a long, shaky breath. It sounds like he's trying not to cry.

I must have seemed so different when we met, at a volunteer clean-up day on foggy Ocean Beach in San Francisco. Empty juice boxes, Doritos bags, and a used nappy littered the sand. The other volunteers and I had no idea where to begin. Then Pete jogged up with a stack of traffic cones. He organized everyone into teams and divided the beach into squares: the first team to clean their square would win a bottle of champagne. "Want to be a team?" he asked me, and I tried not to stare at his full lips and muscular shoulders.

Pete raced about with boundless energy, and I was methodical, gathering every scrap. By sunset, the entire beach was clean, and the triumphant volunteers chugged the beers Pete produced. Later, we found a rock to sit on, away from the others. "I knew we'd make a good team," Pete said. "That's why I picked you."

"We didn't even finish in the top three," I said, warming my cold hands in my armpits.

"Only because we're perfectionists," Pete said. He took my hands and chafed them between his warm ones. His eyes were ridiculously blue.

For our third date, we went camping. Pete pointed out the Big Dipper and told me stories about his childhood growing up in coastal Mendocino: getting up early to feed his pet goats, how great his parents were. He insisted on unzipping our two sleeping bags and then zipping them together to make a single big one, so we could fall asleep entwined.

Remembering this, I start to cry. I no longer know what the truth is, whether I'm sane or not, but I know I've made Pete suffer. "I'm sorry," I say. "I'm sorry."

Pete clears his throat, and I imagine him holding the bridge of his nose for a minute, getting it together. Now that I'm crying, he won't cry, and I feel guilty about that, denying him that relief.

"It's not your fault," he says. "If anything, it's mine. I've been working way too hard and not paying enough attention to what's going on at home. Dr. Beaufort says prenatal depression can be just as bad as postnatal. You had it before Stella was born too."

"No, I didn't."

"You were plagued by negative thoughts. What about Humboldt Redwoods?"

I'd forgotten about that.

When I was seven months pregnant with Stella, we'd flown to visit Dianne, and then we'd taken a side trip, our last camping trip as a couple. After a drive down a dirt road, we arrived at what I'd thought was the campsite. It turned out to be just a trailhead: the site was in the backcountry, half a mile away. We forded a creek and then followed the trail through a tangled mess of forest.

The sun was setting, but there was still just light enough to put up the tent, and Pete made the long trip back and forth to the car to get our stuff. To warn bears of his approach, he belted out "Here Comes the Sun"—he'd inherited his love of the Beatles from his dad. I sat in the tent as the dusk gathered. When Pete finally got all our stuff to the spot, we realized he'd left my Moonlight Slumber pregnancy pillow in the car. I was seven months pregnant and had trouble sleeping. I could only really sleep comfortably with one knee propped on the pillow, so my belly didn't feel squashed. Pete insisted it was no problem for him to go back. I listened as his singing faded into the trees.

Then he didn't come back.

I didn't know how long he'd been gone, because I'd left my phone in the car and I didn't wear a watch. Twenty minutes? "Pete?" I called. "Pete? Pete!" I was panicking now. What if he hadn't come back because he couldn't? He was lost or he'd twisted his ankle. Or a bear had attacked him, a bear made hungry by the drought.

I shouted his name until I was hoarse. When I turned, the trees behind my back seemed to have shuffled closer together. A minute ago, there had been a clearing behind me, and now there was dense forest. I tripped over something and fell forward on my hands and knees. I heaved myself to my feet, whimpering.

I was trapped. Even if I found my way back to the trailhead, it was at least a mile more to a paved road, and there was no chance of a passing car at this time of night. We were miles from civilization. It would be morning by the time I found another human being—if I succeeded. I could easily get lost in the forest.

I got back into the tent before it got too dark to see, and sat there, shivering. It suddenly occurred to me that Pete wasn't lost. Pete had left me because I was too neurotic and demanding. Because I was a selfish tyrant who couldn't sleep without her special pillow. He was gone. Nobody had ever taken care of me the way he did, and nobody ever would again.

Eventually I crawled into our sleeping bag, the one Pete had made by zipping two single bags together. I pulled it tight around me and lay there, shaking. I was alone again, back in that room, radiation coming off my skin, unloved and unlovable.

It felt like hours later when Pete climbed into the tent. He wrapped his arms around me, full of apologies. "I'm so sorry, baby," he said. "I was on my way to the car, and I guess I wasn't paying attention and must have gotten turned around in the dark. I was so worried. Didn't you hear me calling?"

"I called *you*. I called and called."

Pete groaned. "I must have been too far away by then. I just got completely goddamn lost. I thought I was going to be wandering around all night. Then I stumbled into the creek, so I followed it downstream until I recognized the place where we crossed, and from there, I was able to make my way back. I'm so sorry, baby."

"You were gone for so long," I said.

"Honey, it was barely forty-five minutes," Pete said.

"It felt like hours."

Pete gave a shuddery sigh. "I feel like such an idiot. I'm supposed to be the big outdoors guy, and I got lost within a mile of our tent."

I burst into tears. "I thought you left me."

Pete wrapped his arms around me. "Never. I love you. How could you think that?"

I pulled him into the double sleeping bag and nestled against him, and he murmured into my hair. "I would never leave you, never, never."

Now I press the phone to my ear, wishing I could nestle against Pete now. It can't be easy to be married to me. "I still feel awful that I doubted you," I tell him.

"It's OK," said Pete. "I didn't take it personally. You were terrified of your nail polish too, remember?"

"It had phthalates in it." I threw out all my makeup and most of my toiletries, certain that otherwise Stella would be born deformed. That was in the second trimester.

After saying goodbye to Pete, I sit on the bed and lean against the headboard. The raised embroidery on one of the decorative pillows digs painfully into my back. I was in the second trimester when I became convinced the oily bread was harming me.

20.

My doctor ran the probe over my gently rounded stomach. "I'm a little concerned about the size, for twenty-one weeks." She frowned at the ultrasound picture. "You need to take in more calories."

I was stricken. After all this time relaxing and gestating, I only wanted to hear good news. "But the baby is OK?"

"You can feel movement?"

I nodded.

"How's the nausea? Any better?"

"I feel like I'm about to throw up some of the time, but I never actually do." She had a corkboard plastered with baby pictures: girl babies with tulle rose headbands, boy babies with robot onesies. Pregnancy felt like one long battle against nausea and exhaustion. It was almost a jolt to remember I had a baby like these inside me: Stella's brother or sister.

The doctor frowned. "Morning sickness usually fades away in the second trimester. Have you found anything to help with it?"

She glanced at my chart. "You tried promethazine in the first trimester. That didn't work?"

I shook my head. "I only feel better when I eat this one kind of flatbread."

"Pregnant women often get very specific cravings." She smiled to herself. "For me, it was freshly squeezed orange juice. No other kind. Had to be completely fresh." She studied the sharp bones of my hips. "What else are you eating?"

"This bread is the only thing that makes me feel better. Then I sleep for hours."

"A lot of people have trouble with bread nowadays."

A muscle jumped under my eye: it was happening more, recently. I placed my cold fingertips on my cheek. "I've never had trouble before."

"Pregnancy can change your body. What else are you eating?"

"Not much," I said.

The doctor tutted. "No wonder you're so sluggish. You need to choose from all four food groups. When you eat this flatbread, your body metabolizes the sugar in it very fast; then you crash. That's what makes you so sleepy." She handed me a leaflet about eating well in pregnancy. "I recommend you take a break from gluten for a few days. If you're allergic to it, gluten can make depression and anxiety worse."

I sat up, clutching the paper sheet that covered my bottom half. "I'm not depressed. I'm happy. I'm finally having another child. I already have a wonderful daughter. I actually couldn't be happier . . ." I stopped, realizing that I was babbling.

I had to stop eating the bread.

I'd always scoffed at those who gave up gluten, reasoning that most people who claimed an allergy really wanted a shortcut to losing weight. But now that the doctor pointed it out, it was obvious that if I ate a lot of bread—really, nothing but bread—and also slept a lot, there was probably a connection.

When I got home, I went into the kitchen and found the last bit of oily bread in the house, leftover from the previous day. I was hungry, and I could almost taste its delicious, salty greasiness. But I gritted my teeth, stuffed it into a compostable bag, and put the bag in the green bin outside. Then I went to the fridge, determined to devise a lunch that included all four food groups.

But nothing in the fridge appealed. Meanwhile, the bread was still perfectly edible, sealed in its bag. It was wrong to waste food, and one last piece could hardly do any harm. I went back outside and opened the bin, and a bone caught my eye. I thought of how Stella ate meat right off the bone now, eyes alight with gusto, and my stomach twisted. Maybe Pete was right and there was nothing to worry about, but if there was something wrong, I had to stay alert. I tore the bag open and used a broom handle to poke the bread beneath banana peels and old porridge.

Back in the kitchen, I choked down a broccoli floret and then ate chickpeas from the can. Having food in my stomach, food that Irina hadn't prepared, made me feel a little bit stronger. We didn't need her as much as I'd thought. Without the bread, the nausea was back, but my thoughts seemed to come faster.

. . .

When Irina and Stella got home from school, they were excited. Irina held a garment bag. "Irina has a present for me!" Stella announced. "She said I had to wait until we got home to open it."

"Another present?" I was uneasy. As well as the afghan, Irina had given us a tablecloth covered with pomegranates, and several animal figurines. The house was even beginning to smell like her: sensible soap, stewed tea, that heavy spice I couldn't name.

Irina laid the bag flat along the length of the sofa. "Little Wolf, you want to open?"

As Stella tugged at the zipper, I had a sudden vision of it opening to reveal Blanka's face, her round cheeks and thick brows. But then Stella was hauling out a mass of shiny white fabric. A high-necked dress with leg-of-mutton sleeves. A white brocade waistcoat edged with gold braid. A white fez with a veil attached. Every part of the dress seemed to have some kind of decoration: silver embroidery, gold braid, flounces. There was even a pair of lace gloves.

I stared. "A wedding dress?"

"Belong to my mother, then to me. Now I give to Stella." Irina's eyes were bright.

"Oh no," I said. I couldn't imagine Stella wearing this dress, which for a start, looked as tight and scratchy as possible, but also had a lace collar that came up to the chin, and even the sleeves came to the wrists. In this dress, the only skin visible would be the face. It was like a straitjacket. A bride who wore this wouldn't be able to move. "I mean, thank you so much, but I don't think—"

"Will I get married one day?" Stella asked. I stared at her. Once she would have announced that she was never, ever getting married, especially not in this yucky dress, but now she touched the cheap synthetic fabric in a dreamy way—fabric that if you washed it would send toxic microfibers into the sea. "I will have a wedding?"

"Yes, my darling." Irina beamed, like of course every eight-year-old girl dreams of her wedding day.

"Actually, you might never get married," I said. "Not everyone does these days. And of course, there's lots of other things ahead of you in life. So maybe—"

Irina interrupted: "My mother wore; then I did. Now you keep in Stella's room. One day Stella wears."

In "Charlotte Says," I'd written that there is no polite way to refuse a gift, but I couldn't bear to accept this one. "We don't actually have that much storage space," I said. The house was big, but after we gutted the place and knocked down interior walls, we did not have many closets and cupboards. This dress would take up half Stella's closet, just like Irina's black stewpot took up space on the kitchen counter and her afghan ruined my spare esthetic.

"I am last of my family," Irina said. "Now I want to give to Stella."

I turned to Stella: "Honey, go to your room. Go and read—or crochet." She went, like one of those biddable children on TV shows that leave when adults want to talk, even though everyone knows that children never do that in real life. They know when adults are about to talk about something interesting, and they want to stay. Who was this new, malleable child? What happened to freak-out mode? I tamped down my fear and focused on the issue at hand.

I couldn't merely say, "No, thank you," because Irina wasn't offering me a second helping of mashed potatoes. She was offering me a precious gift, a piece of herself. Besides, we'd taken so much from her. I should have insisted on paying her. Now what we owed her was unspecified and so could never be enough.

But if I took the dress, it would bind us to her forever.

"I'm sorry, I can't accept this gift," I said, and Irina shrank into herself. Suddenly, she looked weary and small.

"My grandmother made this dress. Now nobody will wear. I give to charity. Dresses for Angels." She gave me a sidelong look. "They make into gowns for dead babies."

I stared at her. Was there really such a charity? She was going too far. The way she hunched into herself and looked pathetic. It reminded me of a seagull we'd seen once, when at the beach for a picnic. Stella often told us not to feed wild things, and she shooed the other seagulls away, but one hovered on the edge of the group, a scruffy grey gull, when all the rest were white. She limped, and her head was unnaturally close to her body: something was wrong with her neck. Maybe she was malformed or had been injured. She'd die if we didn't feed her. But when we had nothing left to give her, she underwent a transformation. Her head rose as her neck extended. She walked with dainty confidence. Even her feathers looked glossier. She spread her wings and took off. She'd been fine all along, the whole thing an act.

"The outfit will have to go to Dresses for Angels," I said firmly.

"I leave here," Irina said, and I couldn't breathe. I felt like if I didn't draw a line, she would bring more and more stuff, until she was living with us and we were stuck with her forever.

I patted the sofa to get her to sit down next to me. "Look, Irina, I'm feeling better. I really don't feel comfortable prevailing on you."

"Prevail? What is this?"

"You don't need to come every day. You could just visit. That would be more relaxing for you. Maybe once a week."

Irina stroked the dress as if it were made of the finest silk instead of cheap rayon. "I want to come every day."

Charlotte Says: If you want to refuse someone's company, frame it as a positive, rather than a negative. Don't say, "I don't want to have a drink with you." Say, "I've scheduled that night for me time."

"I need time with Stella before the baby comes," I said.

"I pick her up two days," Irina said firmly. "You pick her up three days."

"OK," I said. A gradual transition would be easier for Stella. "There's another thing. It was really kind of you, but I don't need to eat the bread now. I'm feeling better." Or I soon would.

"Fine," Irina said. She took her time putting on her raincoat, seemingly confused by the buttons she'd tackled many times, judging by how old it looked. I hoped that rejecting her bread gift wasn't some kind of mortal insult.

That evening, Pete heated up a veggie tagine from our favorite shop, with couscous to go with it. Vowing to eat a nutritious meal, I spooned it up, trying not to wince: surely the sauce wasn't supposed to be this sour. "It's great to see you eating," Pete said as I worked up the energy to swallow. I realized he was brimming with news.

"What is it?"

"Home Depot are in. They're gonna sign. I can finally pay everyone at the company what they deserve."

"That's fantastic, baby! Does this mean you can relax a little?"

Pete adjusted his glasses. "I wanted to talk to you about that. I didn't really think things through. This deal means we have to ramp up production fast. The time when I can work less is still a while away. I'm just so glad we've got Irina to help."

"Actually, I decided I need more time with Stella," I told him, swallowing a mouthful of couscous. "I've told Irina I'm going to do the school pickup three days a week."

Pete put his fork down. "But Stella's been doing so well. She loves Irina."

"Not as much as her own mother, surely." I put down my spoon, defeated. The couscous looked like tiny eggs, the kind Pete picked off his kale in the spring.

21.

Pete's timer rang. "OK, rub for three minutes and leave," he said. He was kneeling in the middle of the kitchen floor holding a cloth, which he'd been rubbing at the pale blot left after Stella's birthday party. He squinted at the spot. It was barely visible now—a mark you could see only in the right light, if you knew what you were looking for. "Thank god for the Internet," he said in triumph. "I should have done this ages ago." He held up a spray bottle: mineral spirits. "I got the odorless variety on purpose so as not to bother you."

"The mark looks better already," I said.

"So listen, you won't have to do a thing," Pete said. "I've invited people for Thanksgiving." Even though the mineral spirits were supposedly odorless, they reeked like paint thinner. I breathed through my mouth as Pete explained he'd invited people over from work on impulse, but it would be OK because it was a potluck, people were bringing dishes, and so really, I wouldn't have to lift a finger.

"How could you invite people without asking me?" I said. "It's our last Thanksgiving just the three of us. Maybe it would be nice to keep it just us this year."

His face fell. "I thought you'd be pleased it was all taken care of. You love Thanksgiving."

True, I treasured the tradition of spending the entire day cooking and eating with family and friends, and we'd kept it up even after moving to the UK.

"Thanksgiving dinner with three people *is* a little sad," I admitted. And I did have more energy, now I was eating from the nonbread food groups.

"Yes! This is going to be so great. The Brits at the company will get to experience a real Thanksgiving. It'll be a celebration of the Home Depot deal. A celebration of how well Stella's doing too. Thank you, baby." He gave me a smacking kiss on the lips. "Oh, and I've invited Irina. It will make Stella happy if she's there."

This was true. Stella had been sulky when I told her Irina would only be picking her up twice a week. And she didn't seem to be getting much benefit from me doing the other three pickups. I'd thought that if I spent more time with her, she'd get back to her true self. She'd insist we race paper planes, or talk my ear off explaining why a stork's wing was the most aerodynamic. Instead, she just crocheted, or cradled Stick Thing, the doll she'd made with Irina, and sang incomprehensible lullabies under her breath.

As I was finishing the Thanksgiving table decorations ten days later, tying the napkins with rustic twine, Stella clattered down the stairs with Irina behind her.

"What do you think?" Irina said proudly. "She look nice for dinner." I stared, stunned: her hair was in two plaits. Stella had never let anyone touch her hair but me, and she'd never even allowed me to do a ponytail. But Irina had somehow subdued that abundant hair into two skimpy plaits, finished with elastic holders decorated with pink plastic bobbles.

Surely not the same ones that had belonged to Blanka?

"Beautiful, darling," I said stiffly.

We had eight guests, including five from Mycoship: Nathan, the CEO; Kia, who did biz dev—she was American like Pete; and three younger employees. Pete had also invited Nick and Emmy to stop everyone from talking shop all evening (they were leaving their kids with a babysitter). And of course, there was Irina, who bustled around heating up the various things people had brought, even though Pete kept telling her to relax. The collective odor was almost too much. It smelled like a year's worth of leftover school dinners, scraped off plates and boiled down to a concentrate.

Kia's cranberry sauce was the one dish that tempted me, with its waft of orange zest—her mother's recipe, she said. She was muscular from her triathlon training, and her long blond hair was greying naturally. "Your hair is lovely," I said.

Kia tossed her head. "Who has time to get their hair colored, right? I'd rather go for a bike ride." She smelled of magnesium muscle soak and sports deodorant, not unpleasant. "You must be so excited about the baby."

I smiled. "Please. You think we should be paying a carbon tax." Kia had once confided in me that she couldn't have kids because of premature ovarian failure, but at the same time, she'd realized she didn't want them for environmental reasons. "I'm not judging if other people have kids, but for me, the climate crisis is a reason to feel good about not having them," she'd said.

Kia turned to Stella, who was standing at the edge of the kitchen. "Do you remember me? We met a couple of years ago, you were five or six. Are you still interested in disasters? You told me all about the *Titanic*."

"I don't remember," Stella said. How could she not remember? She remembered how many people survived and how many dogs, even the breeds (two Pomeranians and a Pekinese).

Kia smiled. "Are you excited about your little brother or sister?"

"Oh yes," Stella said. I flinched. Was there any way I could reasonably ask her to stop saying two of the most common words in the English language? Pete joined us, putting his arm around me. He wore a crisp shirt instead of his usual California-casual T-shirt. His beard looked more neatly shaped. He'd put some stuff on it, beard balm. I could smell it, fresh and clean like a snowy morning.

"Any names picked out?" Kia asked Pete.

"Whatever it is, it's got to be something I can make into a tattoo. I already have a star for Stella." He rolled up his sleeve and showed the black-and-white nautical star, in the style of a compass rose, adorning his bicep. "I apologize for how cheesy this sounds, but she guides me home. My true north."

My heart squeezed. He hadn't shown anyone that tattoo since the birthday party. Pete picked Stella up, but instead of clinging to him, she just hung there, a deadweight, and he put her down again. "Stella Bella Banana. You're getting bigger. I'm so proud of how well you've been doing at school. Want to go swimming together on Saturday?" She nodded.

I stared. Really? She was suddenly OK with splashing and jostling? What if she found a Band-Aid floating in the water?

Then Emmy came up to us and twirled one of Stella's plaits. "Gorgeous hairdo!"

"Doesn't she look cute?" Pete agreed.

Emmy's gaze flicked to the pristine floor for a moment, and I wondered if she was remembering. She'd been right there when it happened.

At Stella's birthday party, when she'd finally had enough of the animal entertainer tormenting small creatures and the noisy strangers crowding her house, she went into her bedroom and removed her underwear. Then she walked into the kitchen, where the biggest concentration of guests could be found, squatted down, and she— she—well, right in the middle of the floor.

I was in the powder room at the time, splashing cold water on my face. I heard the gasps and rushed into the kitchen. The area emptied in a flash. I took Stella upstairs while Pete pretended to be jolly. He whisked the mess away and cleaned up. But the guests left without singing "Happy Birthday." As they shuffled out the door, Pete told everyone she had an upset tummy. Everyone kept saying they totally understood, it was normal for kids to have accidents, who hadn't been there?

But this wasn't a three-year-old who was poorly potty-trained. This was a child of eight. And this wasn't loss of control of her bodily functions. Stella had shown consummate command of her body, and this was the most disturbing part of it. She wasn't the least bit upset or embarrassed. Her bearing was regal as she stood in the center of the kitchen after this very deliberate act.

Pete knew and I knew that Stella would become the story other parents told themselves to make themselves feel better: "Cyrus might be terrified of movie trailers and have a rash because of his compulsive chin-licking—but he would never take a dump in the middle of his own birthday party." The same people probably got a kick out of saying that she was—literally—a party pooper.

But now Pete was beaming. We were having people over again, and Stella was behaving beautifully, sitting at the table and eating everything on her plate, instead of guzzling the meal in her room. But only because Irina was here. Was this why Pete invited her?

Nathan turned his focus on me. "Pete says you used to write an etiquette column. What is that, like what fork to use?"

"Not at all," Pete said. "It wasn't stuffy. Charlotte was very funny."

I offered, "Thank-you notes shouldn't begin with the words *thank you* because—"

"Thank-you notes?" One of the younger employees, the one with a tongue stud, spoke. "We're way too lazy for those nowadays. I send a text. Or, you know, just say thank you at the time."

"The world is falling apart," Nathan pronounced gloomily. "Eventually all politeness will vanish and we'll all be shooting each other over the last patch of inhabitable earth." He paused. "So, what are you passionate about, Charlotte?"

"I never said I *wasn't* passionate about etiquette," I said. "Won't we need it even more when we're all fighting disaster?"

"Sure," said Nathan. "But seriously. What are you really passionate about?"

"Dude, I thought British people didn't ask each other that kind of question," Kia said. She winked at me. "Isn't that like asking each other how much money you earn?"

I smiled at Kia. "What are *you* passionate about, Nathan?" Let him feel what it was like to be put on the spot.

"Mushrooms," Nathan said firmly. "They're gonna save the world." The conversation moved on to mushrooms' recycling powers—there were even some that could eat plastic—and I sat there, crumbling a piece of cornbread.

Pete stood up and tapped his knife on his glass. "Thanksgiving is traditionally a time to give thanks, so I want to say I'm thankful for my beautiful wife, my incredible daughter, and my second child on the way. I'm grateful for new friends and old ones." He raised his glass. "I'm grateful for all you guys. And I'm grateful I get to be part of Mycoship, this amazing company that's doing some good in the world."

I clinked glasses with the others and took a token sip of champagne. Stella took no notice of Pete. She wolfed her food, and then I let her have her dessert right away so she could go to her room.

"It's fucking great to have a home-cooked meal," Nathan announced. "I've barely had time to boil water for ramen since Home Depot got on board." The employees murmured their agreement.

When the rest of us had our pumpkin pie, Kia turned to Irina, who hadn't joined in with the conversation so far. "So, Irina, tell us about yourself. Where are you from?"

"Azerbaijan," Irina said. There was silence as everyone racked their brains for one scrap of information about this faraway country and came up with nothing.

I'd been wrong: not Kyrgyzstan or Uzbekistan, not that I knew any more about those places. I felt ashamed that I didn't know. I vowed to look up Azerbaijan later.

"And what brought you over to England?" Kia asked.

"Pogrom," Irina said.

Kia took a minute to swallow her mouthful and then said the only thing you could say: "I'm so sorry. That must have been awful."

Emmy ventured, "Wasn't that back in the nineties, Irene? The Russians . . ." She trailed off, having reached the limits of her knowledge.

"Soviet Union collapse," Irina said. "We Armenians live in Azerbaijan many years. We think maybe will be OK, then Azerbaijanis start killing us. They kill Blanka's father."

The railroad-tie light fixture—I'd never noticed how heavy it was before. I felt it was about to come crashing down on our beeswax candles, our handcrafted dishes. "That's terrible, Irina," Pete said. "You don't have to talk about this. We can stop talking about it."

Was Pete respecting her silence or trying to get his dinner party back on track?

"What happened to him?" I asked, sure that she was not finished. I'd always assumed he'd died of something quotidian, like a heart attack. Too much meat stew.

"They shut him in oven," Irina said. "They burn him."

I clapped my hand over my mouth, feeling like it was all going to come back up, the little I had eaten.

Everyone murmured how sorry they were. There was a long

pause, during which people gulped wine. Then Nathan said, "But how do you shut someone in an oven?"

"How?" Irina looked at him, coming back from far away.

"It's too small, isn't it?"

"What do you know about ovens?" one of the twentysomethings said.

Kia nodded. "Right? I doubt he's ever even turned his on."

I glared at Nathan, though I understood why he'd asked the question. The cryptic way she talked. The little house in the forest. The husband shut in the oven. Like something out of a fairy story.

"It is bread oven," Irina said firmly. "Plenty of room."

"And then what happened?" Kia asked.

Irina sat up straight, dignified. "Then I walk over mountains with Blanka, with my daughter. She is three years old. I carry nothing but wedding dress and often Blanka too. For three days, with nothing to eat but dandelion."

"Well, I'm grateful that you are here tonight," Kia said to Irina. "Where is your daughter now?"

"She passed away," Emmy whispered loudly, at the same time as Irina said, "Dead."

Kia placed her hand over Irina's. To her credit, she didn't try to make it any better. I felt awful. I'd judged Irina for being a no-neck seagull. I'd tried to push her away. I'd had no idea of the depth of her suffering.

The guests left soon after dessert, and I slipped up to Stella's room to check on her. Her light was off. I listened for the sound of her breathing, and instead I heard a busy little sound. *Scritch scratch. Scritch scratch.* A mouse? I snapped the light on and caught Stella scrambling to put something under her pillow. I was sure it was the diary. I could see her pen on the nightstand.

"You don't have to write in the dark, honey," I said. "Don't you want your nightlight on?" She'd always hated complete darkness. She shook her head. "Without your nightlight, it's dark-dark," I said.

"I like the dark-dark," she said.

Another change, I thought. "Night night, my precious." She let me kiss her, and I recoiled a little: even though she hadn't been swimming for a few days and had since bathed daily without fail, she smelled faintly of chlorine.

Pete insisted on doing all the clearing up, so I lay on the sofa. I found myself googling "Azerbaijan bread ovens" and learned they made their bread in giant clay pots, with a fire at the bottom. The bakers leaned in to slap the bread to the walls. The ovens didn't look big enough to fit a person. Maybe they cut him in pieces first, but this wasn't a Grimms' fairy tale. That kind of thing didn't happen in real life. Then I read a little about the Baku pogrom and dropped my phone, nauseated.

Irina surely still thought about his death. Now she had to think about Blanka's death too. But she kept on going. How weak I was by contrast. I doubtless seemed absurd to her, too much of a delicate flower to get out of bed some days, stressing because my daughter was only reading at her own age level, because I didn't like her hair in plaits. I should be so grateful for what I had. My child was alive. I fell asleep determined to be nicer to Irina. I could let her be a family member of sorts. You could still set boundaries with family members after all.

In the small hours, I heard a little sound, faint but persistent. I crept to our bedroom door and listened. Silence. I went back to bed and drifted off. In my dreams, I kept hearing that sound: *scritch scratch*, as if some creature were busy in the wall, making its home inside ours.

22.

I went by Irina's after school drop-off the next morning—of course English children didn't have the day off—to tell her we'd keep the wedding dress. She just nodded, like it had been a done deal all along.

"You stay for tea," Irina said, and disappeared into the kitchen. As I sat down, I wondered what on earth we were going to talk about. Other than Stella, we had no interests in common. I contemplated Blanka's school photo, in which she smiled stiffly.

Returning with the tray, Irina caught me looking at the photo, and I felt I was expected to say something about Blanka. "They grow up so fast," I offered.

"Not Blanka."

I nodded. So maybe she did want to talk about Blanka. I'd been so desperate for her help, so ill, that I'd never realized. But here was a chance.

"What was she like as a child?"

"Blanka takes long time to grow up," Irina said. She poured tea from a hideous monkey teapot. The monkey's tail was the handle and its head, resting on the lid, was the knob on top. "She does not—have blood, you know."

"Blood?" I was startled.

"Menstruation," Irina said.

"Right," I said. I'd been expecting to hear about Blanka's first day at school, about the one-eared bear she took everywhere, or about their happy hours crocheting together. Not this.

"No menstruation, her whole life," Irina continued. "We do not know why. But for years, no blood."

I was uncomfortable. I would never have talked to Blanka about this when she was alive, and it seemed like the dead deserved their privacy even more.

"She didn't menstruate," I repeated, falling back on my mirroring technique. But she was in her thirties, a grown woman. "Did you not go to the doctor?"

Irina shook her head. "I ask, but she say no, no, no, is OK."

This seemed strange to me, but then Blanka was a quiet woman whose English wasn't fluent even after nearly two decades in this country. She was so secretive, so private. Perhaps she didn't want to talk to a doctor about something so intimate or, god forbid, remove her long skirt and oversized hoodie and submit to a physical examination.

"But then," Irina said, cradling her teacup, "four days before she die, she is woman."

"Blood? I mean, she was menstruating?"

Irina nodded. The jam seemed very red as she spooned more of it into her tea. I didn't know what to say. All through my teens, I'd never mentioned the word *period* in front of my mother. She replenished the supplies under the sink without comment. It was strange to hear Irina talking about the topic so frankly.

I felt sad for Blanka, not menstruating for years and not knowing why. It was tragic that she couldn't do what a privileged, rich person would do, what I had done for Stella (although it hadn't worked): march straight into the doctor's office and demand to know what the matter was.

"Blanka told you about it?" I said.

"I find blood in her underwear when I am washing clothes."

I shifted uneasily. Wasn't it strange that Blanka hadn't told her mother that, finally, her period had started?

Irina was looking at me, like she wanted something more from me. Maybe she simply wanted someone else to know about this tragic irony: Blanka had in a sense grown up right before she died. Maybe it was enough to share this information with me. Or perhaps she felt guilty that she had not watched over Blanka closely enough. "Do you think there could have been a connection with her heart condition?" I asked.

Irina looked blank. "What condition?"

"The one that, you know . . . killed her."

"Charlotte," Irina said. "She kills herself."

Blood roared in my ears like waves, pounding and crashing. "No, she had a heart attack. That's what you told me. In the hot tub."

She shook her head. "Neighbor has bad back. Blanka is house-sitting. She takes all his muscle relaxants, then gets into hot tub, drinks whole bottle of vodka."

"But you said it was a heart condition."

"She has sickness here," Irina said, placing a fist over her breastbone. "I tell you this. She pass out. She go under. All this I tell you. You hear something else."

"Oh god," I said, thinking she must have thought that my reaction was lacking. She must have thought me callous, shallow. "I'm sorry. That day you took me to the hot tub, I didn't realize what you were saying. I thought it was an accident. I didn't realize she killed herself. I am so sorry, I didn't realize the—the level of tragedy, if that makes sense."

Irina bent over her crochet work, lips pursed. Maybe this was a way to survive: you focused on the next stitch, then the next. That way you could tell someone that your daughter killed herself, and not fall down on the ground and tear your own heart out.

I was too upset to go home. I needed to move. I went to Alexandra Park, where Blanka and Stella had once spent so much time. I walked round and round the duck pond, where brown algae partly covered the oily water. It was cold, the sky grey and low. I found myself at these concrete cylinders of varying heights that were big enough to climb inside. Stella called them the soup pots. Once, I got home and Blanka and Stella were still out. It was past the time that Blanka was supposed to stop work, so I'd run to the park and found them here. Stella crouched inside one of them, and Blanka was making stirring motions with her hand and calling, "And now I put in parsley, chop, chop, chop! Salt and pepper! I am heating up water and boiling you!" Stella was laughing hysterically as she scrambled out and ran away.

Was Blanka depressed the whole time she took care of Stella, for four years, getting worse and worse? But why didn't she *tell* me? If Blanka felt so bad that she killed herself, why did she never ask me for help? We weren't close, we barely knew each other, but I would have helped her if she'd ever asked. I replayed the last few months that I'd known her, the last few months of her life, trying to find a clue in her behavior.

She became sloppier in that time. She took Stella to the park without taking her sunscreen or hat, even though I left the go bag packed and ready by the door. I frequently reminded her to put a drop of bleach solution inside Stella's bath toys to prevent mold growth, but when I squeezed Stella's little blue whale, black gunk shot out.

Still, I wasn't about to look for someone else. Stella was happy with Blanka, and Blanka, in turn, stayed calm whatever Stella did.

The last day she worked for us, I had a deadline and worked late. I emerged from my home office and found Blanka tied to a dining chair. Stella had used loops of masking tape and several colors of ribbon from my gift-wrapping station. Wrapped around her middle was a rope made out of a couple of my bras and a few pairs of tights.

I could never tell if Blanka was brilliant at playing or incredibly apathetic. But I was tired, twelve weeks pregnant, and feeling very sick. I didn't want to deal with this situation. I wanted Blanka to do the job I'd paid her to do. Stella's cheeks were flushed, her breath smelled like chocolate. Blanka had let her plunder my secret stash. I felt a headache coming. "Has she had dinner at least?" I asked.

"She does not want," Blanka said, and I thought, No kidding, why would she bother with vegetables after eating a bar of Green & Black's Salted Caramel?

To be fair, I did tell Blanka not to force Stella to eat. But I also instructed her to put a proper balanced meal in front of Stella each night—whether she consumed it or not—and I saw no sign of cooking.

"Why aren't you in bed, darling?" I asked Stella.

"We're playing Houdini," Stella explained. "Blanka has to escape."

Looking closer, I saw there were knots upon knots upon knots: wool from a pompom-making project in which Stella had lost interest, even the bungee cords Pete used to secure his bike on the car.

I felt hungry but sick at the same time. I found my super-sharp fabric scissors. "I'll have to cut you out," I said. I started at the bottom. Her ankles were tied to the chair legs with kitchen twine. As I slid the scissors inside a loop of twine, Stella said, "No, Mommy! You're ruining the game."

Snip.

"I worked really hard on this," Stella wailed.

Snip. At this rate it could take forty-five minutes to get Blanka free. Stella wouldn't be in bed until close to eleven. Late bedtime meant freak-out mode tomorrow, and I would do anything to avoid that. "Blanka, I'm sorry. You'll have to wait."

"Oh yes," said Blanka.

"Do you want your phone?" I said. Slight head shake. Why wouldn't the woman ever accept anything from me? I would feel better if she would allow me to make her comfortable. "Glass of water? A snack? Wine?"

Blanka nodded at her bound wrists, and I realized, obviously, she couldn't eat or drink. But she didn't seem to mind the prospect of sitting there doing nothing. It was like Blanka had pared down the things she was willing to do until nothing was left except simply exist.

When I came downstairs after putting Stella to bed, I cut her out as quickly as I could, feeling horribly guilty that she'd had to wait, even though she was the one who'd allowed Stella to put her in this situation.

When I finally freed her, Blanka didn't get up right away, not until I prompted her: "Thank you, you can go home now." She gathered her things while I knelt and picked up tangles of wool and twine. Finally, she trudged to the door and paused on the threshold. There was that moment then when I could have asked her how she was, how she really spent her time, because nobody could spend every weekend doing "not much." I should have known that if a person is content to sit alone, bound hand and foot, there is something wrong. Maybe if I'd done something, I could have stopped her: it took so little to stop a person from killing themselves. I'd read that all you had to do was smile at someone as they made their way to the Golden Gate Bridge, and that could be enough to make them turn back.

But I was too tired to smile. She turned as she walked down the path and waved, always that same wave for hello and goodbye, with a circular motion of her hand, as if wiping clean an invisible pane.

She came back two days later, even though it was a Sunday, because she wanted to collect her pay cheque, which she'd forgotten. She often forgot to take it—Was that her excuse to come back on days she didn't work? Did she need us, was she asking for something? But the day she came back for her pay cheque, I was at a prenatal yoga class, and Pete was home with Stella.

And the next day, "I cannot come anymore."

I hated myself for not realizing that Blanka was so depressed. But Irina lived with her and still didn't realize. Maybe depression wasn't always obvious, but Irina knew that Blanka had no periods. The more I thought about it, the more I was convinced that Irina should have pushed Blanka to see a doctor, even if this was uncomfortable. Who knew, Blanka could have had a hormonal imbalance, which could also have caused her depression. She could have got treatment. I thought of Blanka's school photo: her hair had been in braids then, and she'd had the same hairstyle until she died. Perhaps Irina liked having an adult daughter who was like a child, who would never grow up and leave home.

Maybe Irina wasn't the mother I'd thought.

23.

Yoo-hoo! Charlotte!" Emmy came over at pickup time, pushing Madeleine in the stroller. Lulu and Stella were nearby. It was No Uniform Day (a FOMHS fundraising scheme, all the parents donated a pound so their kids could go to school in their own clothes), and Emmy and Lulu wore matching mother-daughter outfits: navy-and-white striped dresses, their hair in ballerina buns. Cherie walked by with Zach in tow and fluttered her fingers at me, and I felt a pang.

"You look great," Emmy said, surveying my figure. "How do you stay so skinny? You barely even look pregnant."

"Hm," I said, thinking that with talk like that, Lulu would be anorexic before she hit puberty.

"Lulu and I are going to try out the new patisserie," Emmy continued. "I know, I know, like Muswell Hill needs another patisserie! But I've heard their gluten-free raspberry croissants are really good. Do you want to come?"

"Thanks, but we really should get back." I didn't want to go to the patisserie with Emmy and make superficial conversation. It was nearly two weeks since Irina had told me about Blanka's suicide, but the last time I'd seen Blanka still played on a loop in my head. If only I'd smiled. If only I'd said something.

But Stella was already nodding, letting Lulu drag her along.

"Looks like the girls have already decided," Emmy said, and I had no choice but to follow. When we found a table, Emmy went to order, leaving Madeleine with us in the stroller. Lulu whispered to Stella, and Stella nodded and began to murmur something under her breath. Stella's hair hung in skimpy plaits, secured with the plastic bobbles. Lulu listened intently. I caught phrases here and there. "Her little old father and her little old mother . . ." Stella continued to mutter under her breath. Then Lulu gasped and clapped her hand over her mouth. A nervous giggle erupted.

"No way. An oven! How did they fit him in?"

My stomach clenched tight, the baby a little fist.

"That's enough," I told Stella. "Not another word." She clamped her lips shut obediently.

"But how—" asked Lulu.

"It's a fairy tale, it doesn't have to make sense," I snapped.

"What's going on?" said Emmy, returning with our order, and I managed to distract everyone by babbling about Lulu's gluten-free croissant. "It's amazing how it looks identical to the normal kind. Same color, same flakiness. It must be really hard for them to tell the difference. Do you think they ever get them mixed up?"

This caused consternation, and by the time it was resolved, Lulu had forgotten about hearing the rest of Stella's story.

. . .

On the way home, I asked Stella, "I heard you telling Lulu how Blanka's father died. How do you know about that?"

"Irina told me."

"Irina?" I was stunned. How could she think the pogrom was appropriate information for an eight-year-old?

"I know what happened to Blanka too," Stella remarked. "She took too much medicine on purpose, so she would fall asleep and drown." She fell silent and trudged along.

My head throbbed. Now that Stella knew these terrible things, she seemed sullied somehow, no longer a child. She spoke of the horror so casually, as if she felt nothing. She was like a disaster survivor who was still in shock. It hit me that of course Stella *was* in shock. She'd shut down because Irina had told her about the worst things humans could do. *This* was why she barely spoke—to me, at any rate—and dragged herself about, why her mind worked at a fraction of its usual speed.

I had to get rid of Irina. No haggling over how many pickups we'd each do. I had to get rid of her for good.

It was Irina's turn to collect Stella the following day. When they got home, she went into the kitchen and began unpacking Stella's lunchbox, something Blanka never did. I turned to Stella: "Can you go to your room? Take a snack from the kitchen."

"Oh yes." She went.

"I need to speak to you," I told Irina.

She nodded, but began filling her black stewpot with water so I had to raise my voice over the sound of the tap. "You shouldn't have told Stella all those terrible things," I said.

She hefted the pot onto the stove. "Children need truth."

"But not the *entire* truth, Irina. She's not old enough for that. Can you not see how much she's changed? You've traumatized her."

Irina nodded, like I was just telling her we'd run out of bin bags, and turned the gas on under her pot. I turned it off, placed myself between her and the stove.

"I'm sorry, but I don't feel comfortable with you taking care of Stella."

Irina took an onion from the basket she kept on the countertop, determined not to hear me. I stood there, hesitating. With my columns, there was always one troll who said, "Just tell it like it is." If your dinner party guests stay too late, if someone serves you a food you hate, if a friend asks if they can come to your birthday party when you didn't invite them, tell the truth. I want you to go now. I don't like this food. I didn't invite you because I don't like you.

But I couldn't "tell it like it is" to Irina. I couldn't "tell it like it is" to anyone, let alone her. I could not say, "Get out of my house. I don't trust you to take care of my daughter, because you failed your own daughter."

She was watching me, shoulders hunched, eyes sunken. I couldn't just "tell it like it is," because she'd suffered too much.

We stood there, frozen, for a moment. Then I emptied the stewpot and thrust it into her arms. I walked to the front door, opened it wide, and stood there. She would have to go eventually, and then all I had to do was not let her back in.

Irina moved towards the door finally, her lips so tightly pressed they were almost folded inwards. It was raining outside. She surveyed my bump. "You have baby in hospital?"

"Probably," I said, wrong-footed by this new tack.

"Bad idea. Very dangerous."

"Hospitals in this country are pretty safe," I said.

"In my country, I help with many, many babies at home," Irina said. "All I need is old shower curtain and scissors." She snipped with two fingers and smiled. "I boil. Good for Stella too. She can help."

"I don't think so." I went upstairs to tell Stella that Irina was leaving. "She has to go away for a while," I said, lacking the energy for a proper explanation. At the door, Stella flung her arms around Irina. "Goodbye, Little Wolf," Irina said. When she left, Stella didn't protest, and this made me more certain I was doing the right thing. Something was very wrong if she could no longer cry or scream.

After Irina was gone, I got a plastic bag and swept through the house, purging it of the afghan, the ceramic spoon rest, the tea caddy, the sticky pot of jam, the packets of herbs and spices. I tied the bag and threw it in the cupboard under the stairs. I'd drop it all by Irina's house at some point. For now, I wanted to get it out of my sight.

I went to the powder room and took my time washing my hands. When I returned to the kitchen area, the cross was back. It wasn't on top of the patch where I'd removed the paint, but higher up. Stella would have had to climb on a chair to draw it. I thought she'd been in her room the whole time, but obviously she'd sneaked out while I was washing my hands. I called her, and she shuffled down the stairs—shuffled, when she used to spring and prance. "I see you've drawn another cross on the wall, even though I asked you not to," I said. "Why did you do that?"

"I did not," said Stella. "I was upstairs."

"Stella, you know all those things Irina told you? How Blanka died, and how Blanka's father died. Pretty upsetting things. Do you want to talk about it?"

She shrugged. "I'm not dead." Again, that puzzling phrase, the one that sounded so callous but surely betrayed a depth of repressed feeling. Unless she really wasn't capable of feeling things, but I pushed that thought away.

I pointed at the cross. "Is this your way of trying to tell me something?"

"Oh yes." Stella dragged over a stool from the breakfast bar. She clambered atop the stool.

"That's not safe," I told her, but she rose to her tiptoes, her nose resting against the cross. "Stop that," I said sharply.

She meekly climbed down, but I didn't tell her to clean the wall. I decided not to clean it myself either. It was clear that whatever I said to her, the cross was going to come back. Maybe she was doing it as a cry for help. Really, that was the only explanation that made sense. In that case, the only way to stop it from reappearing was to actually help her.

Pete got home when I was putting Stella to bed, and when I came out of her room, he was in the garden, on the phone. He was crouched on his heels, digging a dandelion out of the lawn with a weed puller—he refused to use pesticides. While he worked, he murmured into the phone. Nathan was incapable of solving any problem on his own. When he saw me, he ended the call and stood up. He put his arms around me. "What's the matter, baby?"

"I had to get rid of Irina," I confessed.

Pete recoiled. "What? Why on earth would you do that? After all she's been through?"

"She told Stella that Blanka killed herself."

"Poor Blanka," Pete said. I'd told him about Blanka's suicide.

"She also told Stella about the pogrom."

"That is a lot for her to process," Pete said carefully. "But Stella seems OK."

I cast about for a way to convince him I'd done the right thing. "Irina asked about our birth plans. She said I had to have the baby at home."

"You do hate doctors."

"She offered to be the midwife."

"That's so generous."

"It's weird, Pete! And she said Stella could help. That does not sound psychologically healthy."

A vein showed in Pete's forehead. "You know I sometimes get home from work before Irina leaves. Every time, Stella stands in the window and waves until she's out of sight. Have you noticed that?"

"Well, she won't be doing that anymore." I suddenly realized that I didn't like beards, not that I would ever tell Pete that.

"At Thanksgiving, Nick said he couldn't believe how much she's changed. So neat and well-behaved."

I felt like trampling over his careful vegetable bed. "Nick's sex-ist, have you looked at his tweets? I don't want a well-behaved little girl who's all sugar and spice."

"You don't want her to behave?"

"I'm telling you, Irina has damaged her."

"Jesus, Charlotte. Have you thought about how this will affect Stella?"

"I *saw* how it affected her," I said. "She was there when I threw Irina out. She didn't react at all. No emotion. Does that sound like our daughter to you?"

Pete was silent, and I pressed my advantage. "I want to find a therapist for her. She needs to talk to someone. She needs support to process all the horror that woman has fed her."

Pete scratched his beard.

"A few months ago, you wanted to get her professional help. It couldn't hurt," I said.

"I don't agree," he said. "If she talks to a shrink about it, that could make her think it's a big deal. That could be traumatic in itself. It's like when she was little and she fell over. If you picked her up and said, 'Oops-a-daisy,' she was fine. But if you sprinted over and said, 'Oh my god, you poor baby,' she screamed her head off."

I said nothing. I wished I could make him understand how I felt about Irina and particularly about her nutso offer to serve as my midwife. It was as if, not content with messing up both her daugh-ter and mine, Irina wanted to preside over my baby's birth and reach right up inside me where I was most vulnerable.

. . .

Later, when Pete was dealing with work email, I pulled up the Google Doc he'd shared with me, back when he was pushing to take her to get assessed. I found the tab for child psychotherapists, and I felt a stab of misgiving.

When we'd lived in California, everyone seemed to go to therapy, often for the low-grade malaise that was part of life—this person loved his spouse but wasn't "in love" with her, or that person, although a successful doctor, felt she wasn't "passionate" enough about her job. Therapy seemed to be cleansing in a way that wasn't really necessary, like colonic irrigation. In my case, I couldn't see the point of rehashing my childhood after I'd launched myself more or less successfully into adult life.

But Stella was suffering from something much bigger than low-grade malaise. I clicked through therapist web pages, disqualifying anyone who seemed unserious. One woman smiled too widely, flashing teeth I thought had been straightened. A man mentioned "perfectionism" as one of the issues he helped to address—when every job interviewee knows that this is only a pretend flaw.

Wesley Bachman was a fortysomething balding man with a gentle face. He was highly educated, with a lot of letters after his name. He specialized in trauma. He was serious. Over the phone the next day, I told Wesley I believed that the shock of learning about Blanka's suicide, and about Blanka's father's murder, had caused behavior changes in Stella. "I can't get her to talk about it. All she says is 'Oh yes' and 'I'm not dead.' She acts like it's not a big deal, but I know it is. And she'll only eat at the table if Blanka's mother is present; otherwise she eats in her room. Don't you think that's weird?"

"Sometimes children don't have the language to tell us how they're feeling, so they use the tools at their disposal, the few things they have power over, such as where and when they eat."

"Well, I'm hoping you can get her to talk about how she's feeling."

"How old is she?" Wesley said, and when I told him, he continued: "Children don't do well in talk therapy at that age, so I'll mostly be observing her play."

"Stella's a very unusual child. She's hyperverbal." Then I corrected myself: "She used to be."

Wesley made sympathetic noises. "Especially for a sensitive kid, the loss of a babysitter to suicide could constitute a crisis." Wesley told me about a boy he'd treated who'd once been class president, confident, outgoing. But then he was so severely bullied at school that he stayed home and reenacted World War II online all day, obsessed with finding a different outcome. "Trauma can cause a complete personality change," Wesley said. "It can feel like you don't even recognize your child."

Finally, someone who understood.

24.

I was in luck: Wesley had a last-minute cancellation, so I was able to take Stella to see him the following day, after I collected her from school. In the car on the way there, she asked, "When is Irina coming back?"

"She's gone on holiday," I improvised. I'd tell Stella the truth when she was herself again. By then, she would have adjusted to not seeing Irina.

"For how long?"

I shrugged, and Stella slumped into her seat. My heart ached, but I had to do what was best for her.

We'd barely arrived in the waiting room when Wesley Bachman opened his office door, bang on time. He was clean-shaven and shiny-faced, dressed in jacket, shirt, and pressed khakis. He projected competence. I felt underdressed in my old grey jumper and maternity jeans. "Sorry about the drama outside," he said. "They're tree-trimming so the branches don't interfere with a power line.

Necessary work, but I do wish they weren't doing it during office hours."

I said it was fine. It was a pretty office, the walls painted blue with white clouds. There was a wooden dollhouse and a dress-up chest with costumes spilling out of it. There was a craft table, a colorful tent with a flag on top. In a corner of the room, there was a small sofa with two chairs opposite, where adults could talk.

Wesley gestured for me to sit on the sofa. "Stella, you can do whatever you prefer. You can sit with us or play."

Stella knelt down before the wooden play kitchen. I was surprised. I'd never had to encourage gender-neutral play because Stella wasn't interested in the pretend cooking and serving of meals, let alone cleaning or taking care of babies. It had always struck me as a little absurd, the way girls like Lulu and her friends feverishly cooked and served food, playing at the very activities that their moms complained about to each other. Now Stella pulled the sleeve of her cardigan over her hand and rubbed it over the stovetop. "What are you doing, sweetie?" I asked.

"Cleaning," Stella muttered.

"Don't use your sleeve, baby," I said.

Wesley asked me questions about Stella and wrote notes on a clipboard. It wasn't easy to hear everything he said, because the saw revved outside. I kept expecting Stella to put her hands over her ears. Instead, she was intent on removing every plastic saucepan and teacup from a shelf so she could wipe the shelf. She was now using her skirt. The shelf was probably dusty and sticky, but I decided to let it go. Wesley asked some basic questions, and then he said, "How was the birth?"

"It wasn't great, but what birth is? Not that you would know." I left him to interpret the tone of that one. I wasn't about to give this stranger a blow-by-blow account of my episiotomy.

"It's one of the questions I have to ask," said Wesley. "What about friends? Does Stella play with other kids?"

"Not until recently."

"Lulu invites me to her house," Stella contributed.

Wesley smiled. "Great! Playdates are great. Now, tell me. Does Stella have sensitivity to noises, chafing clothes, anything like that?"

I explained that these things used to be challenging but now were not.

"Excellent. Now, eating, sleeping—normal, would you say, or—?"

I admitted that she ate a wider variety of foods now. "And she used to have a lot of trouble falling asleep. Now she sleeps well."

Wesley nodded. "She looks very healthy."

"Hm," I said. Was "very healthy" code for "chunky"?

Wesley clicked his pen. "You don't agree?"

"It's unexpected, the change. We're a skinny family." I saw the look on Wesley's face and explained I didn't care if Stella was on the heavier side, as long as that's how she was naturally. Pete was lean, I was on the slender side, so if Stella was becoming chunky, it likely wasn't natural.

Wesley put his head on one side. "Only being slim is natural?"

"Of course not. I simply want her to be myself. I mean, herself." The playroom smelled unpleasant, sweetish, like apple juice and glue sticks. I placed my hand over my mouth. "I'm sorry, I misspoke."

"Are you feeling OK?" Wesley asked.

"Fine." No need to mention that since giving up Irina's bread, I was back to round-the-clock morning sickness. I didn't want to seem weak.

"What kinds of things do you and Stella like to do together?"

I told him how even when I worked full-time, I'd spent as much time with her as possible. We read, we went on walks, we had secret games. "Like SkyPo," I said. Wesley nodded and twinkled, and I explained.

SkyPo (rhyming with typo) were mysterious enemies in the sky who were out to destroy us. We hid from SkyPo under bushes and trees. The birds were sometimes on SkyPo's side, their brains controlled by SkyPo's birdbrain-control technology, and sometimes on our side, desperately trying to give us messages in their bird language.

I suddenly stopped, seeing Wesley's twinkle fade away. SkyPo always seemed to transform the ordinary stuff of the world—pigeons, bushes, clouds—into an epic drama. But did I somehow make Stella afraid of the world, of clouds and birds? Maybe it wasn't actually such a fun game.

"You mentioned some other changes in Stella that you have concern about," Wesley said. "I mean apart from the eating and sleeping and such."

"She hardly reads anymore, and she talks less," I said. "A lot less. She's always been hyperverbal. Until recently, she read constantly. Talked in elaborate sentences with subclauses. Now, it's like . . . it's like her language is declining. Like she's forgetting it."

Once, Stella would have listened to our conversation and understood every word, no matter what circumlocutions we used. But now, as we discussed her, she polished the stovetop, using her sleeve again, showing no sign of paying attention to us. I felt a sudden urge to quiz her. Did she remember the name of that jellyfish that could turn itself into a baby?

"Tell me, did you have her IQ tested?" Wesley asked.

"There was no need. She was using phrases like *memento mori* when she was five years old."

"Have you heard of asynchronous learning?" Wesley asked. "Different parts of the brain develop at different speeds. Sometimes if one part is developing, the other parts aren't keeping up. That's how you get a child who can use sophisticated sentence structures but who hasn't learned to share yet. It's possible that the verbal part of Stella's brain was developing really fast and now the other parts of her brain are catching up. The playing, the socializing—those are as important as reading books."

"But it's not like the verbal part of her brain is no longer developing as fast. It's shutting down."

"Being a parent can take some unexpected turns," said Wesley. "Our young people are figuring out who they are every day. I've got a client whose daughter was a school refuser, didn't go to school for a year, barely came out of her room. All she did was these incredibly realistic oil paintings of dead fish. Now she's back at school, doing A-levels in geography and computer science. Her mother's over the moon."

"Those fish paintings sound more interesting to me," I said.

"Hm," said Wesley. He looked at his list of questions. "How is your relationship with *your* mother?"

What did that matter? But I didn't want to sound defensive. So I gave my stock response when asked about Edith. "She and I were very different people."

"She passed away?"

"About nine months ago."

Wesley nodded and leaned forward in a way that made me think he'd learned it in therapy school. "Leaning forward at a forty-five-degree angle shows compassion."

"That could put stress on Stella too," he said.

"They weren't close either. It's when Stella found out about Blanka that she started to change. I told you. When she found out about Blanka and then about Blanka's father."

The room really reeked. I wished he would open a window. I pulled out my handkerchief and placed it over my nose and mouth. "Excuse me."

Cherie once sent me a link to that famous essay about adjusting to having a child with issues. The essay compared it to thinking you're going to Italy on holiday and then realizing you're going to Holland. As long as you embrace Holland, you can still have a great holiday. But this wasn't Holland. This was floating on a raft in the middle of the Atlantic. I cast about for some concrete way to convince Wesley that Stella was changing for the worse. "She started keeping a diary. She's always writing in it. It's like a compulsion," I said.

"That makes you uncomfortable," Wesley said.

"Because nobody writes in their diary about how peachy their life is, do they?" I glanced over at her to make sure she was preoccupied, and then I whispered, "She smells different."

Wesley looked startled. "How so?"

I didn't want to tell him about the vanilla and the honeysuckle, about my life's most private, glorious moment. But I told him she smelled of someone else's laundry detergent and of gomgush, even though I used the same detergent I always had, and she hadn't eaten gomgush in days.

"I like gomgush," Stella contributed, "but I'm not allowed to have it anymore."

"We're vegetarian, remember? 'Not allowed,'" I repeated playfully, and rolled my eyes.

Wesley didn't smile back. "What's gomgush—is that how you say it?"

"It's a lamb stew," I said. "Traditionally for banquets."

"Sounds interesting," Wesley said. "How—"

"We're here to talk about Stella," I said. "Not cooking."

"I'd like to hear what Stella thinks. Can you come and sit with us, Stella?" She heaved herself up, shuffled over, and then lowered herself onto the sofa. I wanted to point this out to Wesley: She didn't even move like an eight-year-old. She moved like an overweight adult.

"Your mom says you're interested in birds," Wesley said. "The sky police?"

"The police?" Stella looked alarmed.

"SkyPo," I clarified. "Remember? The baddies in the sky who are out to get us?"

A muscle twitched in Wesley's face. Stella shook her head, apparently nonplussed. "I know you remember," I said. "You have to remember. Do you really not remember? SkyPo?"

She looked blank. The chainsaw revved as it tore through the branch. That poor tree, having one of its limbs torn off.

"So, I hear you lost your babysitter recently," Wesley said. "How are you feeling about that?"

"I'm not lost," Stella said, shrugging. "I'm not dead." She said these phrases in a slightly contentious manner, emphasis on *not*.

I'm *not* lost. I'm *not* dead.

Like we'd been telling her that she herself was dead, and she was contesting this lie: *Here I am.*

I squeezed her hand. Her skin felt cold to the touch, as if she'd climbed out of an icy river. I turned to Wesley. "Please. You have to help us."

"It's very difficult to come to terms with change and death. It's one of the most difficult things, in fact. It's something we work on our whole life long."

What was I supposed to do with that? The revving chainsaw really was unbearable. I leaned towards Wesley and whispered, "You have to help us. I'm desperate. I'd do anything for her. I'd throw myself under a train if I thought it would do any good."

Wesley took a breath. "Stella, can you go and look at the books in the waiting room while I wrap things up with your mom?"

When she'd left the room, he said, "I have to ask you some questions, Charlotte. Do you feel that you may harm yourself or anyone else? Are you having suicidal thoughts?"

I stared at him. "What are you talking about?"

"Sometimes the best way to help your child is to help yourself. I think perhaps you could benefit from therapy."

I got up. "I've heard enough."

Wesley stood between me and the door. "Do you not like me?"

"That's not a fair question," I said. Obviously, I didn't like him.

Wesley studied me. "Maybe this *is* helping Stella."

"Telling you that I don't like you?"

"Bingo. Explain."

I didn't have time for this. It was like a one-night stand asking you to have an in-depth breakup conversation. But I also felt that if I didn't explain why I didn't like him, it would look like I was an unhinged woman who hated any therapist who suggested that she, not her daughter, was the problem.

I took a deep breath. "Because you say incredibly obvious things as if they're profound insights. Because you've told me private stuff about your clients that I don't think they'd want you to share. Worst of all, because Stella's problem doesn't fit into any boxes, instead of trying to solve it, you're taking the easy way out, which is to act like *I'm* the problem. Or my mother is." I paused. "Or her mother."

I felt pleased that it took Wesley a minute to compose himself. When he recovered, he nodded and said, "Now we're being honest."

I stood up and opened the door to the waiting room, where Stella scribbled intently with a crayon. "Stella, we're leaving."

Wesley couldn't help me work out what was wrong with her. But as I marched Stella down the stairs, I figured out a way: the diary. It had to contain her secret thoughts and fears. It would explain why she'd changed so much.

That evening, while Stella was downstairs crocheting, I stole into her room. I'd promised Pete not to read the diary, but Stella's well-being hung in the balance. It sat right there on her desk.

Almost like she *wanted* me to read it. I opened it at random, partway through. The room seemed to tilt, and the diary fell to the floor.

Then I heard the front door opening and Pete coming up the stairs, two at a time. I put the diary back on her desk, but I didn't have time to get out of her room.

"Just doing a sweep for dirty cups and plates," I told him as I met him in the doorway.

"She didn't have any?" Pete said.

I shook my head, but he was looking over my shoulder: that morning's porridge bowl was on the floor by her bed, next to a half-full juice glass.

His face darkened. "Were you reading her diary? Is that why you were in here?"

I looked at the floor. Pete was livid. "We talked about this. We agreed we wouldn't read it even if it was open. She needs her privacy."

"From me?"

He stepped into the corridor. "Let's go into our room so we can be more private." I followed him, and he continued, "I saw Stella downstairs. I asked her what you did this afternoon, and she said you took her to see someone called Wesley. I'm guessing that is Wesley Bachman from my Google Doc? We agreed therapy is not a good idea for her right now."

"*You* agreed. I didn't," I said. "I'm sorry I went behind your back. I was planning to tell you." At the right time. "I thought if I went, Wesley would confirm that she needs help."

"And did he?"

I was silent, and Pete took a deep breath and blew slowly out through his mouth. "I'm worried about you, obsessing about Stella. Can you not just take a break? You need time for yourself. Do some more coloring, you're good at that."

He hadn't even meant this as an insult, and that hurt more. "I'm also good at being a mother," I said.

"Maybe I should call my mom, since you're still feeling sick this far on in the pregnancy. You need to feel better and start eating. She could come and stay for a while."

"I don't want another person in the house right now." Judging me and how I parented Stella. Pete's mom, Dianne, would surely say that Stella was "looking great." Then she'd lay a hand on my arm and invite me to do some chakra-opening breathing with her.

Pete flexed his hand, made it a fist, flexed it again. "This would be so much easier if we still had Irina."

"I told you why I got rid of her."

"But you didn't even bother to ask me what I think. You make your parenting decisions unilaterally."

"Because I'm the one who's with Stella all the time! If you want to have an equal share in the decision-making, you should have an equal share in the childcare."

Pete took my shoulders. "Then let me do more. The school's closed tomorrow—that teacher training thing. I'll take her for the whole day. You go and see Cherie, or something. Go to yoga."

I thought about how I'd tried to convince Wesley by focusing on her changed smell. Of course, Wesley was in no position to judge this, but Pete was there when she was born. He'd smelled the caramelizing sugar, the honeysuckle.

"What about her smell?" I said. "You must have noticed the change. How do you explain that?"

Pete scratched fiercely at his beard. "Her *smell*?" He sounded confused, almost afraid, but what did he have to be afraid of? That made me even more desperate to convince him that I was right. But the more I tried to sound calm and rational, the more I sounded like I was protesting too much. I thought for a moment.

"Look, I know you don't have my pregnant sense of smell, but it's so obvious. I can smell it in here right now." Lamb and chlorine and something sweetish, not in a good way. "Can't you smell it?" I pleaded.

Pete inhaled doubtfully, and I said, "Remember how she smelled, that first night? So wondrous. I lay awake all night breathing it in."

"The first night? I did notice the smell, yes." Pete looked sheepish. "I always thought she smelled like, um, the birth canal. Maybe it was your hormones that made her smell so good to you."

I stared at him. Pete clearly didn't understand what I was talking about at all. That night was the closest I'd got to the molten core of love at the center of it all, to my true purpose in the scheme of things. It was more than just oxytocin. I'd always assumed we loved Stella the same amount, but I now saw that his love for her was not as powerful as mine

Pete stayed up late to work, and I went to bed alone. When I closed my eyes, I could see her handwriting, so small and careful, like someone was going to whack her hand with a ruler if there was a pen stroke out of place. But few of the letters she had formed were ones I recognized. Stella didn't care about leaving the diary in plain sight, because she wrote in code.

25.

The fruit bowl now contains mottled red-and-yellow pears, and they look real. I scan the room, but the ceramic green Bartletts from this morning are nowhere to be seen. I take a bite out of each pear to check: real, real, real.

I sink into the chair by the window. I know this doesn't matter and I should let it go, but I can't. Maybe someone put the fake pears in the fruit bowl by mistake and they noticed it when they came in to make my bed. They added the red-and-yellow pears and removed the ornamental Bartletts. But why wouldn't they put them on the window ledge? They would have looked perfect.

Or maybe the fruit was all real in the first place. There never was any test, that was just paranoia. I mistake reality for an imitation of itself. Panic rises inside me: Can I trust my perception of anything?

I should pump to encourage my milk to come in, but I need to relax to pump. I go to the bathroom and fill a glass with water.

When I look in the mirror, for a moment I just see a jumble of features—a nose here, a grim mouth there, two wild eyes all the way over there—and it takes a moment to organize them into my face. Maybe it's just because I'm not wearing any makeup. I have the dizzying thought that the person in the mirror isn't me, and maybe I'm not real either. I can't be alone anymore. I have to talk to someone.

I listen at Dr. Beaufort's door and can't hear any voices, so she's not with a patient. I knock and enter, and she's sitting in her armchair, scrolling through something on her phone and eating a slice of Christmas stollen, which looks much more tempting than the apple-parsnip muffins on the buffet table at lunch. She stands up, brushing icing sugar from her poncho. "Charlotte, now's not a good—"

I sit on her sofa. "I have to talk to you."

She remains standing. "I know your concern about your daughter feels urgent, but perhaps we need to take a break for the rest of the day. The best thing you can do right now is take care of yourself. Proper sleep, proper meals."

"Please—I'm not some entitled rich bitch who expects her therapist to be available on demand. I'm—" My whole body is trembling. I put my face in my hands.

Her voice is gentle. "Things will look different when you've had some rest."

"How can you be so sure?"

"When you're depressed, your mind plays tricks on you."

"I'm not depressed. Why do people keep saying that to me?"

Dr. Beaufort returns to her chair, sighing. "Having a mother who suffered from postnatal depression is a major risk factor. I've been reading through your file."

I take my hands away from my face. "My mother wasn't depressed either."

Dr. Beaufort consults my file on her phone. "Your husband informed us that your mother was hospitalized three weeks after you were born. She also had major depression later in life, and was hospitalized several more times."

"She had a lot of academic conferences," I say. "My husband must be confused." But I press my fist to my forehead. When I was little, I hated the feeling of the teaspoon scraping the shell of my boiled egg. Now I have that feeling inside my head, something hard scraping at the delicate inside.

My mother's academic conferences never appeared on any calendar. She always remembered one right after she'd lost her temper. She never threw birthday parties or made proper meals. She thought saying, "You're welcome," was unnecessary. Who but a depressed person, a person who can barely get out of bed, would think that saying, "You're welcome," is too much effort?

"My mother *was* depressed," I say, trying it out.

"Perhaps it affected the way she parented you."

My mother treated me as if I were not Charlotte, not the daughter she expected. She made me feel that I didn't act right or look right. Maybe I didn't smell right either—just like Stella is not Stella and doesn't smell right to me.

Maybe I'm the problem, not Stella.

Dr. Beaufort is looking at me like she knows something, but she wants me to realize it on my own. I do know it, but I don't want to say it: my mother and I are not so different after all.

I go up to my room and call Pete for the second time today. "How do you know my mother had postnatal depression?"

Pete sighs, like we've already been over this. "She told me when you were pregnant the first time. It wasn't a big heart-to-heart. She just said she'd had to go to hospital several times for 'trouble with her nerves.'"

"Why did she tell you and not me?" I ask, though I know the answer: it would have been too much like apologizing. My head still hurts, and I press my forehead against the wall. "Why didn't *you* tell me?"

Pete's voice is soft. "I did tell you, baby. You must have forgotten."

The phone slips from my hand. Maureen tried to tell me too, when I went to visit her in the home that time, and she mistook me for Edith. "Sharon's got the baby blues. Just like you, she's on her own."

But now I think what she said was "Sharon's got the baby blues, just like you. She's on her own." Maureen forgot who I was, but she remembered what I needed to know. I just didn't want to hear it.

I was so certain I knew Stella inside and out—who she was and who she wasn't. But hormones *had* addled my mind. Nobody can see into their child's heart.

26.

The next day, Pete said he'd take Stella swimming. As soon as they left, I went to Stella's room to look for the diary. It wasn't on the desk anymore. It wasn't under her pillow or her mattress. I rifled through her drawers. I pulled out the books on her shelves and shook them.

I sat back on my heels. It wasn't here, because Stella hadn't hidden it. Pete had. I searched our room. Nothing. He'd hidden it somewhere crafty, and I wasn't going to find it without tearing everything apart.

I went down to the kitchen, planning to make some tea, and then I thought, Cherie. If anyone would understand that I had to keep fighting for my child, it was her. She fought for Zach all the time. I texted Cherie to ask if I could drop by. OK, she texted back. One word, no smiley face. At least she answered. I picked up chocolate éclairs from one of Muswell Hill's three patisseries.

When Cherie saw me, her gaze took in my body, and she said, "You look . . ."

"Haggard?" I explained about the nausea, how it made it hard to eat. Still, the baby was OK.

"You look good," I told her. For once, Cherie's hair was down, instead of in a ponytail. She'd colored it too, got rid of the grey.

"About before," I continued. "When you pushed for Stella to get assessed, I got defensive. I'm sorry." The question whether Stella should see a doctor now seemed trivial, and my apology came easily. I had much bigger problems now. "And I didn't mean to insult Zach," I said.

Cherie hugged me. "I'm sorry too. I pushed you too hard about Stella. That first assessment can be a psychological hurdle, especially if there's a chance the parent is on the spectrum."

"Wait, now I'm autistic too?" I bristled. Autism was more broadly defined now, but that didn't mean she had the right to go around diagnosing everyone around her. But then I thought about it. "I guess I have some signs," I said.

Cherie sighed. "Or maybe I'm a hammer, so the whole world looks like a nail, or whatever the quote is."

"Well, right now I don't have time to think about it," I said. Cherie nodded. We didn't entirely understand each other, but she was trying. I could try harder too.

She led me into the kitchen, where Zach was pounding soap in a mortar. He looked up and met my eyes. I was surprised. His were the vivid green of young ferns. I realized that even if he never responded, I could still greet him. "Hello, Zach."

"Hello, Charlotte," Cherie prompted.

"Hello," said Zach. He had never spoken directly to me before. Cherie smiled to herself.

"Is that some more slime you've got there?" I asked.

He nodded. "I changed the activating agent, and it created a super-sticky substance, like, industrial-level sticky."

"Amazing," I said. It seemed poignant that someone who struggled to connect to others was so interested in sticking things together.

Cherie was glowing. She brought our tea to her living room. "We got him a social-skills therapist, and we've been doing these exercises."

"I'm glad he's doing so well."

"How's Stella?"

I told her how Stella had changed. Cherie was delighted. "That's fantastic."

I took a bite of chocolate éclair. It tasted at once too bitter and achingly sweet.

"But?" Cherie said.

My hands shook. I put down the éclair. "I'm scared. The way she's changing—I know it sounds great, but it's really not. I'm terrified, to be honest."

"I don't understand," Cherie said. "Stella is getting dressed and going to school without complaining? I would kill for one day of that."

I cast about for a way to explain. "I *know* that something is wrong. It's like when Stella has a fever. I don't need a thermometer—I just use my hand. I *know* if she's sick. A mother's hand knows."

Cherie took a minute to wipe chocolate off her fingers with a paper napkin. "I'm not sure what you mean."

"It's maternal instinct. Look at what happened when Zach was little. People said he had a mental disability because he wouldn't talk, and you knew that wasn't true. You alone knew what he needed."

Cherie threw her dirty napkin on the table. She spoke slowly, emphatically. "I knew what he needed because I got Zach *assessed*. And this new social-skills therapist isn't the first. I've read dozens of books, I'm in three different online groups. You would know all this if you ever really listened to me. It doesn't take a mother's hand—it takes a fucking village."

I had a burning sensation in my throat. "So when it comes to Stella, my problem is that I don't listen to other people. Other people know what she needs better than I do. Including you, I assume?"

"Look, forget I said anything," Cherie backtracked. "Let's change the subject."

"It's fine, really," I said, forcing a smile. "But I don't feel that great. I have to go anyway."

Cherie showed me out, trilling promises we would do coffee soon. Maybe Zach was right to be hesitant about learning social skills. Too often, they meant hiding how you really felt. I'd been so sure that the bedrock of my friendship with Cherie was that we were alike: we were committed to doing whatever our unusual kids needed, regardless of what anyone else thought. But she'd been secretly judging me. And I was at fault too. She was right, I hadn't listened closely to her. Or I would have known we weren't alike at all.

. . .

When I was nearly home, my phone pinged with a message from Pete: On way home from Coral Reef Waterworld! Emmy suggested playdate so I invited them swimming.

I cringed. What was he thinking? This wasn't just a swimming pool. There was a pirate ship and five waterslides—it was a sensory nightmare. Yet my phone pinged again, and there they were: Stella with a small smile and her hair plastered to her shoulders and, next to her, Lulu grinning toothily, with her arm around Stella. I stared at the picture, looking into Stella's eyes. Maybe she was genuinely enjoying something that a few months ago, she would have hated. Or maybe she was just pretending, and on the inside, she was furiously composing the diary entry she'd write when she got home.

A realization started to take shape. This change in her wasn't something imposed from outside. It didn't happen because of Irina and the trauma of Blanka's suicide. Stella had changed who she was, or *appeared* to be, through sheer force of will.

But why?

I studied the photo again. Lulu flashed teeth, but Stella's smile was tense. Pete thought it was a real smile, but I could see that it wasn't. She was just determined to give Daddy a great photo, to show Daddy that she was having a good time. Maybe that was why she suddenly loved going to the pool too: Pete wanted her to become a strong swimmer. She'd humiliated Pete at her birthday party, and now she behaved beautifully around his friends. The last time she'd gone into freak-out mode, Pete had stormed out of the house, and now she'd dropped it for good.

It was so obvious that I couldn't imagine why I hadn't seen it before. Stella longed to please Pete, become his true north again. She was pretending to be the daughter that she thought Pete wanted. The diary was the one clue that inwardly she still seethed with thought.

When I got home, Emmy was coming down our front path with Lulu. Pete stood on our front step with Stella, waving goodbye.

Emmy looked surprised to see me. Her striped dress today had thick bands of color—raspberry red, orange, and lemon yellow—and reminded me of a fruit ice lolly. Damp, her hair had a gentle wave, and this made her look softer and younger. "Hello, Charlotte!" she said. "I'm not really here. It was a long drive home, so Lulu and I popped in to use the loo. The girls had a fabulous time."

Pete stood in the doorway waving to Emmy and Lulu. His curls were wet, close to his head, and behind his glasses, his eyes looked very blue, like they used to do when he surfed. He held Stella's hand as she waved goodbye too.

Once Emmy and Lulu had gone, we went inside. "We had an amazing time," Pete said, his face alight. "Stella was great."

"Really?"

"She didn't even mind the wave machine. She was so brave. She put her head underwater. She's totally mastered blowing bubbles through her nose. She loves it down there. She hardly even came up for air."

He wasn't giving her a chance to talk. "Did you have fun, my sweet?" I asked Stella. I studied her face closely for signs of strain.

"Oh yes. The water is nice," Stella said.

"Was nice," I said sharply. "You mean, it was nice. You're not in the water anymore." I looked deep into her eyes, trying to catch a flicker of her old self.

"I'm going to my room," she said, and I was sure she wanted to get away from Pete. This charade must be exhausting.

Pete got Thai takeout—he'd found a place where they put the food into the containers he brought from home—and Stella took hers to her room.

"Does it bother you that Stella still won't eat with us?" I asked as he lit candles. "She's been like this for months."

"She's eaten with us a few times," Pete said. "When Irina was—" He stopped. We both understood that in marriage, you had to understand when to drop it. Irina wasn't coming back.

"She's eating proper food at least," I said.

Pete took my hand and kissed it. "Are you feeling better? How was Cherie?"

"Great," I said. "She—never mind." I didn't want to rehash my conversation with Cherie, because then Pete would know she agreed with him about Stella. That I stood on my own.

"The green papaya salad is so good," Pete said, tucking in. Then he noticed that I was only toying with my food. "Feeling sick again?"

"I don't have an appetite," I told him.

"Poor baby," Pete said, gazing at me with concern. To make him feel better, I spooned some more papaya salad onto my plate. He was so tender, so loving. I could see how Stella yearned to please him too. I just had to make her understand that changing her entire personality was not the right way.

"Bedtime, honey," I told Stella after we'd all finished eating.

"Will you read to me?"

I was surprised. I'd given up reading to her years earlier, at her request. Now she got into bed and actually scooted over to make room for me. Once, she would have felt suffocated having me in her bed. I would have rumpled the cover in a way that was unacceptable, or accidentally sat on a fold of her pajamas, or read too slowly, or too fast. Once I would have given anything to have had this coziness with her.

She chose a book from when she was a toddler: *Sylvester and the Magic Pebble*, a book about a donkey that finds a wishing pebble and foolishly wishes he were a rock. He drops the pebble and he's stuck: a rock forever. Eventually he escapes from his predicament, but I'd almost never been able to read to the end, so I was surprised by her choice now. The description of the poor donkey rock, alone in the snow, subsiding into endless sleep, had brought Stella to tears every time.

Now Stella listened without comment.

The poster of California birds on Stella's wall caught my eye. *Flight: The Complete History of Aviation*, the book I'd bought for her, still sat on her desk, untouched. She was obsessed with flight until just a few months ago. When she found that gannet on the beach, she'd been so thrilled. At last, a chance to strip a bird's wings down and study the biomechanics of flight like her hero, Otto Lilienthal.

Then I had an idea. I didn't need to crack the diary to find out what was really going on inside my daughter. There was another way to tempt the real Stella out.

I spent a couple of hours looking online and finally posted an ad on what seemed like a suitable site. It seemed right, a way to go back to when this all started and take a different path.

Late that night I checked the site, and I had an offer. It was bigger than I needed, and I wasn't entirely sure it was legal, but this was an emergency.

27.

The box took five days to arrive, because the Christmas delivery rush was beginning. Luckily, the box was insulated. When it finally showed up, Pete wasn't home from work yet. "Why don't you go and have your bath, honey?" I told Stella, and she went. Once she wouldn't have been content until I'd showed her what was in the box straightaway.

I grabbed a kitchen knife and took the box to her room. I put it on her bed and slit it open. First, I had to pull out blocks of Styrofoam. It was ironic that the packaging used to send a dead seabird was exactly the sort that choked seabirds—although maybe it wasn't that ironic.

The bird was much bigger than I expected. It was frozen but emitted an eye-watering smell: salty, gamy. It had slate-grey feathers, with a white neck and breast, a yellow beak with the characteristic red spot—a breeding adult—and pink legs, neatly folded underneath. The one eye I could see, red-rimmed in life, was sunken and yellow. I wondered what had killed it. I couldn't see any obvious wounds. The seller had said it was a great black-backed gull that had died "of natural causes," and I didn't want to inquire further.

I'd thought of the bird as a scientific specimen, something for Stella to dissect, as she had longed to with the gannet. I'd say it was a present from both of us, and she would understand that this present meant we accepted who she was, no matter how hard that was for other people. We supported her fierce curiosity, which could seem ghoulish to others. We accepted that we had a daughter for whom a small corpse was a better present than a jewelry-making set.

But as I stared at the bird, sadness filled me. This was a wild thing that had once been alive, strutting along the shore, soaring on updrafts. There were gulls everywhere when Stella and I went to the beach in Mendocino, one day about a year ago. The waves broke in creamy, shallow swathes of surf, and when we stood in it, feeling the water tug at our ankles, it felt as if we were standing ankle-deep in shining waterlilies.

Stella ran around in circles, shouting quotes from *The Art of War*, which she had insisted on reading, at the gulls. "Know thyself, know thy enemy!" "Warriors win first and then go to war!" "Tactics without strategy is the noise before defeat!" Whenever one came near our backpack, as it always did if we strayed too far away, Stella raced towards it, waving her arms and shouting. There were other kids on the beach, building sandcastles, playing volleyball, or running in circles. But Stella was happy being Stella that day, and I was happy with her.

I wanted that girl back.

I pulled the bird out and arranged it on her bed, and then I stuffed the packaging back into the box and hid the whole thing in her wardrobe. I'd have to get rid of it later, without Pete seeing the Styrofoam. Then I went down to the living room and found my coloring book. I tried to lose myself in completing a mandala. Her bathroom door shut and the landing creaked. She was going into her room. I felt fluttery with anticipation.

A little noise of surprise came from upstairs. "Oh!" Then silence.

Was that happy surprise? I galloped to her room. But she was backed into the corner, her hands pressed over her face. Oh no. She didn't like it. How could she not like it? Only three months ago, she went into freak-out mode because her father composted her dead gannet. Now here was a bigger prize, and in better condition too.

"Stella, baby. It's OK. It's a present," I said. Obviously, surprising her had been a mistake. I knelt before her and held her shoulders. "I bought it so you could use it for science."

But she wouldn't take her hands away from her face. She really was terrified, not excited, not curious. I felt sick. Where did my weird, brave scientific daughter go? I pressed my face into her solid, unyielding chest. "Stella, Stella, my Stella. What's happening to you?" I moaned.

"Jesus fucking Christ! How did that get in here?" Pete was home, standing over the bed.

I leaped to my feet. "It's OK, it's fine. Don't use that language in front of her." I was trembling. I wiped my tears away. "I bought it. I put it here. I thought Stella would like it." I turned back to her, sniffing. "Darling, don't you remember the gannet? This is a replacement. It's even bigger, it's better."

But she shrank away from me. Maybe it had to be a bird she found herself, in its natural environment. Maybe there was something wrong, suspicious, about a dead bird in a box—How did it die really? But then I remembered how excited she'd been about the gannet.

"Daddy?" said Stella in a small voice.

"Stella, my love," I said. "Don't look at Daddy, look at me. You don't have to pretend to be someone else. I know you're in there. Moo, I'm a cockatoo. What do you say? Please, Stella, please. Moo, I'm a cockatoo. And you say?" Nothing. "Please, Stella," I begged, but Stella just stared at me.

Her eyes were different. The irises seemed darker, the eyes themselves narrower. I saw, clearly, that she wasn't pretending to be someone else for her father's sake. She *was* someone else. But that wasn't possible. I sank down onto her rug.

"Stella?" Pete took her hand. "Go downstairs until I can clear this up. Look, I'll take you." He returned wearing the rubber gloves and put the bird in a bin bag. I picked myself up off the rug. He started stripping her bed, his face drawn. When he'd got all her sheets in a bundle, he said, "Can you at least explain to me why you thought she'd be happy to find a dead bird in her bed?"

"On her bed, not *in* it," I said. "And obviously, I got it because she loves that kind of thing. You saw what happened when you threw away the gannet. I was trying to make up for that."

Pete picked up the bundle of sheets and then the bin bag with the bird in it. "Look, go and lie down or something. I'll come and talk to you in a minute."

In our room, I got into bed with my clothes on and tried to close my eyes and shut everything out. But our sheets were bamboo twill, supposed to be both sustainable and soft, but I felt every diagonal rib abrading me. When Pete came in, he said, "I'm really worried about you. You're so hostile to Stella. To me too. You correct her grammar, you said nothing about her swimming or about me taking her all day or dealing with dinner. Then this bird. What the fuck."

"Great black-backed gull." I felt like it was disrespectful to its wild, beautiful life to call it "this bird." Like none of that ever happened. "Anyway, I didn't realize taking care of Stella was such a chore."

"Well, it's tiring, however much we love her. Eight-year-olds are tiring. Emmy and I were talking about how hard it is."

I stared. Why was he lumping her in with other kids? Why was he confiding in Emmy? I wondered if he knew about @LittleHiccups, where there were in fact no hiccups whatsoever. Emmy had once rescheduled Lulu's birthday party at the last minute because the light that day wasn't conducive to photography.

I pulled the sheet over my head and curled up, cradling my stomach, wondering how the child inside me could survive this. Maybe the stress would cause me to miscarry again. That might be a good thing. How I could mother a second child feeling that I had lost my first?

The bed creaked as Pete sat down. He squeezed my shoulder through the sheet. "Would you really want to go back to fighting with her over baths and putting on her pajamas? Getting called into school twice a week? Taking her to the emergency room because she's screaming so much?"

"Yes, I would," I mumbled. "She's changed too much."

He cracked his knuckles, a bad habit I thought he'd quit. "From where I'm standing, you're the one who's changed."

He had it all wrong. I sat up and climbed out of bed, pulling a hoodie from my dresser. "I need some air." Pete nodded, even though it was dark and raining. It was like he was relieved that he and Stella could get a break from me.

Outside, Christmas trees twinkled in people's front windows. One in particular caught my eye, over the top with garish tinsel, multicolored fairy lights, and presents piled high. I'd ordered Stella's presents early, as I always did, and they were waiting on the top shelf of my wardrobe: a biography of Earhart, Antoine de Saint-Exupéry's *Flight to Arras*, a copy of a 1940s Spitfire manual, a pocket compass. All gifts for who Stella used to be. I'd had such fun choosing them, imagining her delight. The fairy lights blurred as my tears fell.

Irina gave me a hard stare when she opened the door. "You look terrible."

"I know." It was raining and my hair hung in rattails. Irina's hair was scraped back, but there seemed to be much less of it: she wasn't wearing the hairpiece with which she usually bulked out her bun. "You're not looking your best either," I found myself saying.

Irina shrugged and patted her hair. "So far, this is terrible apology."

"Look, it's really cold out here." I'd tried talking to Cherie and failed. Irina was the only person I had left, even if she hated me.

She led me into the kitchen, which smelled somewhere between stale gingerbread and the back of an old cupboard. "Well?" she said.

The kitchen had unpleasant fluorescent lighting. "You're not to blame for what's happening to Stella," I admitted. "I shouldn't have thrown you out like that."

Irina's shoulders relaxed a little. She gestured for me to sit at the kitchen table, covered with an embroidered cloth. Before, she'd taken me into the living room. This was where she ate her meals. I felt a tiny spark in my chest. Maybe I wasn't a guest now, to be treated formally. We knew each other better than that.

"I'm worried that something's happening to me," I said. "Pete thinks—" I tried for a laugh. "He thinks I'm going a bit mad."

Irina nodded. "You are—what is word—too tight?"

"Uptight." The lighting was giving me a headache. "But that's not what I'm talking about. When Blanka was a baby, or maybe even when you were pregnant, did you ever feel like you were going crazy?"

Irina snorted. "Many time." I waited warily for Irina to say something about how many women had trouble after giving birth, and she soon felt better. Instead, she said, "My mother's mother says bad spirit gets inside."

"A bad spirit." I nodded. This sounded like a way of describing depression, but I preferred the sound of it. If there's a bad spirit inside you, then *you* are not the problem, and all you need to do is get it out, like a tapeworm. "How did you get rid of it?"

"I show you," says Irina, and I nod, my heart lifting. I still thought Stella was the one with the tapeworm, but there seemed no harm in this, and I would try anything.

Irina picked up an ornate brass salt cellar from the table, unscrewed the lid, and dumped out the salt. "You sit right there," she said. I had no idea what she was up to, but I felt relief at putting myself into her hands. Next to the salt, she set a glass of water. "This is not holy, but maybe works anyway."

Her eyes glinted as she traced something in the salt: a cross. She stood and sprinkled water in my hair, making me flinch. She took a pinch of salt, closed her hand, circled it above my head, and muttered something. It was another language. "Is that Russian?"

"Armenian."

"I thought when the Soviets controlled Azerbaijan, they made everyone speak Russian." I'd gathered this from my research after the Thanksgiving dinner.

"We don't forget our own language," Irina snapped. "Besides, after Azerbaijan, Blanka and I live in Armenia for many years."

"I'm sorry, I'll be quiet."

She dusted her hands off. "Doesn't matter, it is finished."

I shook salt from my hair. "That's it? That got rid of the—the bad spirit?"

Irina chuckled, her eyes cold. "Of course not. I'm just—what's the word—"

"Messing with me," I said, to stop her from saying something worse. She'd let some of the salt fall down inside my shirt, and every grain stung.

"You took my wedding dress," Irina spat. "Then like that!" She snapped her fingers. "Just like that, I'm not good enough."

"I admitted I shouldn't have thrown you out of my house."

"Words," she scoffed. "And now I throw you out of my house."

As I got up, something stuck to her fridge caught my eye: some kind of list. The writing was familiar. It didn't look like the English alphabet. "Who wrote that?"

Irina snatched it before I could get a closer look. "Who do you think? Old shopping list, but I cannot throw away." She clasped the paper to her chest, as if it were infinitely precious. My heart filled with dread. The round loops. The careful spacing. I recognized that handwriting. I thought I recognized those symbols too.

28.

Creamy candles crowd the Georgian mantelpiece, and whale song plays through speakers set high on the claret walls. In the fireplace is a big earthenware vase full of budding branches. They must be top-of-the-line in faux flora, because I don't know *how* I can tell they aren't real. But I know.

Rain, my massage therapist, scoops something from a pot and warms it in her hands. "This is a body butter we make on-site, with calendula, aloe vera, and rosehip oil."

"Lovely," I say. But my leg jerks when she touches my calf.

"You're very tense," she murmurs.

"I'm working on that." I keep my voice sweet, but scowl through the face hole in the massage table. After I burst into Dr. Beaufort's room earlier and interrupted her break, she insisted I get a relaxation treatment. "It takes time to build the trust you need to be completely honest," she said.

True. Had I been completely honest in the first session, she would have prescribed antipsychotics without a second's hesitation. I have to build up to it, to make my case. But it's taking too long. I can't wait until tomorrow. I wonder if I can tell the front desk that it's an emergency, demand her number.

"Try taking deep breaths," says Rain as her bony digits poke my flesh.

"OK," I say, but I can only take in little sips of air. This room was designed to be womb-like, but instead of feeling safe, I feel horribly vulnerable, face down and clad only in towels. I don't even know where my shoes are.

"Try to put your shoes out of your mind," says Rain, and I realize I've spoken aloud.

"I just need to know where they are."

"Breathe," she murmurs. Pain stabs my calf, and my leg jerks again. Rain steps back. I think I kicked her by accident.

"Is this supposed to hurt?" I ask.

"I'm barely touching you," she says.

"This isn't working." I clutch my towels around me and burst out of the room, then rush along the corridor to Dr. Beaufort's office. I pound on the door. No answer, and it's locked. A blast of cold air comes from the lobby, raising goose bumps on my arms and legs, and I fling myself towards it. Dr. Beaufort is heading out the front door, bag over her shoulder, clad in a sensible winter coat, a wearable duvet that makes no concession to style.

"Charlotte. Oh dear." She takes in the towel I'm holding around my naked body, but I'm past caring about such things. She looks around for help. Rain pants up and drapes a fluffy robe over my shoulders.

"You told me to relax," I babble, clutching Dr. Beaufort's sleeve. "But I can't relax when I'm so worried about Stella. Would you expect someone to relax when their baby is trapped under a car? But I still tried. Ask Rain." I turn around, and Rain is edging away, but she doesn't contradict me. "Now you have to make the effort to hear me out," I tell Dr. Beaufort.

"I need to send a message first." She unlocks her room for me, and I sink onto the sofa. I'm sure she's texting her partner to tell them she'll be late. I feel a pang as I imagine what she's writing: Don't forget Eddie's got karate tonight. Save me some spag bol! And then smiley face, spaghetti with hovering fork, heart, heart, heart. Does she know how lucky she is to have a normal family life?

Finally, she trudges in, closes the door, and sits down.

"You're right," I say. "I need to tell you the whole story. But how do I know if I can trust you?"

She settles into her chair. Her face is kind, truthful. "I want to tell you about something that happened to me. My mother came back once, after she died."

"Metaphorically," I say. I brace myself for some theory that we all have to exorcise the spirits of our mothers as we grow into our true selves.

Dr. Beaufort shakes her head. "I saw her, at the foot of my bed. She was as real as you or me."

I'm astounded. Maybe supernatural experiences are more common than I realized, but no one ever talks about them, for the same reason I'm having trouble telling Dr. Beaufort about mine. "In fact," she continues, "I know several people who have had vivid encounters with the dead. I don't leap to the conclusion that they have a mental illness."

I gape at her. Maybe it is possible, after all, to tell her and have her believe me. She smiles at me, and I feel myself relax a little. I bet that when her children have nightmares, she brings warm milk with honey and tells them the tale of how they were born until they fall back asleep.

"What if the spirit who returns isn't your mother?" I ask, just to be sure. "What if it's someone who you thought was more of a peripheral figure in your life?"

"I'm here to listen, not to judge," she says, and I launch into the hardest part of the story.

29.

When I came in from seeing Irina, Pete was at the kitchen counter, in a late-night Zoom meeting. I waved at him, glad that he wasn't going to get in my way. I had to see Stella, and if that meant waking her up, so be it. When I got to the top of the stairs, I leaned against the wall to catch my breath. My lungs felt constricted, the baby rammed underneath my rib cage.

Then I pushed open Stella's door. Because this was light-polluted London, her room was never truly dark, and I could see that her bed was empty, the covers flung back. With a jolt, I realized that she was standing in the middle of her room. Was she sleepwalking? If so, I didn't want to startle her by turning on the light. I tiptoed up. Her eyes were open, but that didn't mean she was awake. I laid a hand on her shoulder, wondering if I could guide her back to bed. But I couldn't move her. Surely a sleepwalker wouldn't have this strange density. I pushed at her shoulder: nothing. I felt like even if I shoved her, she wouldn't fall over. She was definitely awake.

"What are you doing?" I whispered.

"Not much."

I shivered. The same thing Blanka did on weekends.

Irina's grandmother believed that a bad spirit could get inside a pregnant woman. Could a bad spirit get inside a child?

"Listen to me. Why won't you eat when it's just me and you?"

"I don't like eating in front of you."

I never saw Blanka consume a crumb.

"Why do you have Blanka's handwriting?"

"My handwriting," she whispered back.

"What language is your diary in?"

"My language."

"Armenian?" I hissed.

The reek of chlorine seemed to emanate from her, stronger even than when I'd visited the hot tub where Blanka drowned. I snapped on the light.

Last year Pete had made himself and Stella up as zombies for Halloween. He used latex makeup to craft realistic-looking open wounds. They'd been convinced I would be terrified, but I'd had to fake it completely. Stella was so very Stella, with her cloud of red hair and her precise little voice. Just as surely as I'd known that it was Stella under all that makeup, I knew now that this *wasn't* her. I swallowed down the urge to vomit. Stella wasn't acting like Blanka because Irina had made her or because Pete had. She was acting like Blanka because, in some way I couldn't grasp, she *was* Blanka.

Breathe, I told myself, just like I always told Stella during freak-out mode. She could never manage a full, deep breath. But now I understood that terror makes you leave your body. I was just an observer, with no power at all to fill my lungs with air.

But Blanka was a person, or once had been. At this thought, I was able to breathe again. She was a spirit now, but I could still talk to her, like a person. I took her by the shoulders. "I want to help you, but you have to help me. Why are you doing this?" When she didn't respond, I shook her, but I could hardly even move her. "Tell me what you want." She looked at me with her stony gaze, and I shook her again, harder. "What do you want? For fuck's sake, what do you want? What do you want?"

Pete thundered into the room. "What the fuck? What are you doing to Stella?"

I stepped away from them, realizing how loud I'd been yelling. I wiped saliva from my chin as Pete scooped her into his arms. "What the hell is going on?" he said.

I shook my head. I could beg him to look at the diary. But he would only read it if her life was at stake. I couldn't convince him of that without proving that Blanka had possessed her, and the only proof of that *was* the diary.

Stella slithered out of Pete's arms and accused me. "You held me too tight. You hurt me." She looked at me, but I could see that although she sounded like Stella at this moment, it was really Blanka in there. Blanka was the one talking, conspiring with me. I understood then that Blanka didn't want Pete involved. This was between the two of us. She would perform "Stella" for Pete while I worked out what she wanted. Fine, I'd play along.

"I'm sorry, darling," I said. "I was just trying to wake you up." I turned to Pete. "She was sleepwalking."

Pete shook his head. "You're not supposed to wake people up when they're sleepwalking."

I was exhausted. But I couldn't fall asleep knowing that Blanka was inside our house, and not only inside our house, but inside our daughter's body. When I thought back, I saw how crafty she'd been. She didn't move in overnight. She moved in little by little. By the time I recognized what was happening, it was too late.

I went downstairs, leaving Pete asleep, and stood at the windows, but the city's dully glowing sky pressed down. I closed my eyes and rested my forehead against the cold glass. Stella must still be inside herself somewhere, sharing space with Blanka. I hoped it was like being asleep and she had no idea what was going on. Or maybe she did have some idea. Maybe she felt more like a patient under botched anesthesia, paralyzed but fully conscious.

Or maybe she felt like she was being buried alive.

I banged my forehead against the glass. Then I forced myself to stop. I couldn't afford to panic. Now that I knew exactly what was wrong with Stella, maybe the Internet would be more help. I sat down with my phone and learned that demons were usually the ones responsible for possession. It was rare for a spirit to enter a person. It was unfortunate that Stella had the spirit kind, because a demon was a lot easier to deal with. Irina's grandmother had more or less the right idea: the main treatment was Bible readings and holy water. I clicked through link after link. People had plenty of advice about demons. But nobody knew how to banish a dead person's spirit from your child.

Outside, the first bird began to sing, even though it was still dark. I realized I was going about this all wrong. I reminded myself that Blanka wasn't merely a spirit. She was or once had been a person. This was more subtle, more complicated. In a way, it was a matter of etiquette, of finding out what she wanted and giving it to her without making her upset. Wasn't I an expert on this very topic?

It was simply a case of getting a lingering guest to leave. But I had to do it—and this was what the trolls had never understood—*without the guest ever realizing they had outstayed their welcome.* "Turn out the lights of the room, and your guest will get the message," a troll said. "Go to bed," said another. No, because I didn't want to hurt the guest's feelings, and especially not when the guest was Blanka.

I paced the house. Obviously, Blanka had come back because she wanted something, and it must be something connected with Stella. Maybe she had a message for us, though that would be strange, given how reluctant she was to communicate when she was alive. She had loved Stella, so maybe something threatened Stella, and Blanka was protecting her. Though I wasn't sure how taking over her body would help with that.

The cross opposite the fridge was still there, but it was in marker now. I could have sworn it was pencil last time I looked. I touched it with the tip of my finger. I thought of what Wesley had said: when children don't have the language to tell us how they're feeling, they use the tools at their disposal. Blanka wasn't a child, but maybe this mark was her way of telling me how she was feeling. When she was a child, her mother had made her stand with her nose to the cross when she'd done something wrong. She stood there until she'd set it right.

Because this cross kept appearing right here in our kitchen, it was only rational to assume that the cross was for someone in the house. It wasn't for Stella, because Blanka loved her. It wasn't for Blanka, because why come back from the dead to punish yourself? It had to be for me or Pete. One of us had wronged Blanka.

With a shock, I saw that it could only be me. Pete hardly saw her, after all. But look what I'd done to her. When she repelled my efforts to get to know her, I took that at face value and left her alone. I thought she didn't want to communicate with me, but her repeated answer, "Not much," *was* the message. When she said nothing but "Oh yes," I should have read volumes in it. Instead, I accepted her intimate service, her labor taking care of my child, and I didn't trouble to get to know her, because deep down, I thought she didn't matter.

Now she held my daughter hostage. This was her way of saying, "I matter."

Charlotte Says: If in doubt, apologize.

I had to do it in style. A note and a gift would hardly work. I had to show Blanka that I did notice who she was. I did care. I had to think hard about what Blanka would like. The darkness was fading as I climbed into bed to catch a few hours of sleep. I had a busy day ahead.

30.

After Pete left for work, I went to Stella's room and told her I was planning a special surprise. "I have to leave you on your own while I run errands," I explained. It was the first day of the two-week Christmas break. Normally, I wouldn't leave her home alone, but we both knew that she was only an eight-year-old on the outside.

"I can't take you, because I don't want you to guess the surprise," I explained.

She nodded. "Stick Thing will keep me company." She picked up the twig doll she'd made with Irina.

I went to Muswell Hill Broadway to shop for gomgush ingredients. I'd found a recipe online. I bought potatoes and beer and queued at the expensive butcher, a shop I had never entered before, for three pounds of cubed lamb.

When I got home, I told Stella she had to crochet in her room.

"I'm working on the surprise. When it's ready, I'll come and get you."

The stew was supposed to be made in an unwashed tandir, the clay oven that was also used for bread. I wished I still had Irina's black pot, but all I had was my pale "dune"-colored Le Creuset. I simmered the stew for hours. For the final touch, I poured some Armenian wine, just a splash; I hadn't lost sight of the fact that this spirit—Blanka—inhabited Stella's body.

I set the table for one: folded napkin, spoon, fork, and cup. I heated the lavash bread I had bought. This meal for one was the opposite of the family meals I longed for. People should eat together. But I set the table with care. I wanted to show her that I respected her. Gomgush was for feasts. Fine. Blanka-in-Stella would feast. For the first and—I hoped—the last time, she would eat at our table. She would eat out of a handmade ceramic bowl, not a yogurt pot.

Finally, I knocked on her door. "It's ready." She had changed for the occasion into her favorite dark dress. When we got downstairs, she didn't question that our long table was laid for only one. I wondered if I could read a flicker of something in her impassive face—hope, excitement—but I wasn't sure.

"Before you eat," I said, "I want to say thank you. I want to thank you for everything you've done. I never said that, but I'm saying it now. Thank you for all your hard work. Thank you for everything."

Stella sat down and squinted at me with her newly dark eyes. I realized she wanted to be alone. "I'll—I'll leave you to it," I said.

I sat on the sofa and waited, listening to the spoon clinking in the bowl, her slurp and smack. Was she licking her fingers? But in some cultures, slurping was actually polite, a sign of enjoyment. I hoped she *was* enjoying it, because this was her—Blanka's—last meal with us.

When I came back, her bowl was scraped clean. "More?" I asked, and I grimly dolloped gomgush into her bowl. She ate three helpings in total, alone at one end of our long table, hunched over. One arm cradled the bowl as if she feared I'd take it away. I thought of an etiquette question I'd once answered: "Dear Charlotte, I'm a woman with a big appetite, and friends sometimes say to me, 'Wow, you eat a lot.' Is it rude to comment on how much a woman eats?"

For my answer, I'd interviewed a feminist academic who had said people feared voraciousness in women. "They should not take up too much space, have too many desires." At the time, I'd thought this absurd: when people see a woman tucking into a hearty meal, they hardly fear she's destabilizing the patriarchy.

But now I saw how there *was* something frightening about seeing someone eat so much, too much, more than could possibly fit in any eight-year-old's stomach. Then she rose, heavily. "What now?" she said, and even her voice seemed deeper.

"Now we're going to one of your favorite places," I said. She didn't ask why we were going out in the dark, and she let me stuff her into her parka. I led her to the playground. We walked in silence. She didn't ask where we were going either: I think she knew. I chose our destination out of respect for her, to show that I'd considered her desires, for once. But also, this was between us, and so we needed a place where nobody would interrupt, or watch. As she shuffled along by my side, I felt a kinship with Blanka that I'd never felt before. We were working together towards a common end.

The air smelled of burning leaves, and streetlights made greasy pools of light on the wet pavement. I looked into people's windows and felt jealous of their happy, normal lives in desirable Muswell Hill. They had no idea what terrible rite was taking place outside.

The name Muswell came from Mossy Well, a natural spring believed to have miraculous healing properties. If only I could take Stella there, dip her in it, and wash Blanka away. I took her to the duck pond instead, and we walked around it, our breath clouding before us.

Stella was bulky in her parka with the hood up, her long skirts trailing in puddles, her trainers getting soaked. Her face was stony, resigned.

There was a place where you could leave the concrete path and walk right down to the edge of the water. My heart squeezed as I remembered how we came here when she was little. We scattered oats and millet for the ducks and wondered if SkyPo had a base on the overgrown island in the middle of the lake. Stella had chattered on and on about their dastardly plans, and we hid in the bushes for a while, feeling deliciously afraid.

But I now had to focus all my energy on the task before me. I took her cold hands, and in the dark, they felt too large for a child. I began to speak. "I didn't notice you or think about you. I used your cheap labor. I didn't pay you enough, and I didn't offer you more because you didn't ask and also because honestly, I thought you weren't doing a very good job.

"But I valued the wrong things. It doesn't matter that you didn't clean the bath toys or unpack her lunchbox. You were patient with Stella. You loved her. You didn't have a chance to say goodbye to her. I let you go without finding out why you weren't happy."

In a deep apology, you laid your heart bare. You probed into the insecurity, the pettiness, the self-absorption—whatever shameful or embarrassing feelings had driven you to hurt the other person. You took your time and you parsed the darkness within. Only then could they know that you'd done the work to make sure it wouldn't happen again.

I spoke for some time, I said everything I could think of. The feeling left my fingertips. Inside the hood of her parka, Stella's face was drawn, goosefleshed.

"I didn't pay attention to you," I whispered. "But you've got my attention now. I'm sorry."

She gave a meaty sigh, and shifted from foot to foot. "Can we go home?"

"That's not all." I thought she might react like this. "Words," Irina had said when I tried to apologize to her. I had to show that I was sorry with my actions too.

I took her hand and drew her further around the lake until we reached the café, closed right now, but all I needed was the brick wall. I pulled a piece of pavement chalk from my pocket and drew a cross there about the height of my nose.

"I'm sorry, and now I'm accepting my punishment. See?" I shone my phone flashlight on the wall so I could bring my nose right onto the cross, and then I turned off the flashlight. The brick wall felt rough under my nose. Even in the dark, I felt Stella's gaze on me. With my back to the world, I felt vulnerable, like a child waiting for a smack.

But as I stood there, the fear and shame faded. I felt the satisfaction of accepting a just punishment. Was this how Blanka felt? Maybe there was something safe, comforting even, about standing with your nose on the cross. You knew what you were supposed to be doing. It was not like the rest of life, in a vast grey city where the language was difficult and the food strange. All these people lived in such luxury and privilege, ignorant of a place where people had dragged your father from bed in the night and burned him because he was ethnic Armenian. Irina had such a fierce drive to live that she'd succeeded in bringing Blanka over the mountains, taking her to Armenia and eventually to London, but here, maybe that fierce drive to live was too much, and had left Blanka with none.

"I understand you now," I whispered. "I'm sorry." I leaned my forehead on the wall for a moment, exhausted, and then I turned around.

There was nobody there. Nothing except rain beginning to hiss into the puddles. "Stella!" I called. I turned the corner of the café and walked around to the back. Nobody. "Stella?" I couldn't even see anyone walking around the lake. I slipped on a patch of slimy dead leaves and fell heavily on all fours. My knees and palms burned, my breath came fast, my belly tightened so I couldn't breathe.

Then the pain around my midriff receded. "Stella!" I screamed. "Stella! Stella!"

A dark shape prowled by the railing—no, it was the fallen tree she played on. "Stella!" I ran twice around the pond, screaming her name. She had to be close by. She wouldn't just wander off.

I called Pete. My face was so numb from the cold I could barely form words.

"Jesus Christ, Charlotte! How could you lose her? What were you doing in the park in the dark—wait, never mind. I'm on my way."

The band around my midriff pulled so tight I hunched over, panting. The house lights receded, and I wasn't in a London park anymore. I was in a black wilderness with one or two dots of light on the far horizon, other people who had firewood and shelter, but I didn't. I was so cold. I was cold at my very core.

The pain came again, a squeezing that intensified until I clutched the railings and then sank to the ground. Someone hurried past, and I wanted to stop him, ask him for help, but it hurt too much to speak. Seeing that I was in distress, he politely left me to my private torment.

I staggered around the lake one more time, tears and snot streaming. I couldn't feel my fingers. It felt like a giant pair of scissors had snipped off the tips. And I deserved it. I'd give my fingertips to have her back. I'd give my unborn child.

Then my phone pinged: She's here.

Pete opened the door as I was fumbling with my key. "She came home by herself. Luckily, I hadn't left to come find you yet. What the hell happened? How could you let her out of your sight?"

"Oh my god. Is she OK?"

"She's a little chilled, but she's fine. She's upstairs." But his face was grim. I caught sight of myself in the hall mirror, face pinched with cold and smeared with mud, leaves in my hair.

"I need to see her," I said. But Pete was pointing at the empty bowl and wineglass I'd left on the dining table. "Hold on. Did you give her *wine* to drink?"

I folded my arms. "That's mine." There was no excuse for giving alcohol to an eight-year-old apart from the one thing he wouldn't believe.

"And how did you get separated? What were you even doing in the playground after dark?"

"Blank—I mean, Stella wanted to go." I thought quickly. "We were playing a game, and then she disappeared. We lost each other."

"Well, thank god she was smart enough to find her way home on her own."

"Is she in her room?"

"In the bath, trying to warm up. I offered to sit with her, but she wanted to be alone. Maybe she's getting to the age where she feels more self-conscious about her body."

"I'm going up there." I had to find out if Blanka was satisfied with my punishment. I rushed into Stella's bathroom. She was stretched full-length in the bath, her face underwater. The surface of the water was a smooth sheet, so she had to have been down there for some time. It was like she lay inside a glass coffin.

I screamed and lunged for her, and she sat up and blinked, water streaming from her hair. I dragged her out of the bath, my clothes getting soaked.

I pressed her to me while I tried to stop myself from shaking. I pulled back to look at her face. "Why did you do that? I thought you'd drowned! Are you trying to scare me?"

Pete burst in. "What's going on in here?"

"I was upset," I said carefully. "Stella was completely underwater. That's not safe, sweetheart."

"She was practicing holding her breath," Pete said. "Like her swim teacher told her to. Jesus." He handed her a towel.

My teeth chattered. Blanka was sending me a message: her patience was running out. She wasn't going to drown Stella—not yet—but she wanted to show me that she could. She wasn't here to listen to my apology and watch me hold my nose to a cross. She wanted something else, and I'd better figure it out fast. It was just so hard when she wouldn't speak. But there was one place where she expressed herself in words. I'd been wrong to let it go before.

"If you won't talk to me, let me read your diary," I murmured to her. Her dark gaze held mine.

Pete brought me a tray in the bedroom: a cup of tea, a small pitcher of heated milk with a cinnamon stick, and a curl of lemon peel: *té de California*, we called this. Long ago, on our honeymoon in Spain, a café had served me tea this way, and I'd loved it so much that Pete insisted that I have it that way in every café that we went to after that, always leaving a generous tip.

But despite the gesture, I felt that something was different—perhaps the way his beard hid his face. "I'm not angry," he said. "I'm just worried about you."

"I'll be fine," I said, although my teeth still chattered. I leaned a little closer to him and realized what was different. Gone was the scent of citrus and freshly sharpened pencils. He smelled damp and earthy, the secretive smell of mycelium.

Pete went downstairs to make some calls, and I changed out of my jumper and muddy jeans. As I was getting into bed, another contraction came. It was Braxton-Hicks because it was far too early for the baby to come. Probably it was stress, and if I rested, they would pass. Still, the prelude to labor made me think of what life would be like when I had the baby. It took all my time and energy to find out what Blanka wanted. I didn't know how I could do it if I was breastfeeding and changing nappies. I *had* to make her leave before the baby came.

31.

I want my diary." Stella shook me, her breath hot in my face.
I sat up with a jerk. It was morning. "Where's Daddy?"
"Making breakfast. I want my diary." She pointed at Pete's
wardrobe.

"I already looked there." Still, I climbed out of bed and opened
it. She pointed at the high shelf where Pete kept his suitcase. I
pulled it down. "I looked in here too." Then I remembered the
pouches he used to keep things when he traveled, now neatly folded
in the suitcase's mesh pocket.

The diary was in the smallest one. I'd forgotten that it was such
a cheap, dog-eared notebook. I hoped I wasn't foolish for expecting
it to have the answers. "May I?" I asked her, and she nodded. I
opened it at random: a wall of baffling symbols. This had to be the
Armenian alphabet. Pages and pages that I had to find a way to
translate. I found myself tracing the letters on the carpet, beginning with a *t* and a *u*. There was a gap and then a letter that looked

like an upside-down *m*. After five clumps of these strange letters, I was back at the beginning. She was repeating the same phrase. I flipped to the previous page: the same. I looked backwards and forwards through the book, and it was all the same. She'd been copying out the same phrase for months.

"What does it mean?" I whispered. Why repeat the same phrase over and over—to yourself?

"Stella?" Pete called. "Charlotte! Breakfast!"

I took her arm. "Can I show him?"

But Stella shook her head.

"OK, I won't show him. But can I hold on to it?"

More headshaking. She put her finger to her lips.

I understood: Pete couldn't see the diary, and he couldn't even know that I had done so. Whatever Blanka wanted, it was between the two of us.

"Can I take a photo at least?"

She nodded, and I did so before I zipped the book into its hiding place. Then I put the suitcase back on the shelf, careful to leave everything exactly as we'd found it.

Stella went downstairs to get her breakfast, and I grabbed my phone to figure out how to translate the diary. "Charlotte?" Pete appeared in the doorway, and I shoved my phone under the bedclothes. He presented a tray: oatmeal with sliced bananas. "I'm dropping Stella off at Lulu's, so she'll be off your hands for the day, and then I'm heading to the office. I wanted to make sure you eat something before I leave."

"Great!" I shoveled in oatmeal until he was satisfied, and then rushed to Stella's room. I hustled her through getting dressed and brushing her teeth, desperate to be alone with my phone.

The minute the door slammed behind them, I pulled up Google Translate. I couldn't type in the words from the diary because I didn't have those symbols on my keyboard. But I saw the images button and realized I could just upload the photo. With shaking hands, I did so. It was Armenian, of course. In the English alphabet, those words were *yes atum yem ayd mardun.*

Translation: I hate that person.

I felt a jolt of fear. If Blanka hated someone this much, then whatever they had done, they couldn't atone for it simply by holding their nose to a cross. She wanted them to suffer.

I understood now that Blanka didn't hate *me.* I was her collaborator—she showed me the diary. But she'd written it in Armenian. She wanted me to have some information but not all of it. She wanted me to work to get at the truth. The diary took me one step nearer to understanding what she wanted, but not all the way.

I paced around the house for hours. I didn't have the focus for detective work. My thoughts felt like those little silver balls in a game where you have to tilt a plastic tray in a box to get them into the slots. They rolled around and bounced off each other. I couldn't make them come one at a time, or easily decide which was the most important thing to focus on.

In the early afternoon, another contraction came, and it didn't feel like just Braxton-Hicks this time. It felt like a metal contraption squeezing my whole body. I sank to my knees and rested my forehead on the bed. It was too early, just thirty weeks. I had to go to hospital. I had to lie down. But if I dealt with what was happening in my body, it would be all-consuming. I'd probably be put on bed rest. I wouldn't be able to save Stella, and the time to do that was now.

I needed more information about Blanka. Irina wasn't going to tell me anything more. But if I could go to her house when Irina wasn't there, I could look at Blanka's room, at her things. Maybe she had a laptop with an obvious password, or maybe she'd written something down. She wouldn't let me get to know her in life, but in death I could force the issue. She had to have left some clue about who she hated so much.

Outside Irina's house, I lingered for a while, trying to tell if she was in or not, hoping I might see her leave, so I'd know for sure. I dared to walk past once, quickly, to see if she was sitting in the window. Maybe she'd resumed her job as a hospice nurse, sitting at the bedsides of the dying. There was no point in ringing the bell if she was there. Last time I saw her, she'd made her feelings about me clear.

It was getting dark now, raining again. My hands ached with cold. I was so distraught I'd left the house without a jacket and, I now realized, without my phone. People rushed by with the hoods of their parkas up, the handles of heavy bags of festive groceries cutting into their palms.

I rang the bell, and rang it again. If Irina was there, I didn't know what I'd say. The pavement was black with rain now. I rang the bell a third time. No answer. The house was dark. I tried the front windows: locked. I looked around for a hidden key. There wasn't even a pot of geraniums out here.

But then I noticed the alley down the side between Irina's house and the neighbors'. The gate at the back wasn't locked. I went into the backyard. I could see over their fence to the neighbors' garden.

They had removed the hot tub, and there was a half-finished wooden deck in its place. I felt outraged. When summer came again, were they planning to grill rosemary pork chops and sit on indoor-outdoor furniture on the very spot where Blanka had sunk into oblivion?

I prowled the gloomy back garden. A plastic table and chairs stood in the middle of a square of concrete paving stones. A mass of brambles hid the back fence. I checked the back door: locked of course. As I turned away, I stubbed my toe on a broken concrete paving stone and cursed as pain shot through my foot. My midriff squeezed, tighter and tighter, and I crouched on hands and knees, a moan escaping me. I had to get into the house. I had to get this done quickly so I could get to the hospital. I dug my fingers under the broken paving stone, and a chunk came away. I scrabbled and scraped until I'd worked it loose.

I took off my jumper and wrapped it around my right hand. I picked up the chunk, and went to the back door. The glass shattered decisively. I dropped the concrete and pushed away enough glass with my jumper-covered hand to reach my hand through, feel for a key inside. The key wasn't in the lock, because what idiot leaves their key in the back door? I picked up the rock again and bashed at the lower pane of the door until I'd got rid of most of the glass. I laid my jumper on the floor on the other side so I had something to protect my hands from the dagger-strewn floor.

I got down on my hands and knees. It wasn't a big space to squeeze through, but even with my pregnant belly, I was a small woman. I crawled forward. I felt pinpoints of brightness on my scalp and knew that glass had fallen into my hair and cut me, and then pain flashed in the meat of my right palm as glass poked through the sweater. Then I was through. I was in the kitchen, and I almost felt safe for a moment. I could use the lights: who would know I wasn't Irina? I found a tea towel and pressed it against my bleeding hand.

I went through to the living room. Photos crowded the mantelpiece, pictures that were either new or that I hadn't noticed before. Wait—was that Stella? Half a dozen photographs of a round-faced, solid little girl in ugly long dresses, hair tightly braided, face unsmiling. I grabbed the nearest one: a vast grey lake in the background, a pebbly beach. When had Irina taken Stella to visit such a lake? Then I blinked and saw of course it wasn't Stella. It was Blanka as a child. No photographs of Blanka looking older than eighteen. But hadn't she been in her thirties when she died? It was like Irina didn't want to acknowledge that Blanka had grown up.

Could Irina be the person Blanka hated so much?

A door off the hallway led to a bedroom with a double bed with a patchwork quilt, like someone had made it using all the ugliest possible clothes; a bureau with a mirror; a huge, heavy wardrobe; lace curtains dimming the light; a crucifix on the wall: Irina's room. Where had Blanka slept? Surely not in the front room, on that tiny velour sofa?

I went back out to the hallway. Then I spotted a smaller door. I hadn't noticed it because it was under the stairs. I opened it, and concrete steps led down. Cold air streamed out, a whiff of damp, of the earth itself. An iron fist squeezed me, and I had to stop for a moment. When the fist let go, warm wetness trickled down my leg. But I couldn't pay attention to that now. I was too close to discovering something at last, I could feel it. If I was ever going to rid my daughter of Blanka, I had to go down those stairs.

They led to a basement bedroom with a small window at ground level, a carpet smelling of mildew. A chair piled with clothes. A child's bed: maroon sheets with a white arrow on a yellow circle that I thought was a Star Trek logo. It was a child's room, for a grown woman.

On the wall hung a *Doctor Who* poster: the TARDIS floating in space, a door open, light beaming from within. *"Allons-y,"* it read. "Let's go." I studied it, desperate for a clue. Was that what lay behind her dull expression: dreams of adventures to the fringes of the universe?

"Get out." Irina's voice was matter-of-fact, but her anger was like a wall of heat. Something trickled down my leg, and for a second, I thought I'd wet myself in fear, and I was ashamed. But of course, it wasn't that, there was too much of it, splashing onto the carpet, soaking my shoes. I needed to get to the hospital, but she blocked the stairs. She was perhaps twenty years older than me, in her late fifties. But she was tough, a survivor, and I was an emaciated pregnant woman whose water had broken ten weeks early.

I placed my hand on the wall to steady myself and realized there were faint lines there. They swam into focus: a swarm of crosses. I blinked. "What are these marks?"

"From when she is little. I tell you this once already. If she is bad, she must stand with nose to cross until I say."

I shivered. How long did Blanka have to stand there as a child? How harsh was this penalty? Did Irina make her stand there for hours, hungry, needing the toilet? Maybe that was when Blanka began to think, I hate that person.

I sank onto the bed for a rest, but it felt cold and damp. It was the bed Blanka had slept in as a child, the same sheets, even. Irina should have bought her new sheets, or encouraged her to buy them herself. Small things like taking care of your surroundings could make you feel better. "How could you let her be like this?" I said, gesturing at the child's bed, the posters.

Irina snorted. "Nowadays, you people tell your kids they can do anything. This will not help Blanka. She does not speak good English, bad with people. She does not have big choice of job."

I looked around the room. The light was dim, I realized, because the recycling and rubbish bins were partly blocking the window, which was at ground level. It would have been so easy for Blanka to move them, but she didn't do it. She couldn't. "What did she do all the time?" I whispered. It hurt so much I could hardly talk.

"TV shows. She watches same ones many times. Looks on computer and learns many things about this Doctor Who." If this was Blanka's life, then surely, she was depressed. At some point, years before she died, she had stopped living. Did she blame her mother for that?

Irina touched the poster, the TARDIS floating in space with one door open, glowing inside, so inviting, like a kitchen on a winter's night. "I thought she was happy." She swiped at her eyes.

Irina could have helped Blanka to lead a bigger life, but Blanka had made choices too. She'd chosen to stay in her basement bedroom with faded crosses on the wall. She didn't return from the grave because she hated her mother. So who was it?

I felt like someone had taken a stick and was stirring my insides, trying to rearrange them forcibly. My time had nearly run out. I needed an ambulance. I had to be direct.

I tottered to my feet and clutched her hand so hard I could feel the bones scrunching together. "Blanka's come back. She's drawing crosses on my wall, writing in Stella's diary about hating someone. Who did she hate? Tell me."

Irina shook her head. "If Blanka came back, she would come to me, not to you."

Then the pain came again, and it was the kind of pain that makes you think you could die, that stops you from thinking. More water gushed from me, soaking the rug. "I need to get to the hospital. I don't have my phone. Please, call an ambulance." I wasn't sure I could get up the stairs.

Irina's face set and she disappeared, and I sank onto my knees and let the pain out in a groan. I didn't have the breath for screaming. Of course, she wanted to punish me, even if Blanka didn't, and there were so many reasons, the simplest being that I had my daughter, and she did not. The pain came again, obliterating thought, drawing forth a deep, animal sound.

When that contraction ended, Irina was back in the room, wearing an apron and holding a pile of things. She closed the basement door. I felt hot panic. Why did she close that door? "No, no. Call an ambulance. Call Pete. Please." Those were all the words I could get out before the next wave of pain.

I retched as on her knees, she spread out the shower curtain on the moldy rug. "Listen to me. You must be calm. I do this many times."

"No, no, no," I said in the space between contractions. "I'm not having the baby. I can't have the baby. I can't have a baby until Stella is safe. It's too soon. The baby will die. I'll die."

Irina shook her head. "The water is broken. Too late to go back. Too late for hospital."

"What? No. Please. Get me an ambulance. At least call Pete. Please." Then the pain carried me away on its wave, where nothing existed and nothing mattered except the pain. Even I didn't. There was nothing but the pain and groaning. I came out of it and thrashed as I realized she had removed my trainers and was pulling off my maternity jeans. I protested weakly, but when the next wave of pain came, I let her take them, my underwear too.

I was having my baby too early. I would die and so would my baby. I would bleed to death. The baby would be hopeless lumps of flesh that Irina would shove deep into the compost—my baby in exchange for hers. This was what she'd wanted all along.

The waves of pain came, over and over. I vomited. Irina told me to lie on my left side and gave me water to sip that tasted of dirty coins. "Don't leave me," I begged. She left again, only to return with a pair of scissors wrapped in a cloth.

In a moment of clarity, I saw little raised bumps on the white ceiling, like ringworm. Blanka had looked at this and dreamed of journeys to other worlds. Of going to another galaxy in the TARDIS. I closed my eyes, and I was standing in a red desert with Blanka. Three suns appeared above the horizon: dawn on a new planet.

A slap in the face brought me back to the cold, damp room. Another slap. "Charlotte? Listen. You cannot sleep. You must push now. Now, Charlotte."

"No," I moaned. "I can't, I can't. Please." I closed my eyes to be with Blanka. I deserved this. I accepted it. I just wanted it to be over. My baby was dead; Irina's wedding dress would become its shroud.

She got behind me and pulled me between her legs with super-human strength. She held my hands. "Charlotte. It's coming. Get ready. Now push."

The pain became a blazing white sun, and I was inside it. A circle of women surrounded me, murmuring prayers. Not Edith or Dianne, but Irina and her mother and her mother's mother. I was Irina's daughter, and this was her grandchild. Women from her family moved around me, praying, bringing tea and towels. I smelled flatbread fresh from the oven. I had to keep this line of women going, the women who survived, who would do anything for their girls. Blanka had broken it, but I could make it whole again.

It wasn't Irina's fault that Blanka died. It wasn't my fault. I felt love surrounding me. I pushed. I pushed. I pushed.

Then Irina was snipping in a brisk, professional way, and then holding a tiny baby, greasy with vernix, small enough to fit in my cupped hands. "A girl," said Irina, trembling a little. She didn't hate me after all. But I was afraid to look, afraid of how I'd fail this daughter.

Irina clasped my shoulder. "You are good mother," she said. I looked at her, and something passed between us. It wasn't her fault that Blanka had died. She could have done better, but she did the best she could. And I too was doing the best I could.

32.

I hobbled down the corridor to the NICU. It was slow going. Irina had done everything right, the doctors said, but it took a little work to stitch me up after what she'd done with her scissors. They had removed glass from my scalp and put a couple of stitches in my hand too. An accident, I'd told Pete. Fainted from the pain, and my head hit the glass door. I wasn't sure if he believed this, but he didn't ask any more questions for now.

In the NICU, my baby, one day old, lay in a Perspex tank under a jaundice lamp, with tubes coming out of her mouth and nose and wires attached all over her. As well as jaundice, she had underdeveloped lungs. A nurse wearing reindeer antlers approached me: it was Christmas Eve. "Just sit down in the rocker there, and I'll bring her to you." I brought the baby to my chest, under my hospital gown, so we were skin to skin. But holding her didn't feel the same, with all the tubes and wires attached. And she didn't have the wonderful smell that Stella had had. She just smelled salty and fishy. All she did was sleep, so after a while, I gave her back to the nurse.

Pete was on his way with Stella so she could meet her little sister, and I was nervous about how she'd react. To be precise, I was nervous about how Blanka-in-Stella would react. Blanka was accustomed to getting all of my attention. She might not respond well to this new arrival, who kept me in hospital when I could be helping her. I was grateful that only Pete and I were allowed into the NICU. For now, Stella was only allowed to look at her little sister.

I met Pete and Stella at the entrance to the NICU. I hugged Stella, but couldn't read her expression. I led her up to the NICU's viewing window and showed her which baby was ours. Just at that moment, the baby opened her eyes, and her fists clenched and un-clenched. She had an expression on her face like someone trying to remember a dream.

Stella smiled to herself, and I felt a rush of relief. Blanka was great with little ones. I didn't need to worry. Stella would put this baby at ease, the way Blanka had put Stella at ease when they first met.

I wanted to ask, "Who is this person you hate so much?" But that wasn't how this worked: Blanka was here, inside Stella, but she was still herself. She didn't offer up information or answer direct questions.

We left the baby to sleep and returned to my room. Stella pulled out her crochet project, a complicated-looking blanket with tassels and a hexagon pattern. She had been good as soon as she started— but of course, that was Blanka too. I shrank from the blanket.

A nurse brought us champagne and tea and scones. Pete had put me in the nicest maternity hospital money could buy. It was a forty-minute Tube journey from our house, but the room had a view over Regent's Park.

"What do you think about Luna for a name?" Pete said. I forced myself to focus on him. He looked so well-groomed and manly in the maternity ward, a place of nurses and disheveled mothers, almost like a handsome doctor in the soap I'd watched with Maureen.

Stella and Luna, star and moon. It was a bit too cute, but Luna was a pretty name, and I had no energy to think of alternatives. My stitches stung and itched. My hand throbbed. "Fine," I said. I wondered if he had his tattoo planned already.

Pete poured the champagne. But I didn't feel like celebrating. Before I got pregnant, I'd worried about miscarrying, about losing the baby, but I never dreamed that it was Stella I would lose. She took the clotted cream and all the scones and went into the en suite bathroom—a perk of private maternity care—and shut the door.

"I need to talk to you about her," I said.

"Don't worry, Christmas is under control," said Pete. "The hospital will probably give you a Michelin-starred lunch tomorrow, and Stella and I will make do. I was up late wrapping presents last night."

The previous Christmas, Stella had put her hands over her ears and screamed when anyone pulled a Christmas cracker. But when Edith asked her if she "still" believed in Father Christmas, Stella shot back that obviously quantum physics explained Father Christmas: it was no problem for him to deliver millions of presents in twenty-four hours because he was a particle that could be in several places at once.

Suddenly I sat up. "Pete, how long has she been in the bathroom?"

He was about to nod off in the visitor's armchair, but I seized his arm, my heart banging: Blanka could be doing anything to Stella in there. She could be gobbling my painkillers. Blanka had shown me she would hurt Stella if necessary.

"Get her out of there!" I shoved my tray table aside and heaved myself out of bed.

"Jesus, Charlotte. Calm down. She doesn't like me going into the bathroom when she's in there anymore. She's growing up." Pete knocked. "Stella, honey, you OK in there?" The lock clicked, and Stella's head appeared around the door.

"I'm having a picnic." The door closed again.

Pete stared at me. "She's just eating scones. You scared the hell out of me, screaming like that. What did you think was happening in there?"

I sank back onto the pillows. "You have to watch her, Pete, when I'm not with you. Will you promise me? Don't leave her in the bath alone. Don't let her near anything sharp, any medicines."

Pete frowned. "She's not going to hurt herself."

"She's capable of anything. She's very angry."

"She just ate three scones. She can't be that angry."

"Don't joke about it! I *know* she's angry because she showed me her diary. It was right before I had the baby—Luna—at Irina's. Stella knew where you'd hidden it. She gave me permission to read it. And all it says is 'I hate that person I hate that person I hate that person I hate—'"

"I get the message. So she uses her diary as a way to vent. That actually sounds pretty healthy."

"How can you say that?"

"I know you think she's a genius, but she's eight years old. I don't think we need to freak out because her diary isn't great literature."

"Just look at it." I reached for my phone. Pete shook his head, but I shoved the photo under his nose. "Look at it. It's in Armenian. It is not normal for an eight-year-old to write in Armenian. She would have had to learn an entirely new alphabet."

"She can use Google Translate same as you. I expect she was just messing around."

"Armenian was Blanka's first language," I hissed. "That's not all. This is Blanka's handwriting too. I compared it with an old shopping list Blanka wrote—"

"An old shopping list? Sweetheart, you're frightening me. Let's talk about this again after you've had a rest. I'm going to get them to check your temperature. Meanwhile, I promise you Stella's safe with me." He kissed me goodbye and had Stella do so too. Outside, I heard him murmuring to the nurse.

I thought I'd be alone on Christmas Day, but Pete's colleague Kia showed up in the morning. I was touched. Emmy had sent me a text with a flurry of emojis, and Cherie had messaged a **Congratulations!** with no emojis. Kia was the only one to visit; she'd brought a huge hamper and a pink orchid too. I was surprised: I liked her well enough, but she didn't seem the type to visit a colleague's wife in hospital, especially not postpartum. She'd once laughingly told me she hated baby showers. At one, a friend had handed her a fancy journal and asked her to write a special note to welcome the baby. Other guests had jotted life lessons or gushed about the expectant mama, but Kia stood there paralyzed. "In the end, all I could do was write, 'Welcome, Baby!' in really big letters and get the hell out of there."

"I know babies aren't your thing," I said now, touched. "Thank you for coming. Don't you have Christmas plans?"

Kia smiled. "Well, I couldn't make it home to the States, so I'll have dinner with friends later. I thought I'd stop by and congratulate you first. Pete said the pregnancy was rough and you felt sick the whole way through. He feels bad he has to work so hard."

"It's so thoughtful of you to visit." It was. But I felt uneasy. It wasn't that Pete had confided in a work colleague about my pregnancy woes. I understood he needed a shoulder to lean on. It was the way she seemed to be defending Pete: working so hard, feeling so guilty.

But maybe I was reading too much into it. Something about Kia made me think she was lonely too. We both needed a friend. So I smiled, even though the gift hamper contained something called a jade roller for tired eyes and aromatherapy bath oils. Kia was childless, so it wasn't her fault that she didn't know my future as a mother of a newborn and a young child did not include long soaks while treating my unsightly under-eye bags.

Kia flopped into the chair next to my bed, cheeks flushed from the cold. She had a nose stud and the right sort of perky nose for it.

"God, the birth sounded so dramatic. I mean, traumatic. Well, both, I guess." She took my hand. "Charlotte, you are so fucking brave."

"Thank you," I said. "Though I didn't really have any choice."

"Can I see her?" Kia asked.

"You don't have to, honestly." I smiled. "I'll tell her, 'Welcome, Baby!' from you."

Kia grinned. "I'll never live that down. Seriously, I'd love to see her."

I put on my dressing gown and shuffled to the NICU, where I pointed out Luna through the viewing window. "So cute!" breathed Kia. "I wish I could hold her. I love the smell of babies."

"She smells like the birth canal," I said. I felt tired and ancient. "Like my vagina," I clarified.

Kia laughed. She pointed at a nurse, gently joggling a baby, its head against her chest. "Oh look, the snuggle hold."

"I didn't know that position had a name," I said.

"There are five ways to hold a newborn," Kia said. "I studied up on YouTube before I came."

And she'd made the trip here on Christmas Day. "Listen, really and truly, thank you for the gift hamper and the visit."

"No problem." Kia smiled at me, and I smiled back, although early on in "Charlotte Says," I'd written, "When you say, 'No problem,' in response to being thanked, you suggest that there could well have been a problem and it's lucky there wasn't. For a more positive vibe, just say, 'You're welcome.'"

After Kia had gone, I went back to the NICU and I held Luna. She was still curled into herself, asleep nearly all the time. No matter how hard I tried to feel the sweetness at the heart of it all, I still felt like I was holding an ordinary baby.

I called Pete to wish him Happy Christmas, and he said he felt bad I had to spend Christmas Day alone. "I want to make it up to you. I want to take you out for lunch tomorrow. I'll make a reservation somewhere really nice—"

"Pete, I just gave birth. I'll fall asleep halfway through the appetizers."

"I didn't mean that kind of place. I meant somewhere comfortable, where we can just sit by the fire. That's what I really want: just the two of us, no distraction. We've become so disconnected." His voice was wistful.

"You're right," I agreed, hope warming my chest. "I blindsided you yesterday when I told you about the diary. It wasn't a good time to explain, with Stella right there. Don't say anything now: I want you to hear me out properly. A quiet place, with good food. That's what we need. A chance to talk."

"We're going to figure this out," Pete said. "We're a team."

"And you know what, you could ask Kia to watch Stella," I said. I didn't think I could ask Irina, after she'd done so much.

Pete thought that was a great idea, and I felt hopeful. Time alone, away from her, was a rare opportunity. If we were together, really focused on each other for a few hours, I believed I could make him understand what was going on.

33.

The next day, a nurse wheeled me to the front entrance of the hospital, and Pete pulled up in the car. I gingerly settled myself in, careful of the bandage around my hand.

"I've found the perfect place in the country," Pete announced.

"The country? I thought we'd find a place in town."

"Most places around here are pretty fancy. I assumed you wouldn't be in the mood for that." True. I wore a maternity tunic and leggings. Pete had brought a bag from home, but had forgotten to bring other shoes, so I was still wearing the trainers that I'd worn to Irina's, which had recently been soaked in amniotic fluid.

"I just wanted to get away from everything and be together," Pete said. "It will be good to be out of London, don't you think?"

"I can't walk far." I was still bleeding and had to wear a heavy-duty pad.

"Honey, you just gave birth," Pete said. "I don't expect you to walk anywhere. Relax, I'll take care of you." Pete played Paul Simon on the drive, and the car heater was on. I stared out the window as grey buildings gave way to brown fields and leafless hedges. After living in California, it felt like in the English midwinter, the sky never really got light, even at midday. I fell asleep.

When I woke up, Pete was pulling up to a gate in a large privet hedge. A discreet sign advertised THE COTTAGE. He pushed a button, and the intercom crackled. "Pete Mason, with Charlotte Mason. I made a reservation," he said. The gate swung open.

"What is this place? Seems very exclusive." I was touched. I imagined a special vegetarian restaurant with a biodynamic garden. Pete squeezed my hand.

"It is, baby." His beard was starting to look unkempt—the birth had been stressful for him too. It was so sweet of him to make this big effort to spoil me with a special day out.

The driveway led through manicured grounds to a large Georgian house with paned sash windows and brown wisteria climbing the wall, a fanlight over the front door. Pete parked in the horseshoe driveway, and an older woman in a khaki skirt and pressed white shirt came out of the house. "I'm Rosemary," she said.

"Pete Mason, we spoke on the phone." They shook hands.

"Charlotte Mason," I said, uncertain of the etiquette. Was I supposed to introduce myself too?

"How did you find out about this place?" I murmured to Pete as she entered something on a clipboard. "I've never heard of it. Did you read about it or something?"

"I did a lot of research, that's for sure," Pete said, pulling at his collar. He was wearing a proper shirt instead of a T-shirt. I felt bad that I hadn't been able to dress up more for this occasion.

"Coffee and herbal tea are waiting for you in the conservatory," said Rosemary, indicating we should follow her. The conservatory had cushioned wicker chairs and glass-topped coffee tables arranged in discreet groups, a view of a close-trimmed lawn with a rectangular lily pond. There were a couple of other groups, murmuring quietly, white-haired parents talking to their adult daughter, a woman sipping tea alone, another woman, also alone, discreetly nursing a baby. It was impressive to take yourself out to lunch to a place like this with your baby in tow.

We sat down, and another person in khaki trousers and pressed white shirt brought us coffee and biscuits and an herbal tea "that aids lactation."

I turned to Pete, who was glancing at his phone. "How do they know I'm lactating?" Could they tell by looking at me? I shifted and felt blood pulse out of me, and I hoped it wouldn't soak through my pad and my maternity leggings and onto the pristine oatmeal-colored sofa cushions. "This place is a little weird," I whispered. "Why is that woman going out to lunch alone with her baby on Boxing Day? Why is there no menu?" I glanced back at the parents with their adult daughter and realized that the daughter was weeping. Blackness crowded the edges of my vision. But I wouldn't faint. I dug my fingers into the bandage over the cut in my right palm and the pain made me alert again. "How do they know I'm lactating?" I hissed at Pete. The mother of the weeping woman glanced around, and I realized I'd spoken louder than I'd thought.

Pete's face was that of a stranger. "I've consulted with my mom and a couple of other people, and I think it's best you rest here for a few days. Luna is getting the best care possible in the NICU. You need to focus on getting well."

"What is this place?" I whispered.

"It's a well-being clinic." He cleared his throat. "With a focus on maternal peri- and postnatal health."

A moan escaped me. "You can't do this. You don't understand. Stella is in danger. It's her we need to worry about. She's in terrible, terrible danger."

"Charlotte, this place is the best. You have no idea how lucky we are that I was able to get a spot here. Most people don't even know places like this exist. You'll be comfortable here, get the best care."

I thought of something. "Listen, did you tell Kia about watching her in the bath?"

Pete picked up a biscuit, broke it in half. He looked like he wanted to grind it into powder. "That therapist called. Wesley? He was worried *you* might try to hurt Stella. Cherie was worried too."

Everyone I'd confided in had betrayed me.

The glass-topped tables and wicker chairs with their tasteful cushions seemed to cluster closer. Outside it was getting dark, even though it couldn't be later than three in the afternoon.

Pete shifted away from me slightly, sat up a little straighter. "It's best for everyone if you stay away from Stella until you feel better."

"What are you saying, I'm a danger to my own daughter? She is all I think about, day and night."

Pete seemed to reach the limit of his patience. "You put a dead bird in her bed."

"*On* her bed," I said sharply, causing the white-haired parents to look over. Rosemary was standing discreetly in the doorway, watching our whole exchange.

Pete continued reciting my misdeeds, a litany he had stored up. "You think she's keeping a diary in another language."

"It *is* in another language. Armenian."

"You gave her alcohol and then left her wandering around at night on her own. An eight-year-old. You were physically abusing her."

"I admit I shook her that one time," I said. "But listen, I wasn't really shaking her—I was shaking Blanka." He gaped at me, and I clarified, "Blanka is inside Stella. That's what I was trying to tell you yesterday."

Pete's voice was very quiet. "She's possessed."

"Exactly." I exhaled. "Finally, you get it. We can talk about how to help her."

"You're the one who needs help, baby," Pete said gently. "There's a name for this. Capgras delusion—the delusion that your loved one has been replaced by an exact duplicate."

"You planned this speech," I said, sick at the depth of his betrayal. "Anyway, that isn't it. This *is* her, but it's just her body. She's a vessel." I stopped. My voice would hardly work.

Rosemary was suddenly at my elbow with a clipboard, which she handed to Pete, and he gave me a pen. "Sign yourself in here," he said. "Take a couple of nights and rest. Please. They have massages, a saltwater pool."

"No, no, no. I have to see Stella. I have to save her." My lungs were constricted. Once, when we lived in San Francisco, a friend persuaded me to swim off Ocean Beach, and the cold water caused a gasp reflex, where I couldn't stop gulping air, as if my body wanted to prepare me for submersion. But my friend said if I counted to fifteen and kept swimming, by the end I would be breathing normally. I would be able to handle the cold. And now as I struggled to breathe, I kept thinking, In a minute, I'll be OK. But I wasn't. I felt like I was sinking downwards, leaving Stella on the surface, out of reach.

Rosemary placed a hand on my back and said, "Charlotte, you are doing fine. You're safe here."

The rudeness of her intrusion snapped me out of it. "Will you please step away? We are having a private conversation."

Pete leaned close. "Baby, if you promise to eat, sleep, and rest and stay here for two nights, then I'll listen to what you have to say about Stella. I'm serious: you eat three proper meals a day, not rice cakes, and you get the massages and the therapy and get a good night's sleep. If you still believe . . ." He trailed off.

"Blanka is inside Stella," I supplied.

He flinched. "Right, if you still believe that, I will take you seriously."

"You have to keep her safe until then," I said. "Do you promise?"

"I always keep my promises," Pete said. "You know that."

This was true: he wouldn't let anything happen to her. And he'd been focusing on me, thinking I was the problem. Without me there, he'd have more attention for Stella. She was off school for the two-week Christmas holiday. And this was the first chance they'd had since Blanka's death to spend an extended period of time together. He'd finally see that something was wrong. Staying here for a couple of nights was worth it if that was what it took to get Pete on my side. I needed him. I'd tried to get rid of Blanka on my own, and failed.

"Fine." I signed the form.

Pete got up. "I'll call later to check on you." He started edging away, reminding me absurdly of a parent dropping their young child off on the first day of school, knowing there will be screaming and wanting to be away before it starts.

"Wait, what about Luna?" I called.

"The hospital will take care of Luna. She's still nine weeks premature. She won't even know you're gone."

"I need to feed her," I said. Even though Luna hardly nursed, I pumped four times a day in hospital, and my milk was going to come in soon, just when I was separated from her.

"You can pump. They've got your pump and a bag from home with your things." Of course, he'd brought a bag from home. He'd planned carefully.

"We can courier the milk to your baby," Rosemary murmured. But as Pete turned to go, I stumbled after him, feeling like I was coming apart at my stitches.

"Don't leave, Pete. Please, please, please." I knocked over a vase of winter branches as I threw myself against him. I couldn't believe the way he was treating me, the love of his life. What had gone wrong between us? I thought of all those times I had left things unsaid or saved things up, waiting for when he would be most receptive. Now I knew that he too left some things unsaid and hoarded others until he deemed the time was right.

"Charlotte. I have no choice. My heart is breaking here." But he didn't look like his heart was breaking. He seemed cold and efficient. In his pressed shirt and khaki trousers, he looked less laid-back California surfer, more groomed corporate executive. I understood now that he had dressed up not for me, but so that he would look like the sane one.

34.

Pete's latest text reads, Kids both eating well. Visited Luna first thing this morning, now Stella's asked to go swimming. I message back, Do NOT take Stella swimming! I'm ready to leave as per agreement. When can you collect me? Three dots indicate he's typing a message, but then none appears. I call him, and he doesn't pick up. I leave a message telling him to come and get me ASAP. I call him twice more—nothing. I pump for Luna—still nothing but colostrum. Maybe the stress will stop my milk coming in at all. But I can't think about that now. I go to see Dr. Beaufort.

She looks more put together today, without the poncho, in tailored dark wool trousers and draped cream jumper, her hair pinned up with a tortoiseshell claw. The Peppa Pig plaster is gone. I read her Pete's latest text. "He's taking good care of your children," says Dr. Beaufort.

I shake my head. "He's not taking me seriously. Stella isn't safe around water. How could he agree to take her swimming? She already tried to drown herself once."

"In the bath?" says Dr. Beaufort. "You said. I'm not sure that's even possible. That would take tremendous determination."

"Exactly," I say. "Blanka is nothing if not determined." But I see in her eyes that even though I've now told her everything, she still doesn't share my perspective.

I hunch over my bad hand, which is throbbing crazily. "Last night you told me you've known people who have had encounters with the dead and you didn't think they were mad. You saw your own dead mother. So why don't you believe me?"

Dr. Beaufort looks taken aback. "I did see my mother very clearly, yes. But I think there's been a misunderstanding. I had what you might call a waking dream. It's so common that there's even a technical term: hypnagogic hallucination. My point was that the bereaved can have very vivid experiences of seeing the dead. Grief can do crazy things to your mind."

Finally, I understand that I'm not going to convince her. I misjudged her last night. Even when you present all the evidence, people simply won't believe something that contradicts their deepest beliefs: that death is final, that a spirit can't transcend the limits of the body.

"You gave birth five days ago," says Dr. Beaufort. "Hormones can have very powerful effects on the brain too. They can distort our sense of reality."

"Haven't we covered this? Mothers have hormones, but we also have instincts. We're hardwired to know when our children are in danger."

She says nothing, and I think if she had children, there would be a picture of them in the room. "Are you a mother?" I blurt out.

Dr. Beaufort opens her mouth, and I say, "If you're going to answer with a question, I'd prefer it if you didn't answer at all." I look at the ugly vase of thistles. "Just tell me who made that."

"A patient," she says.

Suddenly I'm certain that she *doesn't* have children. She doesn't get it. No wonder she has a bookshelf full of books about under-standing motherhood: she has no personal experience of it.

I think back to what I'd told Cherie: a mother's hand knows. As her mother, I always *know* when something is wrong with Stella. That same intuition tells me she is in danger now.

"What happens if I just walk out of here?" I ask.

Dr. Beaufort looks disappointed with me. "It would be against medical advice. We'd notify your husband. We might want to put proceedings in motion to ensure you are not a danger to yourself or others."

"Proceedings?"

She sighs. "Your husband might seek to keep you in a psychiatric care facility, whether or not you agree."

"He would never do that," I protest. "He loves me." But I realize now, I can't be sure. He put me in here, didn't he? He promised to take care of Stella, but instead he's taking her near deep water. He promised I could leave after two nights, and now he's not answering the phone.

I reach for a marble egg, weighing it in my hand, and Dr. Beaufort shrinks back. Her office is on the ground floor. I could just climb out the window and run. Dr. Beaufort is watching me, hold-ing the arms of her chair a little too tightly.

But if I run, where will that get me? For all I know, they'll send two men sprinting after me with a straitjacket. Even if I get away, they'll call Pete, and he might try to hide Stella from me. I need to leave secretly and be well away before they discover my absence. I must be cunning, play meek and obedient.

I sit, replace the egg, and watch her exhale. I was wrong about Dr. Beaufort being a mother, but I think my guess about her being fairly new to this was spot-on. She must be a novice, because if she'd had many patients, she would know that moms separated from their children don't want to cradle eggs, they want to throw things. A real therapist would never place a bowl of projectiles within reach of a patient.

"Perhaps I'm not seeing clearly," I say. "I just gave birth. It's been less than a year since I lost my mother. I need to stop worrying about Stella." I continue, repeating various things she's said to me in our sessions, but she acts like I've had a major breakthrough.

"This is a huge step forward," she says, beaming.

I go to a restorative yoga class and spend the rest of the day in my room, staring out the window. Eventually, I get a text from Pete: Can't make it down there today. Talk tomorrow?

Great!!! Feeling so much more relaxed! I type. Person-in-lotus-position emoji, heart, heart.

I have dinner in the dining room with the other moms, about ten of us, plus Kelly, the cheery young woman who is obviously there to keep an eye on us. Our white pajamas look out of place in the Georgian dining room, with its marble fireplace and plaster ceiling roses. We serve ourselves from a sideboard buffet of kale salad studded with pomegranate seeds and quinoa with roasted vegetables.

Some moms came to the Cottage with their babies. These are

now tucked up in bed—babies are not allowed at dinner—but these moms cluster together at one end of the table and chatter about sleep schedules and breastfeeding difficulties. The moms who came here without their babies pick at their quinoa. We're second-class citizens who can't be trusted with our offspring. Chapped Hands from the lounge is here, and she launches back into her story, announcing to the table that her husband's laissez-faire attitude to hand hygiene is endangering her twins.

When I heard Chapped Hands yesterday, I thought she sounded crazy, but as I listen to her talk now, I realize that she doesn't sound much crazier than most of the moms I know. Most of those mothers are afraid. Being a mother is frightening. Emmy is afraid of Lulu touching a dead bird or eating the wrong thing. Every mother goes a little bit crazy in her own particular way.

I almost envy other moms though. All they have to do is let go, stop protecting. Let Lulu eat gluten and discover that it's not always healthy, but sometimes it's worth it so you can have a slice of birthday cake with everyone else. Even Chapped Hands—all she has to do is stop her obsessive handwashing. Let her boys play in the sandbox and catch colds. Let them eat dropped toast, even when it lands jammy-side down. She'll realize that they don't get sick—in fact, they'll be stronger.

If I can save Stella, I vow that I will stop cutting up her fruit. I'll make her go to the group swimming lessons, even though she doesn't like the noise. I will not protect her from ordinary difficulties and disasters.

But the danger threatening her now is one I can't let her fight alone.

I go up to my room, and Kelly knocks and asks if I want anything.

"I'm about ready for bed," I say, yawning elaborately.

"Are you sure? It's only half seven." Kelly frowns.

I smile, making sure it goes all the way to my eyes. I need her to leave me in peace. "I must still be recovering from the birth."

"Some milk before you turn in?" says Kelly.

"Are you going to offer a bedtime story too?"

She laughs politely. "It's not in a bottle! It's golden milk, it's got turmeric and a big squeeze of honey. I have it myself every night."

"Wonderful," I say. More turmeric.

When Kelly brings the mug, I ask if I'll see her again before morning. "If I need something," I continue, not wanting to arouse suspicion.

"Not to worry, my love, I'll pop in around nine and bring every mom an essential-oil burner. Valerian and whatnot to promote deep rest."

Translation: I check on all the moms to make sure they're not trying to off themselves.

"I can take it now," I say. "I'll be dead to the world by nine."

Kelly brightens. "One less room for me to visit." She returns with a ceramic oil burner and matches for the tealight inside.

Once she's gone, the decorative pillows come in handy for making a somnolent mound under the bedclothes. I open the window. It's dark outside now, and very cold. My room is one flight up, but wisteria climbs up a trellis outside. The trousers they gave me don't have any pockets, so I have to hold my phone.

I finger the cashmere throw draped over the chair by the window, longing to cocoon myself in it. I'm scared. Even after two nights here, my body is still exhausted from giving birth. But I push the chair out of the way and suck in deep breaths of the night air. The cold is bracing. I heave a leg over the windowsill and search for a foothold on the trellis.

Because it's winter, the wisteria is mostly dry stems and a thick trunk. If I put one foot on the trunk and one foot on the trellis, I don't need to trust my full weight to the trellis. I feel with my foot for the next foothold. I hold on to the wisteria. I find the next foothold and wince at the pressure on my stitches. I cling to the wisteria for a moment, thinking maybe they'll come apart, my insides will start to fall out, but the pain subsides. A splinter enters the pad of my left thumb, but it doesn't hurt. I feel it, but it doesn't hurt.

The next time I put my foot on the wisteria, the branch gives way, and I slip, grazing my bare forearm, and plunge to the gravel. My legs crumple, and then I'm on the ground, my phone flying. I lie there for a moment, cheek on the gravel; then I hear footsteps, and I sprint round the side of the house and press myself against it. Shaking, I heave myself to my feet. My ankle hurts, but I can walk fine. Just a tiny sprain. The front door opens. Someone takes a few steps into the dark, sighs, and goes back inside.

I brush gravel off my chin. I'm lucky: there's a gibbous moon casting enough light to see by. Miraculously, I find my phone. The screen is cracked, but it switches on, and then immediately dies. Probably the cold. I stick it inside my nursing bra to warm up. I'll find somewhere I can charge it. I set off down the driveway towards the gates, swinging my arms to keep warm, my breath smoking. It's only a quarter of a mile to the gates, but they are shut.

I could try to find someone and scream until they open them, but then they'll call Pete. I could try to climb over the stone wall, but it's eight feet high, and after my ankle sprain, and with my right hand still bandaged from the broken glass at Irina's, I don't want to risk any more climbing.

Is there anyone in the gatehouse? It looks uninhabited. I think they control the gate remotely. I'm stuck. I can't get out this way. I'll have to walk the perimeter of the property, hoping to find a place where I can scale the wall.

But then an approaching car slows, and I know what I have to do. I go as close to the gate as I dare, and then crouch low behind a leafless bush, like a frightened rabbit. I hope the car's lights won't pass over me, that the bush will give me enough cover. Is this why they make us wear white, so we'll be easy to spot if we escape?

As soon as the car is on its way up the driveway, I bolt through the gates right before they close, curling my toes to keep my shoes on without their laces. It's still just after Christmas, and people are at home eating leftovers and watching Christmas specials. Meanwhile, I'm alone on a dark road, and it's late. I'm shaking with cold. I have no idea what to do next. Then a shape slips across the road: a fox. She pays no attention to me; she has her own business to attend to. But the sight of her cheers me: she's managing fine out here. I can do it too. I have to get moving. Left, right? Left. I begin to run, to warm up my body, even though my stitches pull and my legs feel shaky from lack of use.

The road goes over a little hill and winds past houses, and I think about stopping at one of them, but if there is a village, maybe there is a pub. Eventually I find one, the Hare & Hounds. It serves such a small cluster of houses, and it's so soon after Christmas and so late that I think maybe it's closed. But the lights are on. I comb my hair with my fingers and straighten my shoulders. There's nothing I can do about the fact that I am wearing what amounts to white pajamas, with no laces in my shoes and no coat.

Inside, a few older couples are having a quiet drink. Everyone can hear everything I say to the tired-looking woman behind the bar. "Hello, excuse me, please. My phone died, and I need to call a cab. Is there any chance you have a phone I could use? I have money." Though, I suddenly realize, all I actually have to pay with is my phone, and I can't be sure that will start working again, after the fall. I start to panic: How am I going to get back to London?

The woman frowns at me, suspicious. "A cab? Where do you need to go?" Is she wondering if I am an escaped mental patient—and am I?

I wrap my arms around myself to stop myself shaking. No keys, no money, and, it seems, no friends. How did I let my life get to the point where I have no one to call? The woman is looking at me with a worried expression.

"Steady on, you look like you're about to faint. I suppose I can manage a cuppa." She bustles about behind the bar.

The tea revives me. I know who I can call. Five days after giving birth, my belly is still round enough for me to be six months pregnant, so I place a hand over it protectively. "In my condition, I get so forgetful," I say. "Mommy brain, I suppose, silly me. Popped out for milk and forgot my keys, money, everything. I'll call my mom. She's going to laugh when she hears what a pickle I got myself into."

The woman relaxes. "Phone's back here, love. Didn't you think to bring a coat either? You look frozen. You know, I was the same with my first. Couldn't remember what day of the week it was."

I still have no idea where we are, so I ask the woman to write down her address "for my mother to pick me up." We are in Surrey, so less than two hours from home.

I have to phone directory inquiries to get Irina's home number. I need her, the way she once needed me. She wasn't afraid to show it. I won't be afraid to show it either. The phone rings for a while, but then Irina picks up. "I need your help," I tell her. "Can you come and get me?"

"How is baby?"

"She's fine. I'm in Surrey. I need to get home."

"Call taxi."

"I can't. I don't have any money on me, and my phone's dead. But I could pay you when I can get some cash."

Irina gives a disbelieving snort. "This is not my job."

"Please. I've got no one else."

"Yes, I come, little fool," she snaps.

"Thank you," I say, hoping "little fool" is affectionate. It's hard to tell with her. The woman behind the bar is hovering, and has doubtless heard every word of the conversation. Believing that I have a grim relationship with my mother, she plies me packets of peanuts that I don't want and insists on lending me an old fleece to keep warm. "I keep it for taking the bins out." Now that it's warmed up, my phone shows the low-battery icon, and the woman even finds me a charger. The pub closes at eleven, and she and her husband go to bed upstairs, but they tell me I can stay downstairs and wait for my ride.

I feel a little better as I begin to warm up. But in the mirror in the pub toilet, I see a madwoman, pale and thin, though with a still-swollen belly. My hair sticks out in all directions. The bandage on my right hand has a red stain on it. Blood must have started leaking through when I climbed down the wisteria. I wet my left hand and run it through my hair to stick it down. I have to keep it together.

Irina shakes me awake. I've fallen asleep on the greasy banquette in one of the booths. "What time is it?"

She points to her eyebrows, carefully drawn on. "You think this face happen just like that?" She snaps her fingers.

"I wasn't complaining," I protest. "Thank you for coming to get me."

"I'm not your chauffeur," she mutters as I follow her outside to her car.

"Thank you for coming," I say again.

Even though there are few cars out, Irina is a crazy driver with no regard for the rules of the road. She runs stop signs and accelerates whenever she sees a traffic light. The second time she runs a light after it turned red, I ask, "Is this how they drive in Azerbaijan?"

"Of course," she says. "Back home, we use both sides of road, both directions, no traffic lights. If you do not get out of way, crash." She takes her hands off the steering wheel to clap her hands dramatically for emphasis, and I reach out to steady it, but she slaps me away and takes control again. "Though we are not driving cars, only donkeys and carts." A muscle in her cheek twitches, and I realize she's made a joke, which I don't remember her doing before. "My car, my rules. You don't like, you walk."

"I feel a little stressed, that's all," I say.

"I do not do stress," Irina says. "Now, eat. Open tin at feet." I open an old cracker tin in the passenger footwell. It contains brown, cookie-like rectangles. "Ter khalvasy," she says. "Good for energy."

I eat one; it is intensely sweet and tastes like cinnamon and something floral, perfumed. I feel the sugar ignite my brain. She doesn't "do" stress. Is this the key to who she is? This could explain how she survived so much, how she keeps moving forward, embracing whatever comes.

You can care about your child and not be destroyed by their loss. You can love your child and destroy them too. Still, although Irina's love might have warped Blanka, it wasn't enough to make Blanka take her own life.

I pull up the photo of the diary on my phone. I can't read the Armenian alphabet, but I've memorized the words. "*Yes atum yem ayd mardun.* I think it means 'I hate that person'?"

Irina snorts as I mangle her language. Then she glances down at my phone and abruptly pulls over, without signaling. She stops on the hard shoulder and grabs the phone. She studies the picture. "This is Blanka's handwriting. Where did you get this?"

"I found it in Stella's room," I hedge. "It just has this one Armenian phrase, I hate that person, over and over again."

"That is one translation," Irina says. "Can also translate like this: I hate that *man*."

I stare at her. That narrows it down a lot.

"Why is Blanka's book in Stella's room?" Irina demands. "Why does she leave it there?"

I think of the little house in the forest, the husband shut in the oven, the journey over the mountains. If anyone can handle a difficult, fantastical truth, it is Irina. "It's Stella's book," I say. "But she writes like Blanka now. In Armenian."

I wait for Irina to draw the obvious conclusion, that Blanka has possessed Stella. "She maybe see Blanka writing and copy," Irina says, and my heart sinks. "And she is very smart girl, sharp like knife. She can find Armenian online. Why, I don't know."

It's just like with Dr. Beaufort. I thought I had unassailable evidence that Blanka was possessing Stella. But of course not. No evidence can ever prove that, not even an eight-year-old learning to crochet almost overnight, not even keeping a diary in someone else's handwriting. The only person who can ever truly *know* that Stella is possessed is me.

The car shakes as a lorry drives by. I hastily put the hazard lights on. Irina stares into the winter darkness as we listen to them clicking. Then she says, "Who is this man she hates so much?"

"Exactly," I say, feeling better. Even if she can't grasp the truth, Irina can still help me. "What man?" The horrible thought occurs to me: If he harmed Blanka, will he harm Stella too? Maybe Blanka has been trying to warn me.

As Irina pulls back onto the road, I decide I must go and see Stella and ask her or, rather, ask Blanka-in-Stella. She's not a fan of giving direct answers to direct questions, but maybe she'll give me another clue.

"Where to?" Irina said. "Home?"

"I can't have Pete see me," I say.

"What is matter?"

"Pete thinks I'm not well." How can I explain this to her? When she showed me the hot tub where Blanka died, she said Blanka "has sickness here" and thumped her chest. "He thinks I've got a sickness here," I say, tapping my head. "If he sees me, he might try to send me back to—to where I was. But I don't have that kind of problem. I'm fine."

"Hm," says Irina, not the woman to offer false comfort as Cherie would have done. She doesn't tell me I'm fine, and she doesn't tell me I'll feel better soon. She doesn't live in that privileged world where "no doubt the universe is unfolding as it should." Cataclysm is possible, and she isn't about to tell me anything different.

35.

Irina makes up a bed on the sofa, but throws me a towel. "Shower first. You smell like old cheese." She nods at my hand. "Then I fix that mess."

I forgot about my cut. The bandage is filthy. After my shower, Irina unwinds it and throws it away. She replaces the dressing and covers it with a fresh bandage. Then I doze for a few hours on her velour sofa. At half past six, I'm up and she makes tea. The staff at the Cottage still think I'm asleep in my bed. They won't notice my absence until I don't show up for breakfast. I zip the pub lady's fleece to my neck and walk from Irina's house back to our neighborhood. I turn onto the defunct railway lane that runs along the bottom of our garden and is now used by joggers and dog walkers.

There's a gate in our back fence, and if you reach over the top, you can undo the bolt, something I always meant to fix. I slip on the muddy path leading up to the gate, but dust myself off and let myself in. It's a dull, drizzly morning, and at this time of year, it's not even fully light until half past eight at the earliest, but I crouch behind a bush anyway. Because Pete insisted that the back wall of the main living area be glass, with no blinds to spoil the look, I can see straight into the house.

Kia is sitting on the kitchen island, clad in a vest and running shorts. She's bundled her grey-blond locks on top of her head in a messy bun. How nice of her to interrupt her morning workout to check on Pete and Stella. But the thought is gone almost as soon as it comes, because suddenly I know the truth. What other explanation can there be for her sitting on our counter—her sweaty thighs unhygienic on our food-preparation surface?

Pete, my Pete—this can't be happening.

I feel unable to move, drained of all the energy that had driven me to escape from the Cottage and get myself here. I don't have proof that anything has happened between them. At the same time, I know that everything has happened. You don't sit on your co-worker's food-preparation surface in shorts otherwise. That messy bun, those little shorts—that isn't postworkout. That is postcoital. She is more than the woman he confides in. She stayed the night.

Pete smiles as Kia offers him a piece of kale. He's probably making one of his tofu scrambles with "secret sauce." This is a random blend of various things in the fridge door—soy, chili, sesame oil, whatever—which always ends up being delicious. Pete will take a plate to Stella in her room, and he and Kia will have breakfast à deux: they will talk about how protein is good for muscle building, how tofu is good for the planet. Pete won't worry about why Stella likes to gobble her meals alone.

With a shock, I see Stella is standing in her bedroom window, looking out into the garden, so very still that I haven't noticed her. Can she see me? Is she waiting, watching for something? From this angle, she seems even bigger, even wider. A standing stone that has stood for five thousand years and will stand until the end of time.

She is the child Pete wanted now, a child I don't understand. What if I can never get rid of Blanka? As I shiver outside my house, I realize that I can walk away right now. I can leave Stella to him. I can leave Luna too. She isn't bonded to me yet. I can go now. I can be done with this. I can stop trying to find out what Blanka wants. I could take a train to another city, and then— But my imagination falters. I can't envision a life without Stella. Even if she never comes out of this, I can't leave her. My breasts prickle: my milk, at last.

I may as well pump at the hospital while I work out what to do next. Then they'll have my milk to feed to Luna. I call an Uber and arrive at the hospital by eight, where I collect my wallet and keys from the front desk. Pete calls, and I let it go to voicemail. He calls twice more. Then my phone dings with one text after another.

> Where are you???
> I'm really worried about you. Are you OK?
> The Cottage has people searching the grounds.
> Please call me. I need to know you're safe.

If I didn't know better, I'd think I was his top concern. I can't bring myself to message him. But I don't want employees at the Cottage to spend half the day searching for me, so I leave a quick message, informing them I'm fine. They can pass on the good news to Pete.

In the NICU, Luna's little squashed face is all pink, as if she's holding her breath. She's asleep as usual. There are a couple of other mothers in the ward, whispering to the nurses about how many ounces their babies have gained and when they can come out of the incubator. Luna lies with arms and legs flung wide, as if sprawled on the grass on a summer's day. I open the porthole to her incubator and brush her cheek with my finger. She has no idea how vulnerable she is, and that makes me want to protect her.

Once out of the NICU, I sit on a chair in the corridor to make a plan. I'm still wearing the white uniform from the Cottage, and have no other clothes. I have no family members to turn to, no idea where to go now. Find a hotel?

I'll call Pete, I think stupidly. Then I remember with a jolt.

I get a message from Emmy: **U ok?**

I snort. Pete obviously enlisted her in the search for me. I text back: **Why are you asking?** If she asks where I am, I'll know she is trying to track me down. But she shoots back: **Need to talk ASAP. It's about Pete.**

> **What about him?**
> **Something he did.**
> **Kia? I already know.**
> **Kia?? I don't know any Kia. When can we meet?**

I'll come to you, I write.

Hope you don't mind mess! Emmy responds, though I know her house is perfect, because it serves as the @LittleHiccups stage set. She follows this with a winking Father Christmas emoji, and I remember with wonder that it is still the Christmas holidays.

Emmy's house isn't exactly messy, but it's far from perfect: crumpled Christmas wrapping paper is still strewn across the living room floor. She waves a hand at it. "I had the girls for Christmas, then Nick took them on Boxing Day, and I haven't had the energy to clear up."

I'm confused. "Where did he take them?"

Emmy isn't her usual perfect self either: baggy cardigan, glasses instead of contacts. She pulls her sleeves over her hands. "You haven't heard? Nick and I are splitting up. He's a colossal dick."

"I'm so sorry. Are you OK?"

"I'm so tired of people asking me that. Do you want a drink?" She leads me into the kitchen, where a roasting tray sticky with meat juice sits on the draining board and a sour odor hangs in the air. "Sorry about the smell, the dishwasher isn't working." It's barely lunchtime, but Emmy finds a half-full bottle of wine and waves it in my direction. "Wait, are you breastfeeding?"

"I can manage half a glass." I forgot to pump at hospital, and I need to do so soon. Although, I now realize, my pump is at the Cottage. "Did you have something to tell me about Pete?"

Emmy fills two glasses to the brim, and we sit at her kitchen table. She pushes aside a pink plastic bowl containing a pacifier in a pool of milk, and a box of Unicorn Froot Loops. "Don't judge me, OK?" she says.

I want to point out that she had no qualms about judging me back when she booted me out of FOMHS. But I need her to get to the point, so I just smile.

She says, "Listen, I will understand if you never want to speak to me again."

The seat of my chair feels gritty. "Go on."

Emmy pulls her cardigan around herself and stares into her wine. "It was right when everything was coming apart with Nick, and I was in free fall. I know that's no excuse."

Carefully, I stand up and brush the seat of my chair off. I sit back down and keep my voice steady. "You and Pete?"

Emmy presses her fingers to her lips for a moment and then says, "Pete kissed me. I mean, we kissed."

It's remarkable how I feel nothing at all. It's less pain than a splinter in my thumb. "When?"

"Right after we took the girls to Coral Reef."

When I ran into Emmy that day, her damp hair had that gentle wave. She wore that striped dress like an ice lolly. "You kissed him at my house," I say slowly. "With the girls there. I can't believe it."

Emmy squirms. "They were playing. We were in the bathroom upstairs."

The Unicorn Froot Loops box is open, and the cereal will get soft and damp if left like that. I roll down the top of the plastic bag and close the box.

"I'm a horrible person," Emmy says. "I know that. I'm not going to make excuses."

"Why are you telling me? You could have just kept quiet."

"You deserve to know. I was going to tell you earlier, but I wanted to give Pete a chance to do it. I told him if he didn't tell you by Christmas, then I would."

I'm still trying to process this. "The bathroom where you kissed—was it the master bathroom? The one off our bedroom? Or Stella's bathroom?"

Emmy closes her eyes. "It was your bathroom." I take a big gulp of wine. How did it happen—Did he push her against the door? Did he lift her up onto the sink and kiss her while she wrapped her legs around him? In the same place where I lean when I'm taking my contacts out?

Maybe doing it in our home is part of the thrill. Grinding against another woman in the very place where I stand with my electric toothbrush, letting another woman's bare thighs rest on the place where I cut up fruit for our child. Seeing how thin he can make the membrane between his regular life and his forbidden one.

The room lurches suddenly. That camping trip, the one where I suspected him of leaving me. I long ago accepted that was hormonal paranoia. But I only had Pete's word that he'd been gone for forty-five minutes. I'd left my phone in the car and had no way of keeping track of time. He could have been gone for much longer.

I remember now that when I nuzzled his neck in the morning, his hair smelled of burned toast, even though we hadn't lit a campfire the night before. And I ran into a young woman at the trailhead. I haven't given her a single thought since, yet somehow, I can recall her perfectly now, as if my brain had stored her image away, knowing this moment would come. She had a scrubbed face and dishwater-blond hair in a ponytail and was a little on the chunky side, clad in plaid pajama bottoms and a UC Santa Cruz T-shirt. I didn't ask her how her night had been, but she volunteered that she'd gone to bed "super early" the night before, and I thought, Why is she telling me this? "I got up super early too," she said. "I saw the sun rise. The sunrise was inspirational."

Then Pete came huffing out of the woods carrying a cooler, the tent, and the sleeping bags, and the two of us quickly became absorbed in the *Tetris* puzzle of how to get all our camping stuff back into the Prius. He didn't even acknowledge her. But there was the smell of someone else's campfire in his hair.

Why do I remember her so clearly? I must have suspected on some level, but also, on another level, I really and truly had no inkling. Both things are true.

I squeeze my wineglass, which I've emptied without noticing. I was pregnant with Stella then. Pete has been cheating on me for her whole life. Does she know? She's so intuitive, so sensitive. She too might know and not know at the same time. Perhaps living with that contradiction was too much for her. When I read about possession, I learned about "soul wounds," which make it easier for a spirit to enter you. Pete's treachery could have made Stella more vulnerable to possession.

"You're going to break that," Emmy says, peeling my fingers away from the wineglass. My hand throbs, and I think the wound is bleeding again. "Try to breathe, sweetie." She pats my hand over the bandage. "What happened there anyway?"

"Long story."

"I'll get you a glass of water," Emmy says.

"It all seems so obvious now," I tell her. He took his phone everywhere. He went out for bike rides at night. Took all these work trips, even on the weekend. But he was so devoted—the foot rubs, the *té de California*—it never occurred to me not to trust him. The only time I wavered for a moment was on Christmas Day, when Kia seemed to know too much about our life together.

"I'm really sorry," Emmy says. "I don't expect you to forgive me."

She did a bad thing, but her apology was good. I tell her, "Coparenting with Nick for the rest of your life is probably punishment enough."

Emmy laughs. "I'm not happy that Pete is a shit too, but at the same time, it's nice not to be the only one in the trenches. Look, I want to help you. What can I do?"

Nothing, I think, which is why it's so easy to ask that question, why that question is worthless. But then I think, Wait a minute. I can *ask*. For once, I can ask. Blanka thought she couldn't ask, because I wouldn't help her. But I would have helped her. So maybe Emmy will help me. "Actually," I say, "I need to borrow a change of clothes, and maybe something to sleep in too, because I need to stay the night."

"Stay as long as you need," Emmy says. "Nick's got the kids for the rest of the holidays."

"Any chance you still have your breast pump?"

"I saw it when I was getting out the Christmas decorations," Emmy says. "No idea why I held on to it. I guess I always thought me and that bastard would have baby number three. Glad I dodged that bullet." Suddenly her face crumples, and she covers her eyes with her hand.

I don't know what to do. I don't know her well enough to give her a hug. And she's sick of people asking her if she's OK. Then I think of something. "You're not OK," I say.

She stares at me, her eyes red. "What?"

"That's what people should say to you. Not 'Are you OK?' but 'You're not OK.' As in 'I see it. I acknowledge it. You're not OK.'"

She manages a smile. "*You're* not OK, Charlotte."

"You have no idea," I say.

I take a long shower. Emmy provides me with leggings and a striped jumper dress. I pump milk and stow it in her freezer. I eat one of her gluten-free mince pies. Then I call Irina. "You again," she says. She sounds tired. "I take care of Stella for many weeks, I help you at birth of new daughter, I drive in the middle of night to pick you up from sick-in-mind hotel in country. Now you say, help me again."

"You're right. But this is not about me. This is about Blanka."

"She is dead," Irina says. "What new thing you can tell me?"

"I think maybe I *can* tell you something new. Well, I need to show you."

In the end, Irina agrees to call Pete and arrange to go over and see Stella and congratulate her on being a big sister. Pete will take the opportunity to get some work done, he tells Irina, which I now know could mean anything. Apparently, he's got more important things to think about than tracking me down. Once Irina is sure Pete has gone, she will text me to enter via the back gate.

36.

When Irina texts me, I enter the house through the French doors. I catch my breath when I see her, my darling, my honeysuckle girl, my secret sweetness at the heart of it all. She barely seems to recognize me. Her face is blank, exhausted. She no longer has the sunny, confident manner of a rich white child born into privilege. She seems bloated too. I picture her scoffing food in her room while Pete is with Kia downstairs. I imagine sharp crumbs falling into her sheets, her bed full of tiny daggers, nobody noticing, and as Blanka, she will never complain.

Even though I don't know if Stella herself can hear me, I speak to her. "My darling, I'm sorry I had to leave you." I gaze into her eyes, searching for some glimmer of my daughter. But it's like staring into a well.

"Now," says Irina, "what do you want to tell me? On phone, you have something special to tell me about Blanka." I realize she is excited, hoping I've found some new tidbit of information about her daughter. It doesn't matter what, just that it is something she didn't know before. Then, for a second, it will be like Blanka is alive again, because she learned something new about her.

"Wait a moment." I run up to our bedroom, where even though my super-sensitive smell has gone, I can still smell Pete: the citrus zest, the sharpened pencils, a hint of beard balm. I can't be sure, without my pregnant power of smell, but I think I smell something fresh, sporty, and feminine too. But I have to focus on Stella. The diary is where it was before, Pete didn't bother to move it. I bring it downstairs. I show Irina that this is the same notebook that she saw a page of on my phone. *I hate that man I hate that man I hate that man.*

"Now," I ask Stella. "This is your diary, your handwriting, right?" A nod. "And this is your language," I say.

Stella mumbles something I can't understand. It isn't English. She looks at Irina, and Irina's whole face changes. The lines melt away. Her eyes shine. She looks almost beautiful. *"Blanka jan?"* she breathes. *"Im gandz."*

"What is that?" I ask sharply. "What are you saying to her?" I longed for Irina to see that Blanka is in Stella, but now that she seems to finally see it, I'm afraid.

"Pet name," Irina murmurs. Then she speaks in a gentle voice I've never heard before, a mother's lullaby voice, the voice you use when no one is listening but the one who loves you most. *"Iskape?s da du yes."*

"Yes yem." Stella is completely focused on Irina, and when she speaks, her voice doesn't sound like a child's voice anymore. *"Mamia, yes yem."*

Irina's face glows with wonder, like she too tastes the secret sweetness at the heart of everything. She seizes Stella and presses her close and murmurs strange words into her hair, the same phrase over and over. I don't need to understand it to know what she is saying: "My baby, my baby, my baby."

I back away a little. It feels wrong to watch. I don't know what to do with myself. I don't want to sit, so I edge over to the corner of the room and stand there. I am the outsider now. Irina is the one who still has her child. I feel sick. I haven't thought beyond convincing Irina that Blanka is in Stella. I've been a fool. I never stopped to ask myself why Irina would want to banish her own daughter, right after getting her back.

Irina will never let go of Blanka. And why should she? It isn't fair for her daughter to take my daughter's body. But it also isn't fair that Blanka lost her father and her home, ending up in a place where she never fit in. Here is a way for life to be a little fairer: we can have the flesh of my child, the soul of hers.

I back farther away, towards the French doors, as Irina continues to murmur to Stella and hug her. She keeps pulling away to look at her face, then hugging her again, as if she can't decide which pleasure is sweeter.

I slip out through the French doors. "I cannot come anymore," I think. They don't come after me to question why. They let me go, as if I never existed.

Once back on the old railway line, a cramp buckles my stomach, a feeling of my uterus being folded and folded into an ever-tighter package, no longer needed, and I hunch over. Stella is more lost to me now than ever. I'd been so sure that once I convinced Irina, she would become my ally. But of course, it is Blanka she wants to help.

I make myself walk to the Tube station, put one foot in front of the other. I will get to the hospital and feed Luna, a simple thing that only I can do. I can get a cup of tea and a sandwich there. I have to eat so I can make milk for Luna. I watched Irina crochet her way out of her grief over Blanka: one stitch and then another stitch. I can do the same, focus on the next thing and the next.

When I go to the front desk of the NICU, the receptionist is new. She frowns when I try to sign in. "And you are?"

"Luna's mother," I tell her.

She raises her eyebrows. "That's odd. It says here that Luna's mother has checked in." She scans her computer screen, but I rush to the viewing window of the NICU. Another woman sits in the glider next to Luna's incubator, gently rocking. Her grey-blond hair hangs loose over her toned shoulders, and because they keep the room warm, she wears a sleeveless yoga top with elaborately criss-crossing straps. Out of context, it takes me a second to recognize Kia. She's got Luna in the snuggle hold. Adrenaline floods my veins. She took my husband. How dare she touch my child, the child I've barely held myself?

She doesn't look like she's worried about a child's ecological impact now. Then it hits me: she isn't responsible for this child's carbon emissions. She didn't bring Luna into the world. With Luna, Kia can have a child without the guilt of creating one.

I ignore the receptionist's protests, push past a nurse, and rush into the NICU. "Give me my baby."

"Charlotte?" Kia's voice is uncertain. Should she continue with her California niceness, or should she treat me with caution? She adjusts Luna's position on her shoulder as if contemplating using her as a shield.

I see the nurse with the reindeer-antler headband: "Hey! This woman should not be in here. I'm the mother. She's got my baby!"

The nurse looks shocked. "Give me the baby," she tells Kia. "You shouldn't be in here." She takes Luna, but instead of giving her to me, she puts her back in the incubator. Does she think I would hurt my own baby?

Two other nurses appear by my side, and they escort me out of the NICU, one with a hand on the small of my back, the other with a hand on my shoulder. "Why are you treating me like the crazy person?" I snap. "She's the one who lied to you. She's not Luna's mother."

Outside, Pete strides towards us, and when I turn, Kia is right behind me. With the two nurses flanking me, I am surrounded.

"Let's all take a breath now," Kia says. "Let's calm down."

I once made a "calm-down jar" for Stella, which some mommy blogger recommended as a surefire cure for tantrums: ultrafine glitter in a glue-and-water solution. All my life I've kept calm, but now I think Stella had the right idea when she smashed that jar against the wall. I break free of the nurses and lunge towards Kia. "Stay away from my baby, you fucking bitch."

Kia gasps and steps backwards, and then a woman in a grey trouser suit and hospital lanyard appears. "I want to apologize for the misunderstanding about who is allowed in the NICU," she says.

"It's my fault," says Pete. "I may have given the receptionist the wrong impression. I apologize."

I take a deep breath. The hospital isn't the enemy here. "It's fine," I tell the trouser-suited woman. "Just a misunderstanding. We'll go to the machine down the hall, have a cup of tea, and get it sorted out." I have no intention of following through on this, but the woman is satisfied, and she retreats, along with the other hospital staff. I turn to Kia. "I know about you two." I stab a finger towards Pete's chest. "I also know about you and Emmy."

Kia gives a little laugh of disbelief. "Who's Emmy?"

Pete scratches his beard. "Charlotte, you need to take a breath. You've had a hard time. You're not well."

"Are you going to try to have me committed again? I'll be happy to tell them how you stuck me in a loony bin so you could shack up with your mistress."

"Who's Emmy?" Kia repeats.

Pete takes Kia's shoulder, and I can still read the language of his eyes: "Ignore her, she's paranoid." He turns back to me, and gestures at a row of chairs against the wall of the corridor. "Let's sit down, the two of us, and talk. It was a good idea of yours to get a tea or something. Kia, will you?"

"I'm not going to sit down," I tell him after Kia has headed to the drinks machine.

"I'm sorry—" Pete begins, but I interrupt.

"Save it. It's not just one mistake, Pete, or two. I know about that woman in Humboldt when I was pregnant with Stella. You've been cheating on me all along."

Pete shakes his head. "I loved you, Charlotte. I never even looked at anyone else until you got pregnant. Then you became so anxious about the pregnancy. And when she was born, that was it: you shut me out."

"Sorry you had to share my attention," I spit.

"I thought things would get better as she got older. I thought you'd get back to your old self. But no. You used to be the one who got everyone to come over and party. You became this person who stays up late online shopping for the perfect kiddie pajamas."

"I became *a mother*."

"You expected me to carry you," Pete says. "It was you looking after Stella, and me looking after you. I needed an outlet."

"That's one hell of a rationalization," I say.

He turns towards me, hands open on his knees. "I was always careful not to let you find out."

"And that's a point in your favor?" Of course he didn't slip up: he's so good at keeping on top of details while seeing the big picture.

Suddenly I realize something. He put me in the Cottage because he saw the big picture. When it comes to deciding custody, he wants to be able to say, "My wife has been in an inpatient psychiatric facility and is mentally unfit to take care of the children."

"You want the kids," I say. "You planned this."

"I'm sorry, baby," Pete says. "I have to do what's best for them. I don't think it's safe for them to be around you right now." The expression on his face is so earnest, his eyes so blue, so serious. He actually believes that I am bad for them. I am wrong: putting me in the Cottage wasn't him playing the long game, at least not consciously. He really has convinced himself that I am mentally ill. In his mind, whatever is convenient for *him* becomes the truth.

Down the hall, Kia is stretching her quads as she waits for the machine to make drinks. I can imagine his conversation with her: "Poor Charlotte. She's got postpartum psychosis. Paranoid delusions. Hormone issues, like her mother. This same thing happened after she had Stella, there was a disastrous camping trip, she thought I sneaked into someone else's tent. This Emmy thing is nonsense. Charlotte's convinced I managed to make out with this random woman, the mother of one of Stella's friends, while Stella and the other kid were in the house. I barely have time to take a leak when I'm looking after Stella." And Kia: "Oh, poor Charlotte. She needs help."

Kia returns from the machine and holds out a cappuccino. "Pete likes oat milk, and it just occurred to me that maybe you do too, so I could go back if you prefer that. Careful, it's super hot." She won't meet my eye, but she still wants everything to be nice, a conscious uncoupling, even though she knows my husband's coffee preference. But here we are, in a land far beyond niceness, beyond etiquette. There is no "Charlotte Says" for this situation.

"Just tell it like it is," the trolls always said.

"I don't want you here," I say. "I don't want your coffee. I don't like you."

"I understand you have a lot of feelings," Kia says, in a way that makes it clear she's spent time in therapy.

"He'll cheat on you too," I tell her, feeling something boiling up inside. When I was young, I always let my mother be the one to lose her temper. When she shut me outside in the snow, when she threw flour at me, I stood there and took it. I let my feet get numb, my nose fill with choking particles. I retreated from the edges of my body and went deep inside myself. But not anymore. "He's a colossal shit," I tell Kia.

Pete shakes his head. "You're not well, Charlotte."

"Take the coffee, please," Kia says. "We can talk." She holds it out, too near my face. I *hate* it when people invade my personal space. I stand up and slap the drink away, and it cascades onto Kia's running tights. She screams, plucking at the fabric. "Fuck, fuck! Pete, help me!"

Pete grabs my shoulders and pushes me away from Kia. Hospital security and yet more nurses appear, and I quickly scream, "Don't touch me! Don't touch me!" as loud as I can. The security guards decide it is Pete they want to show out, not a hysterical, lactating mother. Kia limps after them.

A kind older nurse takes me to the hospital cafeteria and gets me a cup of tea with sugar. I am shaking. I look at the plastic stirrer she brought me, the single-use plastic Pete hates so much. Pete talked about making plant-based coffee stirrers at some point, but the real solution is to go back to using spoons. Or have your tea and coffee at home. But there's no profit for entrepreneurs in that.

The tea is terrible, and I remember the tang of lemon peel, the warmth of cinnamon on our honeymoon. I feel a rush of grief.

37.

On the Tube, my phone pings with a text from Irina: *Blanka is not happy.* My heart lightens: maybe, just maybe, Irina will help me after all. I arrange to meet her at a café in Muswell Hill.

She orders tea but doesn't drink it. She's lost the beauty she had yesterday. She looks tired, her face worn. She doesn't bother with any preamble. "Yesterday, I have many questions for Blanka. 'What is happening to you, my darling? How is this happening?' But Blanka will not talk to me. That first time is the only time. No more." She shakes her head, staring out the café window. "When Blanka is little girl, she goes quiet when angry. Very, very quiet. Is just like that now. She does not like this." She waves her hands. "This situation. She wants to go."

I lean forward. "You'll help me?"

Irina purses her lips. "I help Blanka."

"OK," I say, feeling my determination ignite again. I can still save Stella. "We'll find out what's made her so angry. Any ideas?"

Irina taps her fingers on the table. "I am thinking about Blanka getting menstruation. Before, I think, why does she want to give up on life when she gets menstruation at last?"

"Right, her menstruation." I cringed when Irina wanted to discuss Blanka's period weeks ago. It seemed so inappropriate. But now that I've given birth in front of Irina, now she's seen me splayed and oozing, we can talk about anything.

"Now I think maybe this blood, is not menstruation," Irina says carefully.

"What else could it be?"

Irina stares at me. "First time sex, you bleed."

"You think she lost her virginity?" I whisper, my heart aching for her. "Who could it have been? Not your neighbor? Who else did she know?"

"No friends, never had boyfriend in her life," Irina says. "She goes to work, supermarket, home only. I am asking myself this. Now look." She pulls out a battered phone—Blanka's—and taps in a passcode. She pulls up the messages between me and Blanka. They are innocuous messages about what time she was coming and what Stella could have for dinner. Could they be at home by 4:00 p.m. because someone was coming to fix the fridge. Still, I feel something approaching terror as Irina scrolls through the messages. Finally, she shows me one from Blanka: OK if I come to get cheque today.

Sure, I texted. I have a yoga class but Pete will give it to you. It made no sense, but I feel a pang for that ignorant time, when I had no idea Pete was betraying me and Blanka was suicidally depressed.

"Same day as blood," Irina says. "Four days before she die."

My mind stutters, trying to make sense of this. "What does it mean?"

"Fish stinks from the head," Irina says impatiently.

"The head . . . the head of the family? No way," I say. But Maureen told me about my mother's depression, and I didn't want to hear it. I won't take the easy way now. I will pay attention.

Of course, he made a move on our babysitter. It didn't matter that Blanka wasn't sexy. What mattered was the thrill of being able to do it in our perfect home, risking everything.

Stella was at her swim lesson, I'd arranged for Emmy to pick her up because Lulu went to the same class. Pete had to work.

I feel sick with rage at Pete.

What was in it for Blanka, though? Maybe she was in love with him. If nobody had ever tried to seduce her before, she could have mistaken this for love. Could that be why she can't leave—a lovelorn spirit, unable to forsake Pete's chiseled cheekbones and ice-blue eyes? But that is ridiculous. You wouldn't choose that person's daughter as your vessel—that would guarantee you'd never have any sexual contact.

"He hurt my daughter," Irina says, spitting the words out. "'I hate that man. I hate that man.' *He* is man."

"But how? By rejecting her?"

"We must talk to Blanka."

"She's hard to talk to," I say, afraid of what we might learn. But we have to overcome her reticence. Maybe between the two of us we can make it work.

When I get to Emmy's, she has a glass of wine ready as soon as I get in the door. "What did that bastard say?" She has crudités and dips waiting on the coffee table. She pats the sofa. "Sit down. Tell me everything." She sips her wine, eyes glittering. She enjoys my suffering a little bit. She admitted it last time I saw her: "It's nice not to be the only one in the trenches." But she also truly wants to help. I don't mind if her feelings about me are complicated, because she doesn't hide them. Unlike Cherie.

"He has a girlfriend," I say. "I think he's going to try for custody of the kids with his girlfriend. And a divorce, I assume." We didn't even get around to mentioning that.

"Shit," says Emmy. "I've always thought he seemed too nice. This is how he gets his kicks. I read an article about sociopaths—I thought Nick might be one. They have a lower resting heart rate, so the theory is they have to break rules and take risks to get stimulation, to feel something." She pauses. "You don't seem that bothered."

"I'm not interested in psychoanalyzing Pete. I've got other problems."

"Bigger than this?" She stares at me. "I thought Luna's OK. You're not ill, are you?"

"Actually, it's something I can't really talk about."

Emmy's face closes. I've broken a tacit pact. She will help me to the best of her ability, but in exchange, we'll feast on each other's stories. We'll hold nothing back. I've never been good at this sort of thing.

But she confessed to kissing Pete, even though she didn't have to. She's letting me stay and doing her best to help me. For once, she's not trying to hide what her life is really like. So maybe I dare to tell her what my life is like too. But not yet.

"Look, Emmy, I'll tell you someday," I say. "OK? We'll have wine and I'll tell you the whole story. You won't believe it."

"I look forward to that," she says.

38.

Irina arranges to pick Stella up the following day. She tells Pete she is bringing Stella to her house for a crochet lesson, but really, she brings her to the playground to meet me at 6:00 p.m. We choose the evening because we don't want other people watching whatever is going to happen.

Stella shuffles along, her walk painfully slow now. Her face is calm, empty. She doesn't seem like an angry spirit who cannot rest. But when Blanka was alive, she seemed perfectly placid too.

All the time she babysat Stella, I never walked anywhere with Blanka, because if I was paying her, then I was busy with my job. But now I wonder why I never spared half an hour when she was on duty—Why couldn't I have invited her to go to a café with us?

When we get to the soup pots, it is already getting dark and the playground is deserted except for a couple of teenage boys hanging off the play structure, the tips of their cigarettes glowing. Irina marches over to them and says something, at which they shake their heads, drop to the ground, and race off. "What did you say to them?" I ask.

"I say, 'Sexy boys, which one wants snog with Grandma?' Then I go like this." She puckers up her lips.

"Nice."

We climb the steps by the soup pots, and then I take Stella's chilly hand and stand her next to the biggest one. It is hard to balance on the slope. It is really only comfortable if you are either in a soup pot or you're clambering around. But Blanka spent hours here.

I give my phone to Irina and ask her to record it. I won't show it to anyone, because they'd still think I'm mad, they'd think I coached Stella to act like Blanka. But still, even if only for myself, I want proof—as close to proof as I can ever get.

I turn to my daughter, but I speak to the spirit inside her. "Stella loved you," I say. "For Stella's sake, you need to speak to me directly and tell me what's wrong so I can help you rest. This is Stella's body, and you need to give it back to her."

Stella nods. "Oh yes." My skin crawls. Is that an agreement or the other kind of "oh yes," which is a refusal to communicate?

I keep trying. "You must speak up. I should have asked you before if you were OK, I should have kept asking you. Well, now I am. I am listening, and I am not going to stop asking until you answer me. I already know something is wrong. I know you're angry. I know something happened. I know you hate someone."

"I talk, I make you angry." Her accent is strong now. Blanka lived in England for years, but she still had a strong accent. I know now that's because she barely spoke to anyone except Irina.

"I won't be angry, I promise," I tell her. "Whatever happened. I want to help you so that you can rest. I can't help you until you tell me what you want. We found the diary. I think you wanted us to read it. *Yes atum yem ayd mardun.*"

"Pete." Stella says the word with utter disgust, a contrast to Blanka's normal singsong utterance. And suddenly I know that I am talking directly to Blanka. The last vestige of Stella melts away, and Blanka is here with me. It is an unearthly, vertiginous feeling, talking to this creature. A glimpse of another realm.

My legs are weak, and my knees knock. But then I feel a surge of energy. I've been right all along. This is not Stella. Finally, I've got the spirit to talk to me. I've made this creature of the deep rise to the surface. And we are doing something we never did when Blanka was alive: having a proper, honest conversation.

"That day you went to pick up the cheque," I say through chattering teeth. "What happened?"

Stella considers. "He say nice things at first. He say I look pretty today." She is silent, staring over my shoulder, into the past.

"Stella's dad," I say, to be clear, though I feel sick. "Pete? That is who we're talking about."

"Father of Stella. He has brown drink in glass."

"Whiskey." He sometimes has one when he really needs to unwind. "Then what?"

"I am mysterious, he says. He wants to get to know me. I do not know what to say. Then he comes close. He kisses me." She closes her eyes, remembering. The expression on Stella's face is one I'd never seen before—an adult expression, that of a grown woman remembering her first kiss. It was a little sour, that kiss, I can see, but sweet too. Unexpected.

Stella continues: "I try his whiskey. Then he puts his tongue in my mouth." She makes a face, as if she is sucking saliva into her mouth to wash away the taste. "Then he grabs me, squeezes." There is anguish on her face as she wrings the air, the most emotion I've ever seen Blanka show. "I do not like. I want to go home."

"Did you say that aloud?" I ask.

Stella is silent, and I am afraid that Blanka didn't protest. This is a woman who couldn't ask for a glass of water. I am not sure if she had the power to ask someone not to assault her, especially not her employer. And in her mind, not speaking might have seemed the safest course of action. Maybe she was just allowing the inevitable, the cormorant surrendering to the hawk.

"Then what?" I say, though I know.

Stella speaks in a rush. "Stella's daddy does not listen, forces me to floor, brings up my skirt, opens my knees. All the time, talking, how pretty I am. He pushes inside me and it hurts. . . ." She covers her eyes.

My heart hurts as I imagine her lying there, limp, unresisting. But inside, maybe she was somewhere else. Inside, the whole time it was happening, maybe she was busy being her hero, Doctor Who, fighting monsters throughout space and time.

"I'm so sorry," I say. "I'm so, so sorry. It wasn't your fault." If only Blanka had told me this when it happened, but of course she feared I wouldn't believe her, thought I might blame her perhaps. She was probably right. I would never have believed this of Pete back then. Tears run down my face. I weep for Blanka, for Stella, and for Irina, who has to listen to her daughter's story.

Now I understand why Stella—or, rather, Blanka—takes her

meals to her room and won't sit at the same table with him. I understand why when he picks her up for a hug, she turns to dead weight, and when he holds her after the bath, she slithers away. I know why she closes her bedroom and bathroom door against him. He thought it was because she's growing up, but in fact, he makes her skin crawl.

I feel a sort of pride in Blanka, despite my grief and horror. She's mastered her revulsion so she can return and get revenge.

"Does he touch Stella?" Irina asks sharply. I start. I haven't thought of that. The Pete I love has stepped aside, replaced by a second man, a serial cheater. Then a third, worse Pete appeared, the man who assaulted Blanka. Is there an even more terrible man behind him, a man who assaulted his child? That time Pete dangled Stella over the bath and she screamed so hard— Was that weird? But no, that was just Pete thinking you could overcome Stella's issues by using force, and before me, Stella is shaking her head firmly. "No. Not Stella."

I know Pete hasn't touched Stella, because Stella wouldn't shut up. She would tell me if Pete ever laid a finger on her. You couldn't silence Stella, back when she was still herself, and Pete knows that. He likes to play with chaos, not unleash it.

Irina addresses Blanka. "What do you want? What shall we do for you, my darling? What do you need so you can be free?"

Stella's face hardens. "Make him leave."

"Oh, don't worry about that. He is leaving," I say. "Or I am. We're not living together anymore."

Her voice is harsh. "Not enough. Get Stella away from him."

"You mean stop him from seeing her?"

"He can never see her again," she says, and it makes sense. Pete took Stella away from her, and now she is taking Stella away from him.

"But I can't do that," I say. "He's her father." If I get rid of him, somehow, Stella will have no father, and no matter how much Pete has hurt Blanka, he hasn't hurt Stella. He loves her.

But he also won't let her be herself. Maybe that is part of why Blanka slipped into Stella so easily—that pressure from Pete to change. Still, he has a legal right to see her. "He will never go," I say. "I can't do that."

Stella shrugs. "Then *I* will never go." I shiver at the thought of being stuck with Blanka forever. She is setting me an impossible task, like in a fairy tale. Find the ring I dropped in the sea. Spin hay into gold.

But as in a fairy tale, there has to be a way.

I make up my mind: I will do what Blanka wants. I will find a way. It is the first thing she has ever asked me for, after all. "If Pete goes, you'll be satisfied? This will be over?"

Stella nods. "Oh yes."

Irina says she'll take Stella home and they'll wait until I come up with a plan. But I don't feel good about leaving Stella alone with Pete. "Aren't you scared, after what he did?" I ask Stella, or rather Blanka.

"What more can he do to her?" Irina asks, her face grim.

I go to the NICU to drop off my pumped milk for Luna. The nurses there are on edge around me, after yesterday's fight with Pete and Kia, but they can't deny me access to my own daughter, and the kind older nurse from yesterday provides me with a new breast pump. Then I take the train to my mother's house in Oxford. I need to be alone, somewhere I can think. I have no idea how I am going to do it, but at least I know what I have to do.

I inherited the place on Edith's death, but haven't had the heart to come here since. I've had it cleaned, but it smells of damp, and of course it's freezing. The kitchen cupboards still contain her meagre supplies: tins of baked beans and a packet of digestives. A plain white eggcup is inverted on the dishrack. Her sad last meal: a boiled egg.

I hold the eggcup and look out at her bird table, which has a shelter on top like a miniature Swiss chalet. She kept it stocked with suet balls, which she bought in bulk, rather than making them. Even for her beloved birds, Edith wouldn't cook from scratch.

It probably baffled her that I liked to cook so much. All that effort for something that was going to disappear in a few minutes. Maybe I frightened her a little too, in my otherness. I wasn't possessed, but I was still very different from her: look at how differently we'd reacted to giving birth.

Edith had to endure a grueling two-day labor. She was alone, since my father was dead by then. The doctor dragged me out with forceps, and, Edith said, I'd resembled "a skinned tomato, rather horrifying." She told me this when I was pregnant with Stella. Why did she have to tell me that?

A robin lands on the bird table and finds it empty. He looks at the house with an impatient air, as if wondering why his dinner order is taking so long. Maybe Edith stood here and watched this very robin.

I can't find suet balls in the kitchen, so I rummage around, and in the cupboard under the stairs, on a shelf by themselves, I find a child's faded sun hat, a small pair of yellow binoculars, and a notebook that says *Charlotte's Bird Log* on the cover. Inside: lists of birds I wanted to see, a crayoned drawing of a woodpecker. I trace my finger over its wing. My mother could have binned this stuff. But she kept it to hand, as if any day, we'd go birding again. I pull down her blue waterproof, hanging on a peg on the inside of the cupboard door, and press it to my face.

She used to spread this waterproof out so we could sit on it when it was time for our lunch. She hated being in direct contact with the grass. A list starts to take shape.

Sensory issues
Extreme focus
Bluntness
Meltdowns

I know what Cherie would say. Maybe she's right. I turn out the waterproof's pockets as if they might hold the answer, and not just a few shreds of Kleenex. Then I sink to the floor and sit there for a long time, sifting through memories of my mother. I hated how hard it was to get her to look me in the eye. I thought it was because she wasn't paying attention to me.

It doesn't matter what her diagnosis would be. I understand now that her mind worked differently from mine. When she told me I was "horrifying," I don't think she meant to hurt. She thought she was passing on helpful information: I might not love my baby on first sight. It probably baffled her when my eyes filled with tears.

I go back into the kitchen. I wish I'd thanked her properly for the two pots of mustard she gave me. I think now that they weren't an insult. She simply thought that, like her, I would be happy to receive a gift of mustard, which took up little space in my house and worked perfectly well on fish fingers.

Outside, the robin is still waiting. Suet balls are best, but the damp digestives will have to do. But when I go outside, he flies away. I crumble the biscuits onto the bird table anyway, my eyes streaming in the cold. If only I'd understood that, when my mother wouldn't look at me, it was because meeting someone else's gaze was hard. We could have stood here and watched the robin instead.

A few hours later, I am hungry, for the first time since the morning sickness hit, ravenous in fact. I order Indian food and gorge myself on saag paneer and chana masala. I feel warm and full, especially because the food comes in single-use plastic containers, which will probably be burned overseas, or be dumped in a landfill, or, worse, end up in the ocean in an island of trash the size of Texas. I wish that I could dump Pete in the middle of the Pacific trash vortex for eternity. But I can't do that, and I can't kill him, because I'll end up in prison and then I won't be able to take care of Stella and Luna.

If I can't be with Stella, I'll die. But if I have Stella, I could survive losing Luna. When I gave birth to her, I didn't feel horrified, as Edith was when she first saw me. But I didn't feel overwhelming love.

I can offer him Luna in exchange for Stella.

Pete might take that deal: he'll have a fresh start, with Kia, and they'll be rid of Stella, the difficult party pooper. Luna can still have her life this way, whereas if Blanka stays, Stella's life is over, one way or another.

But no. I tried so hard to have this second baby because Stella needs a friend, or at least an ally. Besides, I can't leave any child to be raised by Pete. I thought Pete was a good father, but you can't be a good father and a cheater and rapist.

I don't have anything else to offer him. But maybe I can offer him a negative inducement—threat rather than reward. How can I terrify him so much he'll do whatever I want, even give up his own children? And then I realize: it is so simple.

I message Pete and tell him to set up a meeting with a mediator for the following afternoon. I tell him I want to "discuss next steps and get the ball rolling," which I think sounds important and Nathan-like, but also nice and vague. I'll keep him guessing as to what I want to discuss—separation, divorce, custody?—and that way it's harder for him to prepare.

39.

hil, the mediator, is an older man with grey hair. His office is in an Edwardian terraced house on the fringe of Muswell Hill. "You're a couple of minutes early," he says with a touch of reproach. Once I would have apologized, but now I say nothing and follow him inside. It is obviously his home, though he's removed personal belongings from the hallway and the doors are closed. He leads us through to a glass-roofed extension off the kitchen. The kitchen has also been depersonalized, no magnets on the fridge or remnants of cooking, though the scent of Heinz baked beans hangs in the air. In the extension stands a circular white table with a small bowl in the center that looks as if it contains fluffy pompoms of moss. Even his potted plants are nonthreatening.

I can't help thinking that if your office space is your kitchen and dining room, then you clearly live alone, and if that is the case, what does that say about your ability to negotiate with your own family members?

On the wall hangs a portrait of three Victorian rabbits. Or rather, they are three people, a mother, father, and child, the father in a dark suit, the mother and child in long, dark dresses, and they wear rabbit masks. White cardboard muzzles, perky brown cardboard ears. Maybe they remind him of the happy animal families depicted in children's books. But the picture makes you wonder why these solemn people are wearing rabbit masks and apparently not having any fun.

The doorbell rings, and my heart flutters, not because I am nervous about seeing Pete, but at the thought of what I have to do. Pete is freshly showered and shaven, wearing a soft, expensive-looking T-shirt and jeans. He is so sure he'll get what he wants that he hasn't troubled to dress up.

"Tea, anyone?" Phil says. "Coffee?" We both shake our heads, united in our desire to get this over with. We sit down, and Phil shuffles papers and drones on about sustainable outcomes and respectful processes. He explains, "The goal is to be 'amicable, equitable, and expedient,' or as I like to say, 'friendly, fair, and fast.'" He twinkles: apparently this amounts to a humorous quip in the world of mediation.

I don't twinkle. There is nothing friendly or fair about what I am about to do. Pete asks if he can speak first, and I say yes. I am in the mood to be generous. He launches into his litany of grievances: the dead bird "in" Stella's bed, the night I "abandoned her" in the park, my "obsession" with reading her diary.

"Charlotte, would you like to contribute?" Phil says when Pete is finished.

"Where so much is wrong, there's no purchase for disagreement," I say. "It's like trying to argue with someone who thinks school shootings are faked by crisis actors."

Pete doesn't flinch. "The stress of miscarriages, hereditary depression, and a difficult birth have pushed Charlotte into florid postpartum psychosis. Unless she seeks aggressive treatment, she should not be allowed near my daughters."

Phil looks at us, clearly wondering why we thought we could find common ground in mediation. "Florid psychosis?" Phil ventures.

"She suffers from Capgras delusion," Pete says. "The belief that a loved one has been replaced by an exact duplicate."

"That is a misrepresentation," I say.

Phil looks alarmed. "This is more confrontational than I expected," he murmurs.

"Isn't your *job* dealing with confrontation?" Pete snaps.

Then Phil takes a deep breath and says, "Pete, assuming what you're saying is accurate—we all know there's more than one side of a story in divorce—"

"I can get a letter from a medical professional at her psychiatric facility attesting that my wife left against medical advice," Pete says.

"If Charlotte does have medical issues that prevent her from caring for your daughters—and that would need to be verified by a professional—you'll need to seek primary custody and Charlotte will need to seek treatment—" Here Phil looks at me as if expecting me to wave a rotting seagull in his face. "She will need treatment at once."

"That's exactly what I think," Pete says, brightening. "I'll pay for it. I have no ill will towards Charlotte, I want her to get well."

It is so transparent, really, what he is doing: focusing all the attention on my mental health to distract from his own monstrous behavior. I wait for my turn to speak. When Pete has said his piece, I say, "My husband sexually assaulted our babysitter, Blanka Hakobyan. Four days later, she took her own life."

Pete's eyes widen. I have to hand it to him: he looks genuinely shocked. "That is a complete fabrication. I reject that absolutely."

Phil looks grey-faced. "Let's listen to Charlotte speak now."

"I have proof," I say. "She wrote about it in her diary. Her mother recently discovered it and showed it to me."

Pete blusters. "This is absurd! What did she say exactly? It was probably just a fantasy, poor girl—I mean, woman."

"It says that you assaulted her. I can show it to you." I'm bluffing, but it works.

Pete massages his temples. "OK, OK. We did have a quick thing, which I'm not proud of, but it was just a one-off, it meant nothing. It was a mistake."

"A 'quick thing'? You assaulted her," I say, feeling a little wrong-footed by his self-belief. He isn't lying. He really believes that it was consensual. How can two people see the truth so differently? And it isn't his word against hers. All I have is the testimony of a ghost.

Pete frowns. "She showed up when I was alone at home. I thought she'd done that on purpose."

"She came to collect her cheque," I say.

CLEVER LITTLE THING

"Go on," says Phil.

"She'd been kind of giving me the eye," Pete says. "I'd picked up on a vibe from her. When she showed up, I thought I knew the reason."

"There was no way she would ever have looked at you flirtatiously," I say. But I remember the expression on her face when she recounted their first kiss. Maybe she did look at him. But that didn't entitle him to do whatever he wanted to her.

"How did it happen?" At least he can't accuse her of dressing suggestively.

Pete sits up a little straighter, glad to get a chance to tell the truth, or, rather, his truth. "I said something about her eyes, some throwaway comment, and she really glowed. I'd never seen her smile. She actually did look kind of pretty and I said so. A harmless compliment."

"You're married," I say. "You were her employer."

"I regret the circumstances," Pete says.

"So why did you do it?"

Pete looks at his hands. "I thought it would be a confidence boost, a nice thing for her."

"Being raped would be a confidence boost?"

Pete shakes his head furiously. "No! God, no. This is insane. I kissed her and she kissed me back. She wanted me. Not once did she say no or stop."

"She never had a boyfriend. Did you know that?" I ask. "She had no experience, no idea how to say no."

Pete shakes his head. "She wanted to kiss me. She was totally into it. And—the rest. She was a little passive, it's true, but I thought

309

she wanted it that way. She wanted to have me make it all happen. I was there, you weren't. I'm not going to let you twist the truth."

"This is not my truth, this is Blanka's," I say.

"Look, maybe she thought it meant more than it did, and then afterwards, when I made it clear it was a one-off, she was upset, and she rewrote the whole incident in her diary. But I know it was consensual, because she never once said the word *no*."

"If you knew her, if you paid any attention to her, you would know that she would never have the confidence to say that word."

Pete rubs his temples. "I am truly sorry that after the fact, she came to view it as a bad experience. But I'm not a mind reader. She didn't say no, she went along with it, so I could only assume she liked it."

"But why—why her? You could have other women. For all I know, you were already with Kia then."

"Look, I was a little buzzed, OK? It was the day after the—the birthday party. I was feeling low. I had a couple of whiskeys; then Blanka showed up. The opportunity was there."

I am sickened. This makes her sound like an open bag of cheese-and-onion crisps.

"That was inappropriate," Phil says. He swipes his brow with the back of his hand. He's sweating. "More than inappropriate."

I turn to Pete. "You're not fit to take care of children. I want full custody. Furthermore, I don't want to see you again, and I don't want you to see the girls."

"You are not taking my children away. I will fight this tooth and nail."

Phil holds up a hand. He looks clammy. "I think we should take a fifteen-minute break here. Get some fresh air."

"We're fine," says Pete, and then he changes tack. "Look, I'm sorry I fell for Kia, I can only apologize."

"When you preface 'I apologize' with the phrase 'all I can do is,' you negate the apology."

"I love you, Charlotte. Those other women—I'm really just trying to find *you* again. You used to sparkle."

"I thought all the cheating was because you 'need an outlet,'" I say. "Wasn't that what you said at the hospital?"

"I *really* think we should take a break," says Phil.

But Pete is on a roll, and it seems that he actually believes what he's saying. "Kia, Emmy, whoever—none of them actually mean anything."

"And that woman on the camping trip in Humboldt," I say. "Yes, I figured that one out too. And Blanka. And those are only the ones I know about."

Then I see the pattern: he chooses the women who think they're not good enough for him. He might think he chose me because I sparkled, but he also saw my loneliness.

"You chose me because you thought you could control me," I say.

"I loved you. I loved our life. But after Stella—"

"You couldn't control her, and you couldn't stand that. So you took it out on Blanka."

"Charlotte, please. I've fucked up, I admit it, OK? But I don't deserve to lose my children."

"You know who didn't get what she deserved? Blanka."

"Let's focus on I statements and on next steps," says Phil, who looks greenish.

"Phil," I say. "Could we have a moment? And maybe you should have a drink of water. Or put your head between your knees."

Phil tugs at his collar. "I really need to be here to keep things amicable, equitable—"

"Just give us some space, OK?" barks Pete. Phil starts to his feet and weaves towards the kitchen door.

"I'm sorry, but we need you to actually go to another part of the house," I tell him. Phil nods, looking dazed, and we hear his feet on the stairs. For a moment, I feel like we're his parents and have sent him to his room. I remember what it was like to be on the same team. But only for a moment.

"You're right. I lied about the diary," I say. "She didn't write about being raped in her diary. She confessed directly to me."

"Before she died? Why didn't you tell me?"

"I want you to watch something." I take out my phone and click to the recording of Blanka-in-Stella speaking at the soup pots. I've edited it so it is just the salient bits.

"I try his whiskey," Stella says. "Then he puts his tongue in my mouth. He grabs me, squeezes. I do not like."

Pete stares. "Why is she talking like that? Is this some kind of game—did you put her up to this? Did you feed her these lines? This is sick."

I hit pause. "I think you know that nobody can feed Stella lines," I say. Then I press play again.

Stella says, "Daddy does not listen, forces me to floor, brings up my skirt, opens my knees. All the time, talking, how pretty I am. He pushes inside me and it hurts. . . ." She covers her eyes.

As Pete watches it, he rubs his eyes and face and pushes his flesh around so vigorously that it feels as if when he takes his hands away, there will be an eye on his chin, another at the level of his hairline, nose and mouth mashed together. "It's not possible. You faked this. This is not Stella."

"It is Stella," I say. "But it's also Blanka."

"This is fucking insane," says Pete, and I realize that even if he still loved me and trusted me, he will never be able to understand that Blanka is in Stella. He has many talents, but he lacks imagination. "You know I'd never lay a finger on Stella," he says. "I never fucking would."

I shrug. "The police don't know that. Child protective services don't know that. They will watch this video and see your eight-year-old saying that you assaulted her."

Pete looks sick. "You won't be able to get this performance out of her under questioning. One recording isn't enough evidence."

Maybe he's right: the video won't be enough. The authorities will want to talk to Stella directly. Maybe they'll give her one of those anatomically correct dolls and ask her to show them what happened. Blanka will have to relive her shame in front of strangers, in a strange place. I don't know for certain that she will tell her story again.

But I can't let him see my doubts.

"I'll show it to the authorities, and I guess we'll see what happens," I say.

"You cold bitch," Pete says. I shrug. A family is not happy,

313

playful rabbit people. It is people in masks whom you can never understand.

"Or I can take the girls and go," I say. "I don't want the house. I don't want half of everything. I just want enough money for us to live on."

Pete rubs his eyes, and I realize he is crying, properly crying, for the first time since his dad died. Whatever else he's done, he's also the man who took such good care of me, who held Stella skin to skin when she was born. "Luna. My baby," Pete sobs out.

I would feel sorry for him if he were crying for both girls.

40.

After Pete storms out, I call Phil downstairs. I confirm that mediation is over and our lawyers will take it from here. By the time I get outside, a car is pulling up for Pete.

"Wait!" I want to discuss logistics. It would be easiest if he could stay somewhere else tonight and give me a chance to reunite with Stella and pack our things. That way I won't have to come back to the house. But he jumps in without looking at me.

I'm desperate to see Stella, but when I check my phone, the next Uber isn't for fourteen minutes. It's just over a mile to our house, so I run. It's hard to sprint, only a few days after giving birth, and I didn't consider how much of the route is uphill. But the thought of seeing Stella—as herself, at last—makes me fly.

The front door is double-locked. My stomach lurches: we only double-lock if nobody's home. My cold fingers are clumsy as I fumble with my keys. Inside, the overhead lights are on, as are the copper cluster lights on the Christmas tree. But the house is empty. I run from room to room, calling her name. A tangle of socks and underwear lies on her bed, the drawer upside-down on the floor. Her wardrobe door is ajar, and when I open it, the child-sized boogie board is gone, the one that looked like a blue fish with yellow stripes. I press one of her little socks to my face.

I call Pete: no answer. I call him again and again. I don't have Kia's number. No answer from Nathan. I run downstairs to Pete's office and check the drawer where he keeps our passports. Empty, except for mine. "No," I say, over and over until the word becomes meaningless.

Yet again, I've failed to anticipate what my husband is capable of. If only I had his ability to think several moves ahead, I would have found a way to hide Stella's passport before the mediation session. There's only one place he could be taking her: California. Five thousand miles away. He will get a lawyer. I'll get one too, but his will be better. I might get her back, but it will take months, or even years, and before then, Blanka will end Stella's life. She'll drown Stella to get revenge on Pete because I couldn't pull it off. On their first father-daughter surfing trip, Blanka will pull Stella under the waves, let an undertow drag her away.

My breath comes in little gasps. I have to stop shaking and get it together. Barely an hour has passed since Pete left the mediation session: enough time for him to jump in a cab to Heathrow, but not enough for him to board a plane. I still have a chance. I check Heathrow departures for flights to San Francisco, and for a moment I breathe more deeply: the next one isn't until 7:05 a.m. tomorrow.

But I have to start thinking like him now, shuffling possibilities. He needs to get her out of the country as quickly as possible, which means the next flight that goes anywhere in the US. No, the next flight out of the country: Milan, Vilnius, Abu Dhabi. The nearest airports with international flights are Heathrow and London City.

I think about going to the police and explaining that my child-abusing ex is attempting to take our daughter out of the country, could board any flight at either airport in the next two hours. But how long will that take? I have to pick an airport and go there *now*. My gut tells me Pete is planning to go straight to the US, so he can lawyer up, and you can't fly there from London City Airport. I call Irina because her crazy driving is the fastest way to get to Heathrow. When she arrives, for once she doesn't tell me she's not a taxi service. She just squeezes my hand, hard.

At Heathrow, Irina has barely pulled up to the curb before I leap out of the car and hurl myself towards the revolving doors. Inside, it's painfully bright and busy. Queues snake through the airport: people in puffy winter jackets with ski bags over their shoulders, families on their way home from Christmas visits. Every check-in desk is crowded. But the rich don't have to stand in long queues: he's probably already at security.

I take the up escalator two steps at a time, then sprint towards security, lungs burning. The queue zigzags between belt barriers and then through a doorway in a smoked-glass screen. I thrust myself between and around people, leaving yelps of outrage in my wake. When I reach the official who is checking documents at the doorway,

I have my passport ready. "My husband is taking my child out of the country without my permission."

"Boarding pass?"

I stare at her. "I'm not here to get on a plane."

"You need a boarding pass to enter the sterile area."

She's in her late twenties, wearing makeup so thick that her skin resembles that of a mannequin. It looks like it would be hard to the touch.

"Please. This is an emergency." I peer over her shoulder, searching for Stella.

"You still have to be processed through passenger security screening."

I can't get her to meet my gaze. "My daughter's being abducted. Please help me. My child."

"Ma'am, in that case, you need to call the police."

I draw myself up straight, smooth my hair. I need her to see that I'm just an ordinary respectable person who happens to be in a terrible situation. "Please let me see if she's there. You can watch me. I don't even have a bag. I'm not going to try and sneak a bomb through."

I know what I've done wrong as soon as the word leaves my mouth. She flings her arms wide across the doorway and starts barking into her radio, calling for support. I raise my hands to show I'm backing down, stepping meekly away. Then I duck underneath her arm and into the throng of people on the other side.

The blue-and-yellow boogie board is about to pass through the baggage scanner. Stella is shuffling through the metal detector nearby, head bowed. Pete must have already gone through—he didn't think to let his daughter go first.

"Stella!" I gasp. "Stella!" She doesn't turn. I throw myself towards her, knocking over a stack of grey plastic bins. As I stumble to my feet, two police officers in fluorescent vests grab my arms. All around me, people are raising their phones to record, but why won't anyone help me? The baggage scanner has swallowed the blue fish. I can't see Stella anymore.

"Blanka!" I scream so loud it makes my jaw hurt.

"Ma'am, you need to come with us," one of the police officers says, a young man with a carefully shaped goatee.

"That man is taking my child!" I struggle to wrench myself free.

"What does she look like?" says the woman. Her mouth turns down at the corners, like a disappointed head teacher. She doesn't believe I really have a daughter.

But the man is listening to his radio. He nods at the woman, and they escort me to the other side of the screening area. Pete's standing there with another police officer while a woman with a Fair Isle cardigan and a security lanyard attempts to distract Stella with a bear in a Santa hat. "Stella!" I shout, but she won't look at me: she asked me to do one thing, and I failed. The police officer is talking to Pete. No sign of Kia: he left her behind. Even she wouldn't condone him taking Stella out of the country without telling me. He blinks as people point their phones at him, whispering to each other: he must have done something bad if the police are detaining him. His arms are rigid by his side. I stare at him. I've never seen him like this, without a plan.

Then the police officers are rushing us down one fluorescent-lit corridor after another, until we reach a windowless room with two sofas, a coffee table, and several chairs. It's the room of last resort, where the news is so bad that it's pointless to provide a potted plant or a magazine. The police officers introduce themselves as Constables Lynne Rolfe and Ajay Grover. The woman with the lanyard is Mandy.

"I want a lawyer," Pete says.

"You're not under arrest," says Rolfe. "Currently. Let's try to get to the bottom of this situation." She gestures at us to sit down. Stella won't. Mandy wants to take her to another room, murmuring about juice and crayons.

"Please keep my daughter where I can see her," I bark, and Mandy subsides. Grover checks our passports, studying our faces, frowning.

"What's your daughter's name?" asks Rolfe.

"Stella," Pete says.

Rolfe raises her eyebrows. "That wasn't the name she answered to earlier."

Mandy crouches down and asks Stella in a soft voice, "What's your name, sweetie?"

Stella stares straight ahead.

"Is she hearing-impaired?" says Mandy.

Pete sighs. "For Christ's sake, you have her passport. You don't need her to say her name."

Rolfe glances at Grover, and he shrugs and shows her Stella's passport photo, taken two years ago, when her skin was still pale and her curls unruly. I loved that picture—her high forehead, her precise, delicate features—like a face you'd find inside an antique locket.

"This doesn't look like her," says Grover, staring at Stella. Since that photo, her hair has darkened and lost its curl, and her face is rounder.

But Pete scoffs. "She's grown, that's all."

Rolfe asks Stella if she can point out her dad. Stella says something incomprehensible, her mouth twisting around strange sounds.

"What did she say?" Rolfe asks Mandy. Mandy squats down next to Stella and points to Pete.

"Is that man your father, sweetie?"

This time I recognize Stella's words.

"*Yes atum yem ayd mardun,*" she says.

"She's saying, 'I hate that man.'" I clear my throat. "In Armenian."

"Come again?" says Grover

The grooves at the side of Rolfe's mouth deepen. "You should have told us she doesn't speak English."

"She does," Pete says.

Rolfe frowns. "Can one of you try speaking to her?"

I scratch my arms. "We don't speak Armenian."

Rolfe looks from me to Pete to Stella, as if formulating a new theory about what is going on here. I scratch harder. This is going to end up with both of us getting arrested. God knows what will happen to Stella.

"Stella, please," tries Pete. "This is not a game."

Stella gives him a polite, puzzled look. Like he's a foreigner struggling to ask for directions. She'd like to help him—if only he could make himself clear. Pete takes a moment to clean a smudge off his glasses. Then he gets up and lays his hands on her shoulders. "Stella, this is not the time to show off."

"Yes atum yem—"

"Jesus *Christ!*" Pete yells. He places his hands over his face, then chops at the air. He paces back and forth. I realize something: He doesn't want to be Stella's full-time parent. He doesn't have the patience. He likes her better as Blanka, but she's still not his perfect daughter. She's never going to be a crown-braided cartwheel-turner like Lulu. She'll never be simple, easy. He just wants Stella because he doesn't like to lose. I store this realization away. Maybe I can use it. Because the video didn't work, I have to come up with something else, and quickly. Rolfe is fed up.

"You both say this child is your daughter, yet you"—she points to me—"call her by a different name. Furthermore, she doesn't resemble her passport picture, and neither of you speak her language."

"Hold on!" I say. "Her grandmother speaks Armenian. She's just parking the car." I send a quick text telling Irina to ask for us at security. On second thought, I send an urgent question too.

"I would like to talk to my wife privately," Pete says.

Grover looks at Rolfe, and they nod. "Five minutes."

I follow Pete into the passage outside. "Make Stella stop this charade," he tells me. "Otherwise, I promise you, Charlotte, I will make sure we both lose. I will not rest until child protective services know all about your mental illness. We'll both lose custody. She'll go to her nearest living relative." He pauses. "My mother."

"You don't even want her," I hiss. I thought I'd come up with the ultimate trick to defeat Pete, but it didn't work, because I didn't let myself see what he is capable of. I never dreamed he'd try to abduct Stella, or that he'd send her to his mother rather than let me have her. Now, to defeat him, I have to truly *see* him, as I've never let myself before. His eyes look bloodshot in the harsh light, and his beard hides his firm jaw, his best feature, and somehow makes his mouth look greedy. How did I ever think this man was gorgeous?

He looks preoccupied, like he's already conducting cost-benefit analyses, formulating a new plan. But just now, in the security area, when the police officer apprehended him and people held up their phones to record the scene, Pete froze. People profile him for business magazines. Antiplastic campaigners give him awards for his good work. Women hang on his every word. The taste of public disapproval is new.

His mother once told me that when Pete was little, if he hit another kid, she never scolded him in public. She got down on his level and asked him why he did it. According to her, his explanations always made sense. Pete believes that he always has a good reason, and he convinces other people of it too. But if that stopped—if people started judging him, instead of applauding—*that* would be the worst thing. Worse than losing his daughters.

"You're right," I say. "I'm not going to show that video to the police."

"Thank you for being reasonable."

"I'm sending it to Nathan. In fact, I'll send it to everyone in Mycoship. Maybe the video won't stand up in a court of law, but you'll be judged in the court of public opinion. You won't be able to keep your job, and I doubt Nathan can keep the company going without you." Pete looks clammy now. I am a step ahead of him. At last. "I'll send it to the press too. Everyone loves the story of a fall from grace. From green business mogul to child abuser—that's a pretty big drop."

Pete rakes his hands through his hair. When he talks, it's not really addressed to me. It's like he's forgotten I'm there. "I put everything into that company," he mutters. "Plastic is wrecking the ocean, but our packaging actually enriches the soil. It's a revolutionary solution. A game changer." His voice steadies. He's convinced himself: he'll give Stella up, because it's for the greater good. He's safely back on the moral high ground. He fixes me with his bloodshot blue eyes. "You get her. For now."

My phone pings: Irina's answer to my question.

When I go back into the room, Pete is crouched in front of Stella. "Daddy has a plane to catch, sweetie."

"You'll leave once we say so," says Rolfe.

"Let him go," I say. "This was a misunderstanding."

Pete nods and turns back to Stella. "I'll see you." A lie, I hope. He opens his arms wide. But Stella stares at Pete, and the look on her face is enough to pin him to the spot. She doesn't look like a little girl upset that her father is leaving. She looks like a grown woman, filled with righteous, bitter loathing. Blood pounds in my ears, just like the surf the day I learned of Blanka's death: pummeling, smashing, grinding.

Pete staggers back. When he turns to leave the room, he looks like someone who has just opened a door to discover that his world is a stage set, blackness howling outside. Maybe that's just the look of a man saying goodbye to his daughter forever. But I think perhaps, at last, he sees Blanka-in-Stella. I didn't think he was capable of that.

Once he's gone, Stella crumples to the floor, and I rush towards her.

I croon Irina's answer to my question: *"Im yerekha, im yerekha."*
My baby, my baby.

In answer to Rolfe's look, I murmur, "I speak a word or two."

I pull back to look at Stella's face: her eyes are half-closed, only the white showing. She judders in my arms.

Mandy looks uneasy. "Is she OK? Do we need to call a doctor?"

"She's fine. She's going to be fine." But her skin feels as cold as marble.

"Stella! My little one!" Irina bursts in, having miraculously found us down this maze of corridors. She directs a stream of Armenian endearments at us, and then barely takes a breath before berating Rolfe and Grove for detaining her daughter and granddaughter and letting Pete go. "I am thinking this is safe, nice country where child is well treated," she snaps. "Maybe now I write letter to my MP."

Rolfe and Grover let us go after we fill out an incident report, and I follow Irina to her car with Stella in my arms, the sound of her chattering teeth in my ear. On the way back, I take out the ponytail holders with the plastic bobbles, comb out her plaits with my fingers.

When Irina reaches our house, I ask her to stay. I carry Stella up to her room. Irina pulls back her comforter and I lay her down and cover her. Then we sit in the dark with just her nightlight on, listening to her deep, struggling breaths. It almost sounds like the way someone breathes when they are dying. Should I call an ambulance? Maybe Blanka is ready to go now, but she's taking Stella with her. Perhaps, once a spirit has entered your body, it can't just exit painlessly. Blanka's like a knife, pulling Stella's guts out as she withdraws.

I try to push down my panic. My mother instinct tells me noth-ing. I don't think any doctor can help her, but I don't know that she'll be OK. All we can do is wait. We sit by her bed for a long time, listening to that terrible breathing.

At first, I'm not sure, but then I am: her breaths are smoothing out. Irina, seated in Stella's desk chair, grows more and more hunched. At long last, Stella's breathing is quiet and steady. Irina stands stiffly. "I sleep in my own bed. You take care of daughter."

When Irina is gone, I listen to Stella inhale and exhale, just like when she was a newborn, and I felt that the only way she would take another breath was if I was there to listen. She's alive. But is she Stella now? I should let her body rest, but I can't wait anymore. I press my face into her hair. No meat stew, no chlorine, just the scent of ordinary sleeping child. "Stella, honey?" I whisper.

"I was asleep," she says groggily.

"Yes, it's still night. But just look at me for a moment." We gaze at each other. One Mississippi, two Mississippi, three Mississippi. I count. Please let this be the hugging stare. "Quack, there's a saddle on my back," I say, my voice trembling.

"Cock-a-doodle-doo," she replies, "I'm a kangaroo."

My heart feels as if it will burst from my chest. My daughter. She's still gazing at me. "Why are you awake, Mommy?" she says. "Are you having trouble sleeping?" She sighs deeply, as if forgoing something very precious. "You can borrow my book on aviation if you want." I clench my fists with the effort of not hugging her.

41.

"More soup, anyone?" I ask Irina and Stella. I made it out of nettles we gathered together, Stella and I, while Irina stayed at the cottage with Luna.

Irina holds out her bowl, but Stella says, "I've had enough." She only spooned up a little, but I didn't have to serve it as components: progress. "Can Luna try it?"

"Not yet," I say.

"Do they think they will close school?" Irina says.

They're talking about a shutdown to limit the spread of coronavirus.

"Yay!" says Stella.

"If that happens, maybe I'll finally become good enough to crochet a decent sock. Right, Irina?" I nudge her. It's a running joke how terrible I am at crocheting.

It's March now, and I've rented a cottage on the Devon coast. Pete deposits money into my bank account every month. If there's a shutdown, we'll have enough to live on, and the four of us will keep each other company, drive each other crazy, or both.

Meanwhile, Irina looks after Luna so I have time to work out what I want to do. I don't know what I am passionate about, but I am going to find it. I have begun to cook again.

All those meals Stella refused to eat—I never enjoyed cooking them. I told myself I didn't enjoy cooking because she wouldn't eat. But what if she didn't eat because I didn't enjoy cooking? Now I cook what *I* feel like eating, and I enjoy it. Sometimes, Stella does too.

Stella goes to the village school. Her handwriting needs work, the teacher tells me. At break, she mostly reads hefty science books while hiding from the teacher on duty behind a bush, but I'm fine if she doesn't want to socialize. She's changed so much, and she will get there in her own time. Plus, she has Luna now.

"I put wild garlic in the soup," I tell Irina. "Like you showed me the other day. Is that something you gathered when you fled Azerbaijan?"

Irina shakes her head. "For three days, we have nothing to eat but dandelion."

"Where did you sleep?" I ask.

"Were you very scared?" says Stella.

"I walk with Blanka, she is three years old. I carry nothing but wedding dress and often Blanka too. There is nothing more to tell." Irina scrapes her spoon around her bowl.

I once wondered if she was exaggerating when she told us about her life. The little house in the forest. The husband shut in an oven. Could she really have walked over the mountains for three days, carrying her daughter and her wedding dress, with only dandelions to eat? But living with her, I've noticed that she tells her story in the same words every time, and if I press her for more information, she shuts me down. This happens and then that happens and then there's nothing more to tell. I think this is her particular way of making the past manageable.

After dinner, we crochet, or try to. Stella is as bad as me. But we find it calming. Irina inspects my work. "Your stitches are too tight. Relax hands."

"But this sock is going to last forever," I say. "Look how thick it is."

"Perfect for one-legged man," mutters Irina.

"Do you remember the crocheting you did before?" I ask Stella. For weeks, I've been terrified to ask her about her time as Blanka, but I am starting to feel safe. She's been Stella for some time now, her hair ablaze again. "Socks are tricky, aren't they?" I ask her as she frowns over hers. "It's funny, you used to crochet such complicated doilies."

Stella shrugs. "I don't remember."

I've asked her other questions too. Does she miss eating lamb stew, her old favorite? Does she miss writing in a diary? I get the same answer whenever I ask her about that time as Blanka.

"I don't remember."

The reason I ask is to find out if she remembered that time of sharing her body, if she has questions or worries about it. But apparently not. She doesn't remember. And I don't want to probe her further. Perhaps her amnesia is self-protective.

After I've put Luna to bed, I have tea with milk. Irina has tea with jam. Stella has milk with jam. I tell Irina, "I'm learning about Armenia, and I read that they have a saying, 'A cup of tea commits you to forty years of friendship.'"

Irina snorts. "Where do you read this? I never hear one Armenian person say that." Her eyes water as she gulps her tea the wrong way, and I have to thump her on the back.

The next day, we take the grape-leaf tin with Blanka's ashes to the beach. It is cold, but Irina stops and kicks off her boots. Without any modesty, matter-of-factly, she lifts her skirt to peel off her long underwear. "You're going to paddle? You're crazy. It's freezing," I call.

Luna nestles against my chest in her carrier. She never had that honeysuckle smell, and my love for her is different, slower, but growing every day. Her eyes notice everything. Is she too planning, storing it all up?

I take off my shoes and socks and let the sea nip my toes. The air tingles with brine. Irina is already in up to her ankles. She holds out her hands to Stella.

Stella takes off her shoes and socks and walks to the edge of the water. I am surprised. I thought Stella was scared of the sea but apparently not anymore. Blanka has left her, but she isn't the old Stella. She is becoming someone new. I can no longer label her behavior as "Stella" or "not Stella," because that is a way of refusing to see her. I have to let her be whoever she wants to be, unfolding from one day to the next.

The wind blows spray into our faces, and something spooks the gulls, so they whirl overhead. "Did Blanka like the sea?" I call to Irina.

She smiles. "We did not come, but I think yes. I think she would—would have liked." I realize with a jolt it is the first time she's spoken of her daughter in the past tense.

Stella gazes out to the horizon. "Is Daddy still in California?"

There is both an ocean and a continent between us and Pete. Emmy heard that Pete left Mycoship and retreated to the Bay Area. He's back to working with his mother at CannaGauge, their cannabis-testing equipment company. I don't know if he turned what happened into a story in which he was the good guy. Or if seeing Blanka for that one moment changed him—if indeed he did see her.

"Do you miss him?" I ask Stella now. I still feel stricken about the price Stella had to pay for getting rid of Blanka. Despite what he did, Pete is her father.

But Stella shakes her head. "Don't worry, Mommy. I'm happy being with you and Luna and Irina." She looks so perky, and I have to admit she does seem to find life easier without Pete. I think back to her birthday party, which she purposely ruined because Pete threw a party for the child he wanted, not the one he had.

That birthday party was the day before Pete assaulted Blanka. He hurt Blanka because he couldn't hurt Stella.

I stub my toe on a rock and stumble, one arm protectively around Luna in her carrier. My god, Stella was *there* that day. I remember now. Emmy was supposed to take her to the group swim class, but Emmy had texted while I was out: Stella had refused to go, so Emmy and Lulu went without her.

Stella was probably in her room when it happened. I pray that she had on her noise-cancelling headphones, the ones I'd got her for when school was too much. She liked a documentary series, *Earth-flight*, so maybe she was watching that. When Pete assaulted Blanka, I hope Stella was blissfully ignorant, watching gorgeous footage of cranes and snow geese.

But was Stella definitely upstairs? What if she came out of her room while Pete was working downstairs? When Blanka arrived, she could have been in her alone-time cupboard, the door open a crack. Or perched at the top of the stairs. I don't know if she would have understood what was happening, but you could understand that Blanka was in distress without knowing what was going on.

If she'd seen that, what might she do? Perhaps she was afraid to tell me, especially if she wasn't sure what she had seen. But if she said nothing, she was left with her anger. It wasn't acceptable for a daughter to hate her father. Maybe she found a way to channel that hatred. To let someone else do the hating for her.

I take sips of the cold air to calm myself. She is capable of more than she lets on, I've always known that. When she was barely a toddler, she hoarded words for months so that her first utterance was a full sentence.

She could have put Vaseline in her hair to make it limp. She could have force-fed herself, and who wouldn't gain weight on a diet of meat stew? She was quite capable of changing her handwriting. Easy enough to adopt shuffling steps and simple sentences.

Her mastery of crochet as Blanka was impressive, but maybe that was "sudden competence"—the genius child's ability to learn skills seemingly overnight. Like Pete said, she could have used

Google Translate for the diary: it was only one phrase, after all. With her memory, she could have learned enough Armenian for her brief conversation with Irina.

Perhaps it all began as a game, and it got out of hand, to the point where even she no longer knew quite where she ended and Blanka began. Or maybe she planned all of it. She is Pete's child, master of the long game, but more intelligent than her father.

Pete brought Kia home and shut himself in our bathroom with Emmy and who knows what else Stella has been aware of. Maybe she saw what I refused to see. Freak-out mode might have been a cry for help, but it didn't work, so she turned to something else.

My mind teeters: Is it possible? Maybe Stella always says, "I don't remember," when I ask her about that time because forgetting is healing. Or maybe it is the subterfuge of a child who doesn't want to be questioned too closely, for fear of giving herself away.

"Are you having a good time at the beach, Mommy?" Her look holds concern for me in a way I've never seen before. Maybe Stella knew, even if I didn't, that we would be better off without Pete. Luna too.

The winter sun comes out and changes the sea from grey to green and turns every pebble on the beach bright and sharp. Tears prick my eyes. "I'm having a lovely time, my darling," I say, and she smiles. Her skin is pearly again, her red hair a wild tangle. If she masterminded Pete's overthrow, she did it for me. I fought so hard to protect her, but all along, she was protecting me—and herself. She was fighting for *us*. My heart ignites.

Irina opens the grape-leaf tin and offers it to me. I take some ash in my hand. The only time I ever touched Blanka was when I released her after Stella tied her up. Now I am touching her in the most intimate way: the fine rubble of her bones, the powdery dust of her organs and skin. In my hand I hold the remnants of the vertebrae that once formed inside Irina. Now I am releasing her again. The wind is at our backs, and the ash leaves my hand and turns to cloud, a puff of breath in cold air. "Thank you," I murmur. *"Allons-y."* That's what her favorite Doctor Who said when it was time for another adventure. Maybe now she will finally travel to the fringes of the universe.

"Allons-y!" Stella shouts. She is right behind me. She strides farther in, up to her knees, and puts her little warm hand in mine. She's just a child, she couldn't have masterminded such a hoax. And when Blanka finally spoke to me at the soup pots, I *knew*, without any doubt, that I was talking to a being beyond my understanding. I felt such awe, as if I were looking into the eye of a whale, sensing its unimaginably vast strength. That couldn't have been my daughter.

If it was, Stella's not going to tell me. She looks up at me and smiles. A wave sucks our footing away and makes us stagger. But we hold hands tightly, and we find our balance.

Acknowledgments

Thank you to my rock star agents, Emma Leong at Janklow & Nesbit (UK) and Chad Luibl at Janklow & Nesbit (US). Their industry savvy and superb storytelling advice has been life changing. I'm the luckiest of writers to be their client.

It has been a dream to work with my editor, publishing legend Pamela Dorman. Along with her Canadian counterpart, Lara Hinchberger, she has made this book infinitely better, and working with these two has felt like a glorious private master class in how to write.

And it has been an honor to work with Pam's fantastic team. Thank you to Marie Michels for always being on top of everything, and thanks to Natalie Grant for all her help too. Rebecca Marsh and Sara Delozier, along with Magdalena Deniz, are true pros who have worked tirelessly to get the word out, and Molly Fessenden is a marketing champion.

ACKNOWLEDGMENTS

Thank you to all the other fantastic people at Pamela Dorman Books/Viking and at Penguin Random House Canada who helped to bring this book into being, especially Brian Tart, Andrea Schulz, Patrick Nolan, Kate Stark, and Mary Stone. I'm also grateful to all those who worked so hard behind the scenes on my book, including Tricia Conley, Diandra Alvarado, Nina Brown, Matt Giarratano, Nick Michal, Laura Petrella, Jenny Moles, and Katie Rizzo. Many thanks to Nicole Celli for skillfully overseeing the publication process. The stunning and evocative cover is the work of Jason Ramirez and Dave Litman. Claire Vaccaro and Cassandra Mueller did a beautiful job of the interior.

I raise a glass to Bea Grabowska and the fabulous team at Headline in the UK. I'm so grateful for their passion and hard work.

Tash Barsby, deputy editorial director at the Novelry, is this book's fairy godmother. She worked her magic on my submission package and connected me with the perfect agent. Louise Dean, the Novelry's founder, has created an incredible community for writers.

I am privileged to be taken care of by the superb agency of Janklow & Nesbit, and really appreciate everyone there who works so hard for writers on the legal and financial side. Nathaniel Alcaraz-Stapleton championed this book early on and has found excellent homes for it abroad. I am also grateful to all my foreign publishers for embracing the book.

Huge thanks to my film and TV agent, Penni Killick at The Artists Partnership, for everything she has done for the book.

On the personal side, thank you to Kara Levy, Kate Milliken, and Rachel Howard, who read these pages first and gave me valuable feedback. Diana Whitney's early support meant the world and kept me going. David Shelley, best friend of my youth, has shared his publishing expertise and given much good advice over the years. Other friends who have generously offered insight and encouragement include Malena Watrous, Yael Goldstein-Love, Martha Conway, Daniel Gilsenan, and Joe Winkley.

Adam Kuper graciously let me use his house in Muswell Hill and it's been a tranquil haven when I really needed to get work done.

I am grateful to Sophia Grene for advice on portraying autism, and to authors whose books helped me understand autism and neurodivergence, including *Drama Queen* by Sara Gibbs and *Your Child is Not Broken* by Heidi Mavir.

Big hug to Osanna Avanesova for plowing through my book in order help me out with her knowledge of Armenia and Azerbaijan. The following accounts were particularly helpful in understanding the experience of the Armenian refugee from Azerbaijan: *Liminal: a refugee memoir* by Liyah Babayan and *Nowhere: A Story of Exile* by Anna Astvatsaturian Turcotte. Krikor Moskofian, founder and director of the Centre for Western Armenian Studies, generously helped with Armenian translation. Thank you, Suzan Kalayci, for pointing me his way.

I started this book in 2019, and then 2020 happened. I owe everything to my beloved friend Stephanie Grandjacques and the other wonderful women who were there for me in that darkest of years. Thank you from the bottom of my heart to Ruth Whippman, Caroline Paul, Arabella Hester, and Hilda Wang. Dearest schoolfriends Hannah Kuper, Judith Wardle, and Kathryn Crandon, you also had my back in 2020, and helped me survive that time.

My marvelous friend Catherine Kernot, cold-water swim buddy, brings me inspiration during our weekly dip. Lucy Ayrton's fierce productivity spurs me on, and Cindy Skach makes me laugh when we share our life and writing travails.

I've learned so much from my talented fiction students at Stanford and Oxford universities. I'm grateful to all of them, especially the ones who asked the hardest questions.

Support from Megan, my children's beloved babysitter, allowed me to get writing done in their early years, and I am so grateful to her for all the trips to Totland, goldfish crackers, and sewing projects.

Thank you to my kind and loving family by marriage, particularly Carol Wells and Chas Harrison, Cathy Strisik, and Luke, Lindsey, Lucy, and Annaleigh Schreiber. During the pandemic, they put the kettle on and told me I was doing a good job when I needed it most. The late Larry Schreiber, much missed, was a wonderful storyteller and if he was still alive, he'd been telling everyone he knows about this book.

When I was little, I carried a pink suitcase of books everywhere. My wonderful parents, Rose and David Echlin, made sure that suitcase was always full, and, by choosing their own paths in life they gave me the confidence to do the same. Thanks to my beloved brother, Jamie Echlin, for doing his very best to offer support in 2020. When the worst happens, Jamie is there for me. My treasured sister, Kezia Echlin, once told me I should keep writing regardless of whether I ever published a book, because "you're a writer and that's what you do." I pay tribute to her for believing in me, for the loveliest bouquet at just the right time, and for medical fact-checking. (Mistakes are mine.)

Thank you to my beloved children, Griffin and Seraphine, for being so full of stories, jokes, and ideas. There is nobody with whom I'd rather go for a walk.

Over our years together, Jordan Schreiber, the love of my life, has fixed the taps, done the taxes, and made the budget work. He always helped me find time to write, and never told me to get a proper job, even when we were broke. Our passion has buoyed me ever since we met in college and when things fall apart, he can still make me laugh. I owe the greatest debt to him.